MY STORY

MY STORY

Caroline Cossey

faber and faber
LONDON · BOSTON

Published in the United States by Faber and Faber, Inc., 50 Cross Street, Winchester, MA 01890 and in the United Kingdom by Faber and Faber Ltd., 3 Queen Square, London WC1N 3AU.

This paperback edition first published in 1992.

A CIP record for this book is available from the Library of Congress and the British Library.

ISBN 0-571-12909-9

Printed in the United States of America

To my family
for all their love and support

Contents

Illustrations

(left to right) Paulo, Glauco and Pam

Being serenaded in Venice with Glauco

Taken by a friend of Glauco's before a cocktail party

Visiting Pam with my mother in Rome

With Dad, Mum and Pam on New Year's Eve 1986/7 – the last before he died

Cover shot for *Osrati*, an Arab fashion magazine

Modelling for Victor Hromin in Italy

Photo by John Hedgecoe for one of his books

Cutting our wedding cake in the beautiful Lancaster Room at the Savoy Hotel

Kissing and thanking my bridesmaids and pageboys for handling my train so well

Looking happy and relaxed with my little helpers after the ceremony

Posing for friends in front of the old Rolls-Royce that was to take us to the ball

On honeymoon in Acapulco: a photo taken by me of Elias with my hairdresser Owen and his boyfriend Jonathan

A happy honeymooning couple sightseeing in Acapulco

Preface

My childhood was a jigsaw puzzle. All the pieces were there, but there was no one to fit them together, no one to make a complete picture. Nothing felt right. I could trust no impulse. All I knew in those early years was isolation and confusion. I see myself as I was then, a small, anxious boy hiding amongst the bean rows, truanting from school, standing alone in the playground. I could make no sense of the world that ran and skipped and jumped beside me. Life was a game that I could not learn to play.

I would lie on my bed and dream that I was somebody else, somebody respected and admired, somebody who belonged. I had no words for my unhappiness, but, with the blind faith of a child, I believed that there had to be a better life for me. What I could not know then, and wasn't to learn for many years, was that I had been born with a body at war with itself. I was a girl trapped inside a male form.

Had I come into the world a hundred years earlier, I would probably have killed myself. As it was, even in the early 1970s, the problem I faced was surrounded by the mists of mythology and misinformation. Transsexuality was slowly emerging into the light of day, but it was still beset by prejudice and ignorance. Many thought that transsexuals were synonymous with transvestites. Many thought that transsexuals were thwarted homosexuals. Many thought that transsexuals were freaks. Many still do.

As I lay dreaming on my bed all those years ago, I had no way of knowing that I had been born between two sexes, and that one day I would, for the sake of my sanity, have to choose between those warring genders.

I could not know then that the impulse which led me to seek the company of girls, to play their games and to imitate their behaviour, was the irresistible call of my true nature. I could not know then that the force which drove me into the arms of men, which led me to abhor the sight of my naked body, and sent me away from home on a journey that was to lead to London and surgery, sprang from a chromosomal blueprint laid down in the womb.

I now know that I was born transsexual and that I was starved of the formative experiences I needed as a little girl. It took years to fit the pieces together, to understand the past, to make the picture. I wrote this book not as a medical textbook to explain the technicalities of gender reassignment, nor as a legal brief describing the long-drawn-out battle I have fought in the European courts, but as an honest and unadorned account of my life – a life made remarkable by an accident of biology.

I hope that my story may help others who are in search of unity between body and mind, as they struggle to piece together their particular jigsaw in the face of prejudice and ignorance – mankind's greatest enemy.

Transsexuals are in a minority. But it is a larger minority than many might imagine. To date many thousands of sex-change operations have been performed in this country, and many more abroad. And yet the immensely painful surgery that the transsexual has to undergo is the least of his or her trials. When I had my operation in 1974 I imagined that, like a butterfly emerging from a chrysalis, I would spread my wings and fly. Nothing could have been further from the truth. What I did not know then, but have since learnt to my cost, was that as a transsexual in this country I had none of the legal rights of my new sex. I could not marry the man of my choice. I could not alter my now inaccurate birth certificate. If convicted of a crime, I would be sent to a male prison. I could not legally be raped. In those heady days when, rejoicing in my new body, I was accepted by all who met me as female, I could not know what lay ahead. I had no idea that a country which allowed its doctors to perform and perfect this revolutionary surgery would refuse to protect the woman they had helped create.

Once again I was to find myself wandering in no man's land, a target for the snipers from the gutter press. Without my legal rights to protect me I was fair game for anyone, and consigned to a half-life. 'Be a transsexual,' the law said to me, 'but be silent. Be humble. Be grateful.'

I won't be silent. I won't be humble. I won't be grateful. I did not choose to be born the way I was, and I refuse to be punished for something over which I had no control. And so I have written this book not only for transsexuals but also for the many men and women who have no understanding of what it means to be trapped in the wrong gender, who have no idea of the persecution that transsexuals suffer. I hope that it will teach them to show a little compassion, tolerance and understanding. For, in the words of the barrister David Pannick, 'The way in which our society deals with minorities is a guide to our civilization.'

This is my story.

1

Growing Pains

I was born on 31 August 1954 to Robert and Doreen Cossey. My mother had a difficult labour that began at nine in the evening and ended at 7.30 the following morning. 'You were the only one I had trouble with,' she told me. 'The midwife had just produced the forceps, and was threatening to use them, when you finally made your appearance.' I was a pretty baby, but small and frail. I cried continuously and suffered from colic. But my parents and my older brother, Terry, were delighted with me. Mum had waited six years before having a second child. She and my dad had wanted to have sufficient money and a large enough house before they added to the family. Mum soon became pregnant again, and gave birth to a girl just over a year after I was born. She had wanted a daughter, and now she felt her family was complete. She had her children, a house in the quiet Norfolk countryside, and a marriage to a man she adored.

My parents had met at the Samson Hercules Dance in Norwich. They were instantly attracted to each other. Mum was a tall, pretty girl, with big brown eyes and dark wavy hair. The second of four children, she had led a sheltered life in Norwich, and nursed a secret ambition to become a model. But my dad, with his dark Errol Flynn good looks, swept her off her feet, and they decided to marry. Terry was born just over a year after their marriage.

My dad brought his 'city' bride to live in Brooke, a tiny village deep in the Norfolk countryside. His family had lived in East Anglia for several generations, and there was even a rumour that the Cosseys were related to the hero of that area, Lord Nelson. Dad had been born in Brooke. He was the youngest of three boys, and his father was the village blacksmith. He had a rough, tough childhood – shooting, working for pocket money on the local farms, and fishing for eels on the Broads. He was very much a countryman, and he spoke with a broad Norfolk accent. Although he didn't have a great education, he was clever, quick-witted and humorous. He had a strong sense of personal integrity and placed great store on honesty. As a child I looked up to him, but was always afraid of his anger. It wasn't that he was a disciplinarian, far from it; he was firm but always fair. However, I was a highly sensitive child, and felt even the slightest reprimand keenly. Dad had no idea of what I was going through during my early years, and I had no way of explaining. He was aware I was a troubled and unhappy little boy, but very often his concern manifested itself as disapproval. I felt that I was a disappointment to him, and this placed a constraint on our relationship. We loved each other, but lacked the language to express that love. In later years, when I was able to share my understanding of transsexuality with him, he showed a compassion and tolerance that was remarkable in a man of his background and nature. It was his acceptance and his courage that inspired me to fight for the cause I believed in.

Dad had served as an ambulance driver in the Second World War. The four years he spent driving the sick and the dying through the battlefields of northern France had a profound effect on him. He saw terrible suffering, but, like so many of his generation, he kept those sights and sounds a secret. He would never talk about the war when I was a child. He had a little box in which he kept all his mementoes of that time – photographs of friends, postcards and letters. I suppose he wanted to protect his wife and children from his memories.

Mine was a country childhood. I remember long, hot summers spent playing in the fields and woods. I slid down hayricks, raced my bike along the flat Norfolk roads, and swung on farm gates watching the cows driven in for milking. From the front of our house you could see for about five miles to the villages in the distance. Their church spires offered the only landmarks in an otherwise flat landscape.

My home and the land around it have remained important in my life. I have always returned to Brooke whenever I felt cornered or low. Its tranquillity helps to calm my mind. Although many of my childhood experiences were troubled,

Norfolk has never ceased to offer comfort. Much has changed over the years. When I was small it was still possible to walk to the village across the fields. You could climb over the fence at the bottom of our garden and then run through the corn to Brooke. But later an old people's home was built at the back of the house.

Our home was set slightly apart from the village, at the end of a small lane. The lane led off the main Norwich road, where, when I was at secondary school, I would wait for the bus. Norwich was only seven miles away, but it seemed like another world. Walking in the opposite direction to that distant metropolis, you passed the church, and the farm where Mum would send us for eggs or extra milk, and arrived at the centre of Brooke, where there was a mere, two village pubs and the local primary school. Opposite the school was the forge where my uncle John worked as the village blacksmith. He's retired now, and the forge is deserted – boarded up and empty.

We were not a poor family, but with three children my parents had to work hard. My dad left the house each morning at seven to travel to Norwich, where he worked as a coach-builder for Eastern Counties Garage. He was employed there for thirty-nine years, and his work was very important to him. When the story about my transsexuality broke in the press he suffered terrible anxiety about how his workmates would react. He was a private man, and found it difficult to confide in people outside the family. Luckily his colleagues were supportive. Dad was popular at work, and had earned their friendship and admiration.

My mother was a traditional mum. While we were young she stayed at home and devoted herself to our welfare. She liked us to look smart and fed us on good, healthy country food – lots of soups and stews in the winter, to stave off colds and influenza. In the summer she would take us fruit picking to earn a little extra money. As a small child I hated to be separated from her, and followed her wherever she went, sitting at her feet while she cooked and cleaned.

Pam, my sister, I adored from the moment she was born. Terry was too old to be a real playmate, but with only just over a year between us, Pam and I became inseparable. She never made my being a boy a reason to exclude me from her games, and even shared her toys with me. She gave me one of her dolls, which I named Cynthia. Pam's favourite doll was Susan, and we would dress Susan and Cynthia in their finest clothes and play make-believe with them.

From the very first, there was an air of secrecy about these games. Both Pam and I knew instinctively that Mum and Dad would not approve of my playing with dolls. We took an oath never to tell them, and from that moment Pam became a fellow conspirator. She accepted me as I was, and treated me exactly as if I were a sister, but she was careful never to tell Dad about Cynthia and our playtime.

I still have Cynthia. She sits on my dressing table – old and bald and adorable.

Our favourite game was dressing up. We loved climbing into Mum's best dresses and staggering around the room in her high heels, our faces covered in powder and our mouths red with shiny lipstick. Grown-up women seemed such elegant, mysterious and glamorous beings. I would become so engrossed in my make-believe that I would lose all sense of being a boy – I felt like any little girl posing before the mirror in her mummy's clothes. But as I approached my fifth birthday I was in for a rude awakening. School loomed on the horizon, and with it came the growing awareness that I was not like the other boys. The rough world of the classroom was to teach me some harsh lessons. The real traumas of my childhood were about to begin.

I loathed school from the very first day. My mum walked me to the gates, and I clung to her and wailed. I didn't stop crying all day, and my face was still wet with tears when she came to collect me at 3.30. The teacher told my mother not to worry. 'They're often a bit upset to begin with,' she said. 'He'll soon get used to it.' She was wrong. Every day my mother had a battle to get me to school. It was a battle she fought on her own. She didn't like to worry Dad with stories of my hysteria, and so she would sit me on her bike and wheel me to school each morning. The following year, when my sister joined me, Pam would sit in the bike basket and Mum would push us both the short distance to the gates. The other mothers were puzzled. 'It's only a little walk,' they said. 'Why don't you let them go by themselves?' My mother made some excuse, but

4

the truth was, if she hadn't taken me, I would never have gone at all. Until I was eight, when Pam and I began to walk there by ourselves, I cried each and every morning when Mum left me. I can still remember the distress I felt as I watched her walk away. I would shout and struggle to reach her. Many mornings I was not the only one with tears pouring down my face. It hurt Mum to see me so unhappy.

Terry had been a successful and popular boy in his class. He was good at sports and quick to learn. As his brother, much was expected of me. I disappointed those hopes at every turn. I was small, painfully shy, and terrified of sports. From the first day I knew that I was a misfit, and in such a tiny village school it wasn't possible for me to melt into the crowd. I stuck out like a sore thumb. Even in the infant classes I failed to integrate. In the nativity play at Christmas I was utterly humiliated to be playing the part of a shepherd, dressed in a tea towel, or a wise man with a false beard, carrying a cardboard box covered with gold foil. I longed to be cast as Mary, or at least as one of the pretty angels all in white with wings and tinsel haloes. I identified entirely with a female world, but in Norfolk in the 1950s, boys were very much boys and girls were girls. It was not acceptable for boys to play girls' games. As I got older the sexes drew even further apart, and my confusion became even more apparent.

I was bullied. The bane of my life was the headmaster. He knew I was shy and under-confident, yet he was forever calling me out to stand in front of the class. He'd ask me to read, or to perform some calculation on the blackboard, and when I made a mistake, he slapped me round the head, or threw the board rubber at me. I lived in a state of perpetual terror, and would often go home at night with my ears red and stinging from his smacks. There was one other boy in the class who got picked on; his name was Matthew and, like me, he was small, weak and lacking in confidence. The headmaster had it in for both of us. I suppose he despised what he saw as our 'weakness' and thought it was his job to turn us into tough little boys. In our peer group the ability to fight for yourself was a vital part of attracting friends. Needless to say, Matthew and I stood alone and ignored in the playground.

I longed for the afternoon bell, when I could escape and run home to the safety and security of my family. Soon I wasn't even able to make it through the day. I began to play truant.

My uncle's forge was directly opposite the school. My desk was by the window, and I could see the people coming and going with their horses. If my mum came to call she would lean her bike against the wall and take the path down the side of the forge to my gran's house. The sight of that bike would set my heart racing. I would ask to be excused, sneak out of the door, and creep past the classroom window. Then, running like the wind, I would dash across the road and hide behind my uncle's big, black dustbins. When Mum emerged from the bungalow, I would plead illness and beg her to take me home. Other times I would find my way back to our house, and hide in among the bean rows at the bottom of the garden. One day I was spotted by a neighbour, and my mother hauled me out and dragged me back to school. The headmaster was always very understanding while she was there, but the minute she left he would whack me across the legs.

I was no dunce at school, but the headmaster did ask to speak to my parents. 'Barry has trouble concentrating,' he told them. And he was right. Most of the time I felt too intimidated by him and by my classmates to focus on my schoolwork. My sister became my protector. I believed that she had magic powers and, by repeating certain spells, could shield me from the terrors of the day. We walked to school hand in hand, and I would beg her to 'spirit the day away'. 'Make it go as quickly as possible,' I pleaded. 'Don't let anyone pick on me.' We developed a ritual, and I made her repeat certain magic incantations over and over, checking that she didn't omit anything and leave me vulnerable to attack.

If primary school was bad, secondary school was a nightmare. I was forever getting beaten up. I was punched and kicked, and often sported a black eye or a split lip at the end of the day. 'What happened to you?' Dad would ask when I got home. I would lie. 'I tripped,' I'd say. 'I fell off my bike.' If I told him the truth, he would try to toughen me up. But it was no use. I couldn't fight; aggression made me feel sick.

I began to bribe my way out of trouble. My dad collected coins and the cards from cigarette packets. I stole them and offered them along with money, in the hope that the bullies would leave me alone. I pretended it was no big deal.

'I've got plenty of money,' I said, handing out my savings from my paper round. They took the 'gifts', but the persecution continued. On autumn nights a small gang of village boys would wait in the lane leading to my house. 'Cissey Cossey,' they chanted. I can still feel the terror today. Even when I grew a few feet, they wouldn't leave me be. I may have been tall, but I was skinny with it, and no match for their strength.

It was in sports that I suffered the most. The other boys had begun to develop hairy chests, but I stayed smooth and girlish. In the changing rooms I was pushed and shoved. Boys would run past me and give my balls a sharp squeeze. I was a disaster at football. If the ball came towards me, I'd run the other way. 'Kick it, Cossey,' the teacher screamed. 'Kick the bloody ball, you imbecile!' When I did make an effort, and got the football, some large, sweaty boy would descend on me, kick me swiftly on the shins, and disappear with the prize. I hated it.

All through secondary school I remained a solitary child, eaten up by my sense of shame and failure. If it had not been for the love I found at home, I might have gone under. Mum and Dad may not have understood what I was going through, but they worked hard to provide a good life for Terry, Pam and me. We were a very close family, and I have happy memories from my childhood as well as sad ones.

At home, insulated from the pressures of the outside world, life became more bearable. Pam and I would wander through the fields lost in games of make-believe. In her company I felt relaxed and accepted. On Saturday mornings we raced down to the church to watch weddings. Afterwards we collected up handfuls of confetti in paper bags. We rushed home, wrapped ourselves in Mum's lace curtains, and tossed the confetti up into the air.

Pam had a friend called Jennifer, with whom I became close. Jennifer lived on a farm at the opposite end of the village, and I visited her. I suppose she thought of me as a kind of boyfriend. We were very young, and it was entirely innocent. Going to her house was a real treat. I loved farms, and she had a black pony that I was allowed to ride. But, best of all, she had an older sister. Jennifer's sister was heaven. She wore bright-red lipstick, hairspray and stilettos. In the farmhouse was a boxroom where Jennifer and I played, and, tossed among the boxes of old clothes, were a pile of her sister's discarded high heels. We would try them on and clatter up and down the room. I loved the clicking noise they made on the bare floor.

As we both approached puberty, dressing up became a more serious business for Pam and me. I loved Helen Shapiro, and we had all of her records. Dusty Springfield and Cilla Black were also favourites. We'd put the records on the gramophone, stand on the table, and mime to them. Pam wound a long, black scarf around her head in imitation of a beehive. I found a brown scarf and imagined myself to be Ms Shapiro. We dressed in two of Mum's pretty summer dresses, and covered our faces with make-up – lipstick, false eyelashes, rouge. Giggling like mad, we would wiggle our hips, flutter our eyelashes, and sing our hearts out.

'Don't tell Mum,' I warned Pam afterwards. But I didn't need to say it. We shared a secret pact.

'You're going to have to watch that one, Bob. He could grow up funny.' I remember these words, spoken by a well-meaning uncle one Christmas time. They filled me with dread. The fear that I would turn out to be gay must have been in my dad's mind. He was a conventional man, and in the 1950s homosexuality was a great taboo, and the thought would have alarmed him. If I was showing signs of effeminacy, it was his duty to toughen me up, and if I was physically weak, he must teach me to defend myself. To Dad's mind, the male world was a tough place. He wasn't going to stand by and watch a son of his persecuted. He encouraged Terry to teach me boxing moves. 'Take him outside,' he said. 'Teach him how to punch properly.' Reluctantly I followed Terry out into the garden. 'So you can look after yourself,' explained my brother, putting up his fists. It was hopeless. I would never defend myself, and I'd get clobbered and start crying. Mum would come running. 'Leave him alone,' she'd shout. It wasn't Terry's fault. I know he still feels bad about it to this day, but he was only trying to help me get by. He was my older brother, it was his job.

Dad had a licence for two guns and, like most countrymen, he'd walk over the fields looking for rabbits and pigeons. Terry loved to go with him and, when I was old enough, Dad took me along too. I hated everything about those expeditions: the smell of the cartridges, the sight of the dead and bloodied pigeons, the crack of the shotgun. In the fields the young bullocks would come crowding around us, their eyes wild and their nostrils flaring. I would run away in terror, with the sound of Dad's laughter ringing in my ears. Myxomatosis was rife at that time, and Dad killed the blind, diseased rabbits to put them out of their misery. He didn't like to waste valuable shot on them, and clubbed them to death with his stick. I would turn away, sick to the stomach.

At home Pam and I kept pet rabbits and, of course, they bred. Dad was a practical man with a family to feed and so, when the baby rabbits grew up, he killed them for the pot. I was appalled. One time I caught sight of his silhouette on the shed floor. He was holding a rabbit by the back legs and chopping at its neck with his hand. I can still hear the rabbit scream. To the other village boys all these things were perfectly normal. They liked to hunt, they adored football, they even enjoyed a brawl. I couldn't seem to adapt to the world in which I found myself. I felt as though I were being brainwashed.

Dad earned a little extra money on a Sunday by cutting men's hair. It was a skill had learnt from his father. He'd put down some lino in the shed at the side of the house, and on it placed an old dressing table. He set out his brushes, combs and electric clippers with neat precision, and we were told never to touch them. It was a place of great mystery and dread to me. The local farmers and men from the village would come along in the morning, and sit smoking and laughing in the shed while they waited to be trimmed. Dad kept a pile of pin-up magazines to amuse them, and I'd hear the deep and secret laughter of these adult men as I lay hiding in my bedroom. I always felt profoundly inadequate, and the idea of speaking to them terrified me. Terry had no such qualms. Dad would invite him in and boast a little about his son's academic and sporting achievements. When they caught sight of me their faces fell. It was probably my imagination, but none the less, I was crippled with a sense of failure and shame.

With the advent of puberty, my isolation from my peer group became even more pronounced. In my last year at school

I had begun to experience dizzy spells that were close to black-outs. I lost my vision, shook, and had to grip on to something to stop myself falling. The dizziness would pass, but it left me drained and drenched in sweat. Initially Mum and Dad thought that this, like my other illnesses, was a way for me to grab attention. But when these 'spells' continued they took me to a local doctor, who referred me to a specialist in Norwich. They took tests, asked a hundred questions, and even stuck electrodes on my head. They asked me about my sexual feelings, but, with my mum present, I didn't feel able to express myself. The conclusion of the doctors was that it was something to do with 'growing up' and 'hormones'. 'It'll cure itself in time,' they said. Looking back, I now see that those dizzy spells were the first signs of a hormone imbalance in my body, rather like the hot flushes that some women experience during the menopause.

My first sexual experiences were with boys from the village. I must have been about thirteen years old. Ben was older than me, and he had a dog which he took for regular walks. I liked his company. He was a good-looking boy, with a cheerful and frank nature. When I saw him pass our house in the direction of the fields, I called my dog, Tiger, and ran to catch up with him. His dog was a bitch, and she and Tiger would sniff around each other, growing ever more excited. The bitch had been spayed, so it wasn't necessary to separate the two animals.

One time Ben began to play with himself as he watched the dogs. He turned to look at me. 'Don't it turn you on?' he asked. 'No,' I replied, staring in fascination at his erection. He let me watch while he continued to masturbate. I had no urge to touch myself, but couldn't take my eyes off Ben. It was as though I had never seen a penis before.

The next time it happened my sister and one of her friends were with us. I nudged Pam, my eyes alight with innocent enthusiasm. 'You've *got* to see this. It's incredible!' But Pam was not impressed. She and the friend bolted, their faces white with shock, and I was left with the unabashed Ben, wondering what it was I'd said to upset her.

The second incident was with a local boy called Robin. Again, he was older than me, but we were both still very young. This experience was more explicitly sexual, and as such was fraught with guilt and secrecy. My brother had a rather tattered copy of a nudist magazine. Like my dad's magazines, this was less pornography, more pin-up. But at that time the mere sight of the naked female body was enough to send any country lad into spasms of ecstasy. Any lad but me, that was. To me women seemed familiar and safe. They were certainly not the objects of curiosity and desire. Boys were the focus of my erotic imaginings.

In a bid for Robin's attention, I stole the magazine, and we took off into the fields to read it. In the camouflage of the waist-high corn, Robin lay down and began to masturbate. 'Why don't you do it, too?' he asked. Desperate not to lose his friendship, but utterly incapable of touching my own body, I told him that I hadn't had an erection as yet. Innocence was my cover as I exclaimed about the size of his penis. 'I hope mine'll grow that big,' I said. Flattered, and lordly with the wisdom of his few extra years, Robin lay back, closed his eyes and graciously allowed me to play with him.

My arousal disturbed me. I knew that it wasn't right for me to want to touch other boys, and I felt guilty and ashamed. Running against these negative feelings was the thrill and excitement I had felt. I had initiated a pattern that was to run throughout my adolescent sexual experiences; as I touched Robin I thought of myself as a girl touching a boy. I looked down at his face and imagined that the hand he felt caressing him was a woman's hand. It was that fantasy, of me as the female offering sexual pleasure to the male, that gave me my own erotic thrill.

At school we started sex education classes. They were an innovation of the new curriculum, and caused much excitement. The teacher pinned two large pictures on the black-board: one of the male genitalia, the other of the female. The facts of life were news to nobody; we were country children after all, surrounded by fields of procreating animals. None the less, there was a great deal of giggling and shuffling as the teacher stepped back from the anatomical diagrams. I stared with fascination at the picture of the adult male genitalia. It didn't strike me as strange that I displayed almost no interest in my own penis. When I did masturbate, I did it lying face

11

down on the bed, rubbing myself against a pillow. The idea of actually handling myself repulsed me. I even sat down on the toilet to urinate in order to avoid contact.

When I got home, Dad questioned me closely about that class. 'How did it make you feel?' he asked. Instinctively I lied. 'It made me feel excited, Dad,' I told him. 'Good,' he replied. 'That's good. It's natural to feel that way.'

I did have one heterosexual experience around this time. Cathy was a friend of my sister's, and I'd known her throughout my childhood. She found me attractive and made no secret of the fact. She was sexually precocious and, one day when my parents were both out, she took me upstairs to my bedroom and closed the door behind us. We ended up having intercourse with her lying on top of me. I find it hard to relate to the memory of that sexual encounter. I do remember that she produced a Durex that seemed to me to be impossibly large! I didn't climax, and remained distant from the entire event. I do remember being intrigued by her breasts, however. She was a chubby girl and, compared with my sister, had a well-developed chest. I felt envious. It was a brief encounter, and I mimed pleasure, sustaining an erection by role reversal – I imagined that I was her being made love to by a man. We were both tender and gentle with one another. But, after it was all over, I felt sad, confused and disappointed. Once again I stood outside conventional experience. I was on my own.

At school my behaviour became more and more singular. I was obsessed by hair – hair on legs, hair under arms, pubic hair. The gym master had a wonderfully hairy chest, and I would stare at him longingly, aching to reach out and touch his dark curls. Teased by other boys about my own lack of body hair, I had tried to encourage it to grow. I shaved my legs with Dad's razor, and, being unfamiliar with the process, had cut my leg, leaving a deep scar. But I soon began to relish my smooth skin. I liked to imagine that men were admiring my long, hairless legs.

I began to make subtle and then not so subtle adjustments to my school uniform. I wore a shirt with a large, floppy collar instead of the regulation kind. 'Why are you wearing that?'

demanded one master, pointing at the offending garment. 'My other one's in the wash, sir,' I lied.

I was desperate to have breasts, and convinced myself that they were growing. My nipples were larger and more sensitive than most boys'. I stuffed the top pocket of my school blazer with pens, pencils and erasers, to create a 'bust'. I liked the sensation of weight, the feeling of movement against my chest.

My hair became a battleground between Dad and me. 'Get your bloody hair cut,' he would moan. 'Cut' meant short back and sides, but I hated to show my ears. When I reached my eleventh birthday, I persuaded him that it was fashionable to have longer hair. Secretly, I longed for hair like Pam's, that would reach down below my shoulders, but for the time being, just getting Dad to agree to a length that covered my ears was a big enough battle. When Mum had her hair cut, I collected up the clippings and created my own idiosyncratic fantasy. I would tie up the strands with an elastic band, and then attempt to grip it under my own locks.

Pam was beginning to wear make-up – despite Dad's complaints – and I copied her. I put a little mascara on my lashes and darkened my eyebrows with kohl. There was no sexual thrill for me in this, nor had there been in dressing up. In fact, the make-up, the long hair, and the refashioned school uniform cost me dear in taunts and bullying. But my instincts to be female, to behave and be accepted as a woman, were so strong that I had no choice. Being a 'boy' and all that that entailed was far more painful than trying, in my own rather stumbling and inarticulate way, to be a girl.

While I was still at school, I started a part-time job at a butcher's in the next village. The butcher was a quiet and rather gentle man, and I quite enjoyed the Saturdays I spent in his shop. I cleaned out the displays, stocked the shelves, and, best of all, made the sausages. I put the meat into the top of the machine and then watched it emerge as one long, smooth sausage. Then, one hand's length at a time, I twisted the meat and tucked it through. I liked the sensuous feel of the cool meat. I think I must have found it erotic, for my sausages grew steadily longer each week!

One day at school, our teacher asked what we intended to do when we left. It was possible to leave at fifteen in those days, and although I would be fifteen that summer, I was hoping to be allowed to finish my education at the end of term. Everyone had a definite idea of what they wished to do: some were staying on and going into higher education, others were joining family trades. As usual, I hadn't a clue. One by one the teacher went round the class, and I knew that whatever I said would be met by sniggers and laughter. Then I had an inspiration. 'I'm going to be a butcher, sir!' For a moment there was a stunned silence. Cissie Cossey, a butcher! The giggle started, but I felt I had surprised them. They expected me to say, 'Hairdresser, sir' or 'Fashion designer'. To their minds I was the epitome of camp.

Mum and Dad encouraged me. 'If you like it well enough, why don't you stay?' said Mum. So it was decided. I would be taken on full-time as a butcher's apprentice.

It was so obviously a bad idea – a last-ditch attempt to prove myself a normal adolescent boy. I didn't last more than two months. It was horrendous. No more shelf stocking or sausage making – now I had to learn how to butcher meat properly. I had to know how to dissect a pig's head, cut it in half and dig out all the meat from the various sections. I remember holding this head, the glassy eyeball staring straight at me, and with one or two sweeps having to sever it in two. I used to perform the operation with my eyes shut! It would have been only a matter of time before I lost a finger.

As an apprentice you had to have your own set of knives. These were bought for me, and deducted from my first week's wages. That Friday I went home with less money than I had started with! The only compensation for working was the thought of the financial gain. Now all I had was a set of repulsive knives, and blood under my fingernails. I began to look around for something else. Norwich was the obvious place to start.

2

Escape from Brooke

Norwich was the big city, and offered an escape from the tiny world of Brooke. Every day I scanned the newspapers looking for a job. I was a little over fifteen years old, with no qualifications and no particular skills. But when I saw an advertisement for a shop assistant in a men's boutique, I thought it was worth a try. At school I had been mocked for my interest in fashion; now that interest might be of use.

The shop was one of a chain of three. Not exactly high fashion, it sold army surplus alongside the tie-dyed T-shirts and flares that were the style of the 1970s. Workmen bought their overalls there, and they even stocked wellington boots. I wasn't about to complain. After the butcher's shop, with its trails of blood-stained sawdust, this was Mecca. Taking a deep breath, I marched in.

'I've come about the job.'

The manager, Mr Hunt, looked surprised. 'I'm sorry,' he said. 'We're looking for a young boy.'

'But I am a boy!' I exclaimed, blushing fiercely. He apologized.

'With that long hair and all, I took you for a girl.'

I didn't know whether to feel elated or ashamed.

He must have liked the way I looked, because he offered me the job on the spot.

And I loved it. Dad was none too pleased. 'Bit of a cissy job, isn't it?' he grumbled. But after the traumas of the butcher's shop, he was relieved to see me smiling again.

I got myself a bus pass and caught the Norwich bus every morning from the bottom of our road. As soon as I was out of sight of the house, I would take out a small hand-mirror and 'do my face'. My make-up was very subtle: a little mascara, eye pencil, and a touch of rouge. But it gave me the confidence

I needed. Opposite the shop there was a building site, and the workmen would whistle as I passed. Perhaps they were sending me up, but since so many people mistook me for a girl, I liked to think their admiration was genuine.

I worked hard at my new job, and was popular with customers. After a few months the manager transferred me to a smaller branch, specializing in army surplus. I was given the key to the shop, and entrusted with the task of cashing up at the end of the day. It was quite a responsibility for a boy of fifteen, and my self-confidence began to blossom.

The assistants at the main branch were all a good deal older than me, and, to my young mind, they seemed remarkably sophisticated. When I delivered the takings at the end of the day I would often hang around and listen to their chat. It was on one of these occasions that I first heard the Mischief Tavern mentioned.

The Mischief Tavern was Norwich's one and only gay pub. Homosexuality was a great mystery to me. I knew no gay people, and at home the subject was rarely mentioned. When it was spoken of, it was in tones of the fiercest disapproval. The Norfolk I knew was very working class, and homosexuality was a taboo subject. The pub in Norwich was probably the only gay meeting place in the entire county, and it was under constant attack. The windows would be smashed by gangs of youths, or the police would threaten a raid. Most homosexuals at the time were closet, and that was how society wished them to stay; silent and ashamed. I remember that there were two gay men who lived together in a nearby village. They were pointed out to me as 'dirty queers' or 'disgusting bastards'. 'Don't you ever speak to either of them,' Dad warned me. I was never left in any doubt that homosexuality was unacceptable to my father, and would shock even my more lenient and understanding mother. As my dad got older, and was able to understand more about the subject, he became increasingly tolerant, but when I was fifteen, to have been gay would have brought disgrace to the family.

I was left with a dilemma: my sexual desire for men led me towards the homosexual community, but my fear of exposure urged me to stay clear. In the end any thirst for knowledge won the day. I had lived in isolation so long, not understanding my sexual urges, that I was hungry for the society of others like myself. All adolescents need to define themselves socially, and I was no exception.

I walked past the Mischief Tavern a number of times before I plucked up the courage to go inside. It was a quaint pub by a bridge, and I saw hardly anyone going either in or out. There was a bar at the front of the building, but it was the lounge at the back that was designated a 'gay bar'. To get to it you had to walk down an alleyway and through a side door. The minute you turned off the main street, it would be obvious where you were headed. I stood there one lunchtime, my heart pounding, working up the nerve to open the door to this new world. I looked up and down the road, anxiously scanning the passers-by for any familiar faces. 'My dad'll kill me,' I thought. It felt like that moment when, standing on the edge of a pool of freezing water, you steel yourself for the dive and the rush of cold on your skin.

Well, I did it. I don't know quite what I expected. Scenes of wild debauchery? Loud music? Drag queens? Inside, it was quite an ordinary little pub. The decor was tasteful but slightly theatrical, with signed photographs of celebrities on the wall. There were one or two men sitting at tables drinking. The landlady, Billy, had a brusque manner, but she must have realized that it was my 'first time', for she softened her tone when speaking to me. She was a Londoner, and had been quite a society girl in her day, running a nightclub. She had retired to Norwich to take charge of this pub. I sat down with my shandy and looked about me. The men in the bar seemed perfectly 'straight', and not the effeminate creatures of my imagination. I was surprised by the discovery. I had thought that all gay men would act like Kenneth Williams.

That was my introduction to the gay world. Despite my feelings of paranoia, I felt safe in the Mischief Tavern. It was a great relief to be amongst people who, like myself, would have been described by society as 'abnormal'. I began to drink in there regularly, and it was there that I made my first gay friend, Adrian.

Adrian was a hairdresser. He was a few years older than me, but we had a great deal in common: we were both tall, pretty and effeminate. We were also terrified of being 'found

17

out' by our families. We started meeting for lunch, and then in the evenings. Adrian owned a car and would pick me up at the top of the lane near my house. I didn't introduce him to Mum and Dad; I was scared that he might seem too obviously effeminate. We went to the cinema together, or, when we could afford it, to a restaurant. There was no sexual relationship between us. We were more like girlfriends out on the town for a night.

Dressing for those evenings was an exercise in diplomacy. If I wore anything too outrageous Dad would protest, but I needed to look my best. I compromised with chest-hugging multicoloured T-shirts and tight white jeans. Dad still complained. 'I don't know how you can go out like that,' he moaned. 'You look like a poof.'

Now that I worked in fashion, I could blind him with science. 'It's the trend, Dad,' I would explain, and he was forced to concede.

As soon as I got into Adrian's car, I put on my mascara, rouge and lip gloss, and we would speed off into the night. We were desperately inhibited, and never actually *did* anything on these trips. We were quite happy sitting in some coffee house staring at the attractive men walking past.

Although Adrian and I got on well, the differences between us soon became apparent. Adrian never wore make-up and couldn't understand why I did. He was a pretty boy, but, unlike me, he had no desire to be taken for a girl. 'If you look too feminine, you'll never meet anyone in the gay scene,' he explained. 'Gay men like men. That's the whole point.' But I enjoyed going to pubs and clubs looking like a girl. I had no words to explain the compulsion, and he was unable to change my mind.

The two of us became familiar in the small and highly secretive homosexual community. We received invitations to all sorts of parties. Traditionally, these celebrations took place on a Friday or a Saturday night, and they were highly clandestine. I felt as though I had joined a new sect. One Saturday Adrian rang me up. 'There's a party tonight in the outskirts of Norwich. It's quite a smart do. Can you come?' I said yes, told Mum and Dad I was 'going for a drink with my mates' and did my best to dress up without incurring Dad's wrath.

The house was set in huge grounds, with tiered gardens, and inside it was spectacular – a blaze of crystal chandeliers. In one room there were men dancing together, and in another, tables loaded with drink and food. The people were amazing – all types, from the camp to the conservative. I recognized familiar faces from the local TV station, hairdressers, shop assistants, and even two very strange-looking women who I now realize must have been transvestites.

I was asked to dance by men who in the outside world would have passed for 'straight'. As I moved around the room, slightly high on wine, I felt as though I were in a dream. There were many things left for me to resolve about myself, but this freedom was dizzying. I revelled in it.

Adrian introduced me to two people who were to play an important part in my life: David, who had been brought up in Norwich and now lived in London, and the host of the party, Neville.

Neville was a wealthy man in his early forties. He owned a chain of businesses in Norwich, dressed immaculately, and liked to be thought of as 'straight' by his business associates. He was to have a profound influence on me, and give me my first taste of a life of elegance and sophistication. That evening he was dressed in a finely tailored Italian suit and a silk shirt. We began talking and got on well. There was never anything sexual between us; I think Neville felt sorry for me. I was young and painfully shy. He took me under his wing. Besides, it did his ego good to be seen with an attractive teenage boy. 'Pretty little chickens' we were called. I became Neville's 'little chicken', and he introduced me to a brave new world.

Neville was not overly fond of the gay scene in Norwich. When he wanted to go clubbing he drove up to London, where he had a flat and a lover. Back in Norfolk, he preferred to drink in the straight pubs. And it was in one of these bars that he introduced me to a friend of his called Alan.

I was sweet sixteen and had never been kissed. Alan was handsome, rugged, and solidly heterosexual. I fell in love at first sight. He knew Neville through business, and often teased him about his homosexuality. So when Alan was as smitten as I, Neville found the situation hilarious. 'But I thought he was a girl!' Alan protested, after he had shown his admiration.

This cut no ice with the beaming Neville. 'There you are,' he crowed, 'I always knew that you were one of the guys!' Perhaps Neville had deliberately set the whole thing up. Desperately flattered, I sat in silence as Alan defended himself from Neville's onslaught.

When Neville got up to buy the next round of drinks, Alan leant across the table and whispered, 'I think you are the most beautiful person I have ever seen. I would like to see you again. Would you agree to meet me on your own?'

'Yes,' I nodded.

We arranged the time and the place. 'Don't say anything to him,' hissed Alan, as Neville returned to the table.

We decided to spend a weekend together in Alan's caravan. I told my parents that I was going to a party in Norwich and would be back late Sunday afternoon. He picked me up near the bus station and we drove to the coast. It was a bizarre experience. We were both desperately shy, and knew almost nothing about each other. I was so engrossed in the Mills and Boon fantasy playing in my head that I hardly stopped to consider how strange a situation it really was. I had never had sex with a man and neither had Alan; we had no idea what to expect. I know now that he was working out some homosexual feeling, but at the time I convinced myself that he fancied me as a girl. In my mind we were a man and a woman embarking on a passionate affair.

I made few demands sexually. The exhilaration of being kissed and held were enough for me. I knew that in homosexual relationships there was an active and a passive partner, and I supposed that I would be passive. But I had absolutely no interest in anal sex. I had tried at home to prepare myself for penetration, and had found it unerotic and unpleasantly painful. As Alan and I drove away from Norwich, the caravan in tow, I didn't know quite what to expect.

He parked in a corner of a quiet trailer park. Since I never stepped out of the caravan for the entire weekend, I have no memory of the landscape of the place. I was terrified of being seen, and stayed away from the windows when Alan ventured out to get food or drink. The sky was overcast, and the caravan small and stuffy. But I couldn't have cared less. I was with a man who found me attractive. A heterosexual man who wanted me!

In the end, the sex was rather inhibited. I so disliked my genitalia that I refused to let him see me naked. I took off my trousers, but kept my pants on. He lay on top of me and rubbed against me. Since this was the way I masturbated, I was more than happy. I was also glad to touch and caress him. 'I'm in love,' I thought, as I nestled my head against Alan's hairy chest and smelt the warm, musky scent of his neck. I felt something approaching sexual happiness for the first time in my life. That night I lay awake and watched him as he slept. He was beautiful, so beautiful, and he found *me* attractive! He wanted *me*!

The dream did not last. We saw each other a few more times after that weekend, but Alan's interest had waned. The episode had alarmed him, and caused him to question his masculinity. It was also obvious that I was infatuated and, as it later transpired, he couldn't afford to get involved.

It was a sobering experience. My involvement with the gay world was by no means over, but that relationship had sent out signals that were, with time, to become ever clearer. I was turned on by men, yet I could not function properly in a homosexual relationship. I was not interested in anal inter-course, and although I fantasized about penetration, that fantasy was of heterosexual intercourse. It was sex in the head. I was stuck in a no man's land. Later Neville told me that Alan was married. I had been lied to and spurned. I felt doubly betrayed.

I lived with the constant fear of exposure, and I began to dream of leaving Brooke. Neville had a flat in London, and he promised on several occasions to take me there. I'd been to London as a kid on school trips to the zoo or Madame Tussaud's, but I was hungry for a very different city. A city that only the sophisticated Neville could show me.

After much pestering, he agreed to take me. We drove to London in Neville's car early one Sunday morning, stopping off at his flat for a late breakfast. 'We'll go to the Pig and Whistle for lunch,' he announced. 'It's a gay pub in Victoria.' I was delighted, and slipped away to the bathroom to fix my face. Neville followed me, and stood at my shoulder as I painstakingly covered each lash with its coat of mascara. 'Take a piece of advice from me,' he said. 'You don't need all that stuff on your face. Men don't like it, and, in any case, you're beautiful as you are.' Normally I listened to Neville's every word, and followed his advice slavishly. But on this matter I refused to be moved. Looking feminine was too important to me. It gave me my sense of liberation.

Nothing I had seen in Norwich prepared me for the cultural shock of the Pig and Whistle. Back at home there were perhaps thirty or forty people on the gay scene, but on that Sunday in Victoria the pub was so crowded that men were flowing out on to the streets. There was another gay pub twenty yards away that was every bit as full. Everywhere I looked I saw gay men – laughing, talking, drinking. I was stunned. There was such an open, easy atmosphere, so different from the quiet paranoia of the Mischief Tavern. Here nobody seemed to mind who saw them or what they thought. They were free to behave as they liked.

I received some admiring glances, and soon got chatting. I was invited to drinks by one man, and to dinner by another. I had to be back in Norfolk that night, so I was unable to accept, but the readiness of these people to befriend me was very significant. I began to see that living in London might be possible. Here was a social life all ready and waiting.

As we drove back up the darkened motorway, I had much to think over. Not least on my list of concerns was the strain of the double life I was leading. Nobody in my family knew the first thing about this secret social life. I needed to explain the very complicated emotions that I was experiencing, but was too terrified to speak out. That evening I made a decision. I would take a risk; I would talk to Terry.

If I had been an ordinary boy, Terry would have been my hero. He was good at sports, rugged, smart and popular. I admired him terribly, but I was also in awe of him. I should have been a proper brother, I thought to myself, instead of which I'm an embarrassment. Terry sensed my awkwardness and took it upon himself to encourage me. He wanted us to become real 'mates'. Much to Dad's delight, we began to make a real effort, and started going out together regularly on a Tuesday night. We went bowling, or for a drink in the pub.

Those evenings weren't easy for me. Terry urged me to chat up girls. 'She's pretty, isn't she?' he would say, eyeing up a passing woman. 'What d'ye reckon, Barry?' Feeling awkward and embarrassed, I was stuck for words. Terry sensed my embarrassment and I felt bad for him. 'If only I had the courage to tell him what's on my mind', I thought. But I was terrified of his rejection. What if he thought me disgusting? What if he told Dad?

Things came to a head when I developed a crush on one of Terry's friends from work. He was tremendously good-looking, and came bowling with us on a number of occasions. He was always polite, but in his eyes I was just Terry's little brother. I was smitten. I couldn't keep my eyes off him, and he became aware of my admiration. He caught my idolizing gaze and frowned a little before turning away. In that one glance I was destroyed. I saw myself with blinding clarity as a pretty, effeminate boy whose attentions were not wanted. I blushed a deep red and longed for the ground to swallow me up. 'What's wrong, mate?' said Terry, noticing my discomfort.

'Nothing,' I mumbled, reaching for my drink.

I began to make excuses to get out of the Tuesday night meetings. Terry was puzzled. He had no idea of what it might be that was troubling me. We had grown up together. He didn't see me as the outside world did. I decided to confide in him. We were sitting in a pub, and I'd had a few drinks to give me courage. I began hesitantly: 'Terry, I want to talk to you about something. It's something I find difficult to explain.'

'Go on,' he encouraged.

It was now or never. 'I'm attracted to your friend . . . in a sexual way!' I had said it. I sat back in my chair and waited for the storm to break. But nothing happened. Terry was looking at me sympathetically. 'Is that all?' he asked. He told me not to worry. 'All boys go through that stage, it's quite normal.'

'No,' I said. 'It's more serious. I fantasize about being a woman, not a man. Are those homosexual feelings?'

My brother reassured me. 'It's nothing, Barry. You'll grow out of it in time.'

His advice may not have been expert, but it hardly mattered. It was such a relief to talk to someone that I felt quite exhilarated. I wanted to believe that he was right, that this was just a phase, and that one day soon everything would slot into place, and I would no longer feel isolated. 'Terry's older than me', I thought. 'He knows what he's talking about.'

'Have you told Dad?' he asked.

'No, I daren't.'

He was reassuring. 'I'm sure he'd understand.'

But I wasn't so sure. 'No, I can't. I really can't.' We left it at that. The conversation brought us much closer, but it failed to make life any easier. Terry had no idea of how involved I was in the gay scene. And he was wrong on two scores: firstly, Dad would not understand what I was doing, and secondly, this was not a phase that I was about to grow out of.

I spent more time with Adrian's friend David. He came home to Norfolk at weekends, and I loved to hear him talk about his wild London life. David kept his homosexuality a secret from his parents but, unlike me, he was free to do as he liked in the metropolis. I lay in bed at night and dreamt of London. There I could wear the clothes I liked, smother my face in make-up, grow my hair down to my waist. I plotted my escape in elaborate nocturnal fantasies. Then two incidents occurred that convinced me that escape might be more necessary than I'd thought. I was living on borrowed time.

One afternoon I was delivering the takings to the main branch when 'Peggy', the bus driver, came whizzing past at the wheel of his bus. Peggy was a friend of Neville. 'Watch out for him,' he'd warned me. 'He's too outrageous for his own good.' He was a big, roly-poly bus driver who seemed perfectly straight until he opened his mouth. His voice was high-pitched and camp in the extreme. Peggy never shouted, he screamed.

He slowed the bus down as he passed me and, leaning out of the window, let out a piercing whistle followed by a stream of lewd jokes. I laughed and waved, but the smile froze on my face as I looked up at the rows of passengers staring out at me. 'What if they are from Brooke?' I thought, and scuttled on, head down, my face as red as a beetroot.

A few months later I had an even bigger scare. Adrian and I had been out for the evening and, as his car was being serviced, I had to catch the bus home. I missed the last bus and was forced to hitch the seven miles to Brooke.

With my long hair and slim figure people were always mistaking me for a girl, and on that dark night it must have been hard to tell the difference. I walked on in silence through the dark, my thumb stuck out hopefully. A car drew up. 'Where are you going, love?' The man at the wheel was large and rugged. I realized at once that he too had mistaken me for a woman. 'Oh, well', I thought, 'a lift's a lift', and hopped into the car.

As soon as he saw me in the light he registered his mistake. But he seemed unperturbed, and carried on chatting. He told me that he had just been visiting his wife in hospital. 'She's having a baby,' he told me. As we drove on the conversation took a more sexual tone. 'A man with a pregnant wife gets very frustrated,' he told me. Shortly before we reached the village, he turned off the road and pulled up in the entrance to a field. He switched the lights out and we sat there in the dark. I was both thrilled and alarmed. He asked me to touch him and, unable to restrain my curiosity, I complied.

Looking back, it seems very sordid. But I was young, only sixteen, and hungry for male attention. I closed my eyes and imagined that I was a woman touching him. I blocked my mind to all thoughts of homosexuality. He's enjoying the caresses of a woman, I told myself. These were elaborate fantasies I ran in my head. I hated to touch my own genitalia – my pleasure was all in giving, not in receiving.

When it was over we sat in the darkness, talking quietly. The peace was rudely interrupted by a sharp rap on the window, followed by the dazzling beam from a powerful torch. We both froze.

It was a policeman, and, as my eyes recovered from the glare, I recognized my local bobby. He lived in the village and had known me from childhood. He asked us to get out of the car. My heart was thudding. I had never felt so scared. All I could think was, 'What if he tells Dad? What if he tells Dad?' He questioned the driver of the car, and asked him where he was from and what had been going on. He was clearly suspicious, but both of us swore blind that we had just been talking. He took down the name of the driver, warned him and let him go.

Then he turned to me. 'Come on. I'm taking you home.

We're going to tell your father about this.' I pleaded with him, my face clammy with sweat, blood pounding in my ears. 'It's not what you think,' I said. 'We were just talking.' I told him that it would never happen again, and that I had a girlfriend. 'Dad'll kill me if he finds out,' I cried. In the end he relented, but he insisted I come to see him the next day at the station.

As I let myself into the house that night, I knew I'd had a lucky escape. The house was quiet, everyone asleep. I looked around at all the familiar objects, the things Mum and Dad had brought together to make a warm and loving home. 'They don't deserve this,' I thought. I knew if I stayed in Brooke I would embarrass and humiliate them. The idea appalled me. I couldn't sleep that night.

The next day I went to see the policeman, who gave me a stern warning. He told me that if it ever happened again he would have to speak to my dad. His manner was harsh and, as I listened to him, I saw the beginnings of a kind of contempt in his eyes. Later that week he saw me walking to the bus stop with one of Pam's friends. I deliberately slipped my arm around her shoulder. I knew it looked good, and that he had taken notice. But this double life couldn't last for long. Hurting my family was unbearable to me, but so was living a lie. I hated my body, I was attracted to men but so far had found gay sex unsatisfactory, and I fantasized about being a woman. I was in a mess. Only one thing was clear – I had to get out of Brooke.

That night I told Dad that I had decided to go to London. Both he and Mum were very upset. 'Why do you want to go to London? You've only just got into this new job.' I told him that I had met someone through a mate at work who'd told me jobs were easy to find and that there were more opportunities. 'I want to see a bit of the world,' I said. 'Make a bit more money.' I had been spending a lot of nights away from home, and I think my dad could understand it when I told him I felt trapped.

It took a good two months to convince them both. I was still under age, and my dad could have forbidden it. But they had my happiness at heart, and finally they agreed. Before I left Dad gave me some advice. 'If you don't like it, or anything bad happens, for God's sake come home. You're not to go short of anything, and you're to call us regularly. Remember, we'll always be here for you.'

With those words ringing in my ears, I set off for London and a brave new world. I had no idea what I would do when I got there, but I did know that I would have the freedom to try to untangle the troubled knot of my childhood. What I couldn't have realized was just how prophetic my father's words were to be. 'We'll always be here for you,' he said. But as a sixteen-year-old, sitting on the London-bound train, I had little idea of how much his love was to mean to me, or how complete the support my parents offered was to be. I had a long journey to make before I could come back home.

3

The Jigsaw Falls into Place

I arrived in London with no job, few friends and £50 in savings. David came to my rescue. He arranged for me to stay in a bedsit in Ravenscourt Park, near Shepherd's Bush. He lived in the same street, three or four doors down.

The bedsit was in a small terraced house owned by an old couple. I had a bedroom upstairs and a kitchenette where I could cook. My culinary skills just about stretched to boiling an egg.

The bedroom was tiny, but I didn't care. It was my first home, and to me it felt like a palace. Now I had to find a way to support myself. In the local paper I saw an advertisement for a job serving in a Jewish delicatessen in the Goldhawk Road. It paid £15 a week and, with my rent set at £8, I thought I would be able to manage. I liked the idea of a shop. In Norwich I had been good at serving customers.

I applied and got the job. I worked behind the cheese counter. They taught me to cut slices from a whole cheese, how to cut smoked salmon, and how to make the counter look attractive. It was hard work, with long hours spent on my feet. But I enjoyed it. Now, when people mistook me for a girl, I didn't feel paranoid. I grew my hair even longer, wore mascara, and invested in a pair of bell-bottoms. I really thought I had arrived.

With David as my guide, I began to explore the gay world. Together we went to clubs and discos. I was amazed at the size of the gay community. Looking for a sense of identity, I was anxious to fit in, to be accepted. But I had difficulties forming friendships. David explained it to me.

'It's the hair and the make-up, Barry. Gay men don't want to look like women. You make them feel uncomfortable.'

Even when I did manage to form a brief attachment to a

man, I always felt less than satisfied. I couldn't enjoy my body, and I was only truly excited by heterosexual men.

It wasn't long before money became a problem. With the rent paid, I found it very hard to survive until the end of the week. It was spring, and the weather was warm, but I couldn't afford a bus pass, and the thought of walking to work on winter mornings was not a pleasant one. Also, my landlady didn't allow visitors to the house after 10.30 p.m. To get to my bedroom I had to pass hers. Revelling in my new-found freedom, I didn't want any prohibitions.

David and I decided to rent a place we could share. We found a bedsit in Fulham for £10 a week. The room was in a converted loft at the top of a big house split into bedsits and owned by an Irish landlord. It was poorly furnished and, with no insulation in the roof, would be freezing in the winter. But we were young and desperate. We took it. It was to be an important decision, for it was here that I met Polly, the woman who was to have such an effect on my life.

We met over the gas meter. I had noticed her a few times in the hallway. She was a striking Eurasian, with long golden hair and an eccentric dress sense. I thought her glamorous, with her bold print blouses, loose cotton trousers, and wide ethnic belts. She had style. But I was shy, and would never have spoken to her. Still, one day, as I bent over the meter in the bathroom, trying to extricate a sixpence, she stopped to help me and we got talking.

The feeling of friendship was immediate and mutual. I suppose she took me for a quiet and gentle gay guy. She must have felt sorry for me. I had few friends – David and I were drifting apart – and I was unused to fending for myself. I learnt that she was a design student finishing an MA and had come from the Far East. She seemed tremendously sophisticated. What I didn't know, and was soon to learn, was that she was a transsexual.

Her birth name was Ronnie. Listening to me speak about the confusion I felt, and about my desire to be a woman, she decided to confide in me. I was dumbfounded. I'd had no idea and was both fascinated and excited at the thought of a man being able to live as a woman. As she told me her story, I realized just how tough her struggle had been.

29

She had been born in Singapore and, like me, had grown up feeling confused and unhappy. She had left home and come to London to study art. It was while she was here and enjoying the freedom of student life that she decided to change her name by deed poll and begin the long process that would lead to surgery and a sex change. Not only did she have to prove to doctors that she could live and work as a woman, she also had to find the money. At that time her mother was supporting her through her education, but there was no possibility of further cash. And she was unable to go home. Her life as a woman had been kept a secret from the rest of the family. In the meantime she worked hard at her studies, lived determinedly as a woman, and tried to survive with dignity. Although her work was admired by her fellow students, I had the sense, as she talked, that they humoured her and looked upon her as something of a freak.

That conversation with Polly changed my life. Until that moment I had never heard the word transsexual, and had no idea that people could have an operation to change their sex. Polly was careful to explain the difference between transsexuals and transvestites: 'Transvestites get sexual pleasure from dressing up in women's clothes, but transsexuals actually wish to *be* women.'

It was as though she had taken an X-ray of my heart, so completely did she describe my own secret thoughts. At last I had found someone in the world who understood what it was I was going through. Polly saw nothing wrong with my wanting to live and work as a woman, and she understood why I could not adapt to the gay community. That night I was unable to sleep. My mind teemed with thoughts and possibilities.

We became the best of friends. In the evening, when I got home from work, I would knock on her door, and she would cook for me while I sat and watched. The windows would steam up and the smell of garlic filled the room. When we could afford it we went out for the evening, mostly to clubs or discos. Restaurants were too expensive. On these outings we both dressed as women, and Polly helped me to choose an outfit from her more extensive wardrobe.

She introduced me to the drag world, and together we bought tickets to the Butterfly Ball. We dressed up and went along to gawp at the extravagant costumes. There were drag queens of every description: burlesque, transvestite, gay. They were all costumed outrageously, with huge hats and layers of make-up. It was not a world with which either of us could identify. There was an air of comedy about the whole event, but Polly and I felt serious about dressing as women. We couldn't think of it as 'drag'. I had to think of a girl's name for the evening, and, on the spur of the moment, I came up with Caroline. The name stuck!

Polly was right. Transvestism is often confused with transsexuality, but they are two entirely separate things. When I dressed as a woman I didn't experience sexual excitement from my attire, nor did I wish to draw attention to the disparity between my gender and my clothing. My dream was to pass through the clubs, pubs and discos undetected. The greatest pleasure imaginable at that time was to sit in a club and be asked to dance by a good-looking man. I was always careful to leave it at that, just a quiet drink and a chat. Somewhere in the conversation I would mention 'my boyfriend' and, going home alone that evening, feel elated at my success.

There were dangers in appearing dressed as a woman. Polly told me that the police could arrest you for female impersonation. One night, at a club in Covent Garden which entertained a mixed clientele (both gay and straight), Polly and I were asked to dance by two men. I had been on my feet all evening and I was hot and tired. I refused their invitation. Out of the corner of my eye I could see the manager, a friendly Spanish guy, gesturing frantically. I nudged Polly and we headed for the ladies.

He followed us in and warned us that the two men were plainclothes police. They had been asking questions and he had covered for us, vouching that we were girls. We were both shaken as we slipped out of the back door. The manager had ordered a car, and we sped away feeling like criminals.

It should have been safer to stick to the gay clubs. But even there we experienced hostility. There were few places that would let us in dressed as women, and those that did were not overly friendly. We belonged nowhere.

I decided to change my job. The delicatessen was too far away, and I was spending a fortune on travel. I wanted to work as a beautician or a hairdresser. There was a job being advertised at a salon in Baker Street. I applied, and they took me on. But the money was not good, £12 a week, and so I started an evening job at a theatre, working as an usherette. I sold ice-cream in the intervals and made a little extra from tips.

It was a hard life! But I was still only seventeen, and I was desperate to prove that I could make it on my own. I often felt lonely. Polly had a boyfriend, and when he was with her I didn't like to intrude. Sometimes he would turn up drunk, and they would have screaming rows. I would lie on my bed, listening to them shout. It made me wonder if I wasn't better off on my own.

I was spending more and more on clothes. I bought myself a pair of high heels and learnt to walk in them. They made me taller than ever, but it was worth it. I had a few dresses but, as unisex fashions were coming in at the time, I could look like a woman wearing shorts or jeans. My legs were hairless and I loved wearing hot pants – the big fashion craze of the early 1970s. But make-up was my real extravagance. Lipsticks, foundations, blushers – to me they were the essence of femininity. I spent hours in chemists looking at all the different bottles, testing fragrances and colours.

When my parents came to visit, all the toiletries were hidden, and the dresses stored in Polly's room. Mum and Dad weren't much impressed with my new home. 'It's a dump,' said Dad. It's so cold,' said Mum. I reassured them that I was fine, but it *was* freezing, and in the winter I had to feed the meter and sleep with the electric fire on.

I was so taken up with establishing my life in London that I'd had no time to learn more about the possibility of a sex change. In my heart of hearts I thought it an impossible dream.

One night Polly gave a party and introduced me to a 'woman' whose decolletage revealed a magnificent cleavage.

'She's a transsexual,' Polly whispered, as I poured myself a drink. I was bewildered.

'But they look so real,' I muttered.

I sat opposite her, mesmerized. I longed to ask about her breasts, but it was hardly a great opening line.

A few days later she came out for the evening with Polly and me, and I was able to get to know her a little better. By now I was convinced that the breasts were real. I asked her. She told me that she was taking hormone tablets, and gave me the name and address of the doctor who was prescribing them.

Since adolescence, when I had so envied the development of my sister and her friends, I had wanted breasts. My nipples had always been large and sensitive, but it was obvious that my breasts were not going to grow on their own. Now that I was dressing and socializing as a girl, I thought that I might have a strong case to present to a doctor. The excitement I felt as I lay in bed that night is difficult to describe. 'I may not be a fully functioning female,' I thought, 'but at least I can look and feel like one.'

The next day I made an appointment to see the doctor (a psychiatrist whose name I've been asked not to reveal) at his surgery in the Edgware Road. I took great care with my appearance. I curled my hair to make it soft and bouncy, and I wore a half-cup bra padded out. Polly wished me luck. 'He may ask a lot of questions,' she warned. 'Don't be fazed.' She reassured me by telling me that he was very understanding, and used to dealing with problems like mine.

'Just tell him what you told me,' she said. 'You'll be fine.'

Despite her kind words, I was very nervous as I sat in the waiting room.

'What if he laughs at me?' I thought. 'What if he says No?'

But Polly was right. The doctor, a small, elderly man, was both kind and sympathetic. I was able to tell him exactly how I felt; how I had always been happier dressed as a girl and thought of myself as female. He listened to me talk, nodding every so often, and watching me closely. When I had finished speaking the questions began. He asked me about my childhood and my early sexual experiences. He particularly focused on my childhood homosexual experiences. Clearly it was vital for him to establish that I was a transsexual and not a transvestite.

'I feel attracted to men.' I explained, 'but to heterosexual men. I have tried anal intercourse, but disliked it. I feel utterly unfulfilled sexually, and torn apart by living a double life.'

I was honest about everything but my age. I told him I was twenty when I was in fact only seventeen. I was desperate that he should think me mature and responsible. I was afraid that if he knew how young I really was he'd tell me to go away and think again, or ask to speak to my parents.

He did neither. Instead he declared that he was certain that I was transsexual; not only would he prescribe hormone therapy but, if I would agree to see him for more counselling, he would be happy to recommend me for gender reassignment.

I was hungry for information. He explained that it was possible to have a sex-change operation done in this country, but that you needed a psychiatrist's recommendation. You also had to prove that you could live and work as a woman for three years before they would consider surgery. 'Do you think this is a path you would want to go down?' he asked me. 'It will not be an easy course of action.'

But I was in no doubt. As soon as the operation became a real possibility and not just a fantastic dream, I knew the direction my life would take. There was not only light at the end of the tunnel, there was a choir of angels singing their hearts out!

As I sat there trying to contain my excitement, he told me more about the hormone therapy.

'You'll need to be on the treatment for a while,' he said. 'And it may make you sick. Also you shouldn't expect too much, or you'll be disappointed.' He pointed out that, since I was very thin and had very little fat displacement, I was unlikely to grow a very large bust.

'Damn,' I thought. 'If only I'd been short and fat.'

I had to go back a few times before the doctor would prescribe the pills. In the meantime Polly had told me how important it was to keep his goodwill. Without his go-ahead it would be very difficult to get surgery. Casablanca was talked about as a place to go and have the operation, but I wanted to keep all options open. Polly told me some real horror stories about transsexuals who had become so desperate they had castrated themselves, or gone to back-street surgeons and suffered from terrible infections. 'Once they've neutered themselves,' she said, 'the NHS is obliged to perform the op.' But I didn't want to get that desperate. With a psychiatrist's letter and the money

I was determined to save in the next three years, I would have my gender-reassignment surgery performed in England.

Finally, I got my prescription. I was to take two pills a day, one in the morning and one at night. I deliberately avoided the local chemist's shop, preferring to go further afield and avoid embarrassment or hostility. Times have changed, but in those days homosexuality had only recently been made legal between consenting adults. Transsexuality was stuck in a shady half-world, hovering between legality and illegality. Most people, including myself, at that time were ignorant on the subject.

The doctor was right, the tablets did make me sick. He changed them to a different kind but to no effect. I still threw up every morning. I tried everything: eating late at night and then taking them, not eating at all, taking them with milk. I felt it was worth the nausea. My breasts did grow, though not as noticeably as I would have liked. But it was psychologically that the hormone tablets made the greatest difference. Taking them brought me closer to my goal, and with every passing day I felt more feminine and more at ease with the world.

I shall never be able to describe the great joy I felt in those first few months in London. I had no money and few friends, but none of that made the slightest difference, for suddenly, after seventeen years of wandering in the wilderness, I had purpose and the hope of a better, brighter future. From the moment I realized that gender-reassignment surgery was a real possibility for me I had no doubt that it was the perfect and only solution to my distress.

I was desperate to talk to someone who had had the operation, and when Polly told me she knew a girl who had undergone successful surgery I begged her to introduce me. She arranged a meeting, and we went together to the woman's flat.

The door was opened by a petite oriental. She was five foot two, with very long, dark hair. I towered over her, feeling large and clumsy. Her flat was immaculate, and everything about her was neat and stylish. We sat and talked about her experiences. She was happy to explain and, without my asking, to display the results of her surgery. I was impressed. She looked utterly female and spoke with glowing pride about her life as a woman. Not only did the operation appear to be an unqualified success, but it was clear that it had also given her a great sense of personal dignity. I left the apartment with my resolve strengthened.

The problem would be money. I already had two jobs and could barely make ends meet as it was. I didn't see how, in the foreseeable future, I would be able to save sufficient funds. I was still working in the theatre in Shaftesbury Avenue. The musical *Hair* was playing and I enjoyed the show. I was friendly with all the staff, and the box-office manager, Nick, named me Myra, after Myra Breckinridge. I discussed my hopes and ambitions with him and the rest of the front of house staff. 'How will I ever earn enough money?' I wailed.

Somebody up in heaven must have been looking after me, for, out of the blue, came the most extraordinary lucky break.

One evening I was standing in the bar with my tray of ice-creams slung over my shoulder, when I noticed a man staring at me. He came up and introduced himself as the choreographer David Toguri. I had heard of him and knew that he was a highly influential man in show business. He came straight to the point.

'Have you ever thought of being a showgirl?' he asked.

I was stunned. 'But, I'm a boy!' I exclaimed, blushing furiously. He didn't even pause for breath. 'Yes, I know that,' he said. 'It makes no difference. You are tall and beautiful.' He went on to explain that in several shows in Paris some of the most successful showgirls were actually boys.

'I've heard you are contemplating a sex change,' he continued. 'That makes no difference to me. I would still like you to consider coming along for an audition for a new show I'm choreographing at the Latin Quarter in Soho.'

I stammered something about having no confidence and two left feet.

'Just think about it,' he said. 'I'll be in touch.'

A week later he telephoned and gave me an audition date. I had talked to Polly and she told me to give it a try. 'What have you got to lose?' she said. I knew that I was no natural performer, I was too shy for that. But the idea of being offered a job as a woman, and such a glamorous job at that, was a great attraction. I needed my ego boosting and I needed to prove my femininity. I wanted to be more of a woman than most women do! I told him I would be there and then began to panic.

'What should I wear?' I asked. 'Do you want me to buy a wig?'

He laughed as he tried to calm me down. 'Just come as yourself. You'll stun them.'

'But what about make-up?'

'You wear enough as it is,' he exclaimed, and we both began to giggle.

The rest of that week I spent in a state of high anxiety. I was terrified that I would make a fool of myself but, deep down, I was desperate for the job. It would mean a lot more money. And more money meant moving one step nearer to my goal.

The big day arrived.

I took David's advice and wore a pair of hot pants and a halter neck. I tried to restrain myself on the make-up, putting on just a little more mascara and lipstick. At the rehearsal studios there were half a dozen other girls, all getting changed. We didn't speak, and the air was electric with tension. Several of the girls were wearing bikinis, and I felt gauche in my shorts. I could hear voices and music coming from the auditorium. My stomach lurched, and I felt sweat prickling on my skin. One by one we were called up on to the stage.

'It's your turn, Caroline.' David took my arm and led me into a pool of blazing light. He gave me a reassuring squeeze and then turned to go. I was left standing alone in the middle of a vast space.

I heard David announce, 'This is Caroline.' From the darkness he told me to walk up and down with one hand on my hip and one held out, in true showgirl style. I could hear people talking, but peering into the gloom I couldn't make out their faces. My knees began to shake.

Then David came back on to the stage and taught me a few simple step routines. Showgirls are not truly dancers – they are there to provide spectacle and to decorate the set – but they do have to be able to move gracefully, perform high kicks, and follow basic dance routines. That day I was all left feet.

David was very patient, but it took me for ever to pick up the steps. I couldn't even manage a smile, I was so nervous.

'I've blown it,' I thought, and was about to call it a day when a man leapt on to the stage and introduced himself as John. 'Hi, Caroline,' he grinned. 'Could you take off your top and hold your arms above your head?' I was a little taken aback by his request, but it seemed rude to refuse.

'Hmm,' said John, chewing the end of his pencil. 'You're right. They aren't too big, are they?'

David nodded in agreement.

'I am taking hormone tablets,' I told them. 'They might get a bit bigger . . .'

John interrupted me. 'It makes no difference. You look amazing under the lights, and you've got the height. You'll develop grace when you feel a little more confident.'

'You mean I've got the job?'

He nodded and smiled.

That night Polly and I celebrated. 'In less than one month,' I thought, 'I will be performing as a woman in front of an audience.'

'Oh God!' I exclaimed, and poured myself another glass of wine. 'I'm terrified.'

'Don't be daft,' said Polly. 'This is just the beginning, Caroline. You're on your way!'

4

The Showgirl and the Sheikh

With the start of my new job, my life changed utterly. I handed in my notice at the beauty salon and started rehearsals for the show. I was now earning as much as both of my previous jobs put together and I could afford to move into a nicer place. I found a room at the top of a house in Wetherby Gardens. It was small, but it did have a private bathroom and a kitchenette – a big improvement on Fulham.

I had introduced myself to my new landlady as Caroline, and now seemed as good a time as any to make a break with the past. I threw away the bulk of my male clothes. I intended to live as a woman twenty-four hours a day. As I parcelled up the remnants of that past life, I felt liberated. The next step was to tell my doctor the good news.

He was delighted for me, but he was also careful to explain the legal position.

'You can appear on stage as a woman,' he told me. 'But the minute you leave the club you will have to dress as a man.' Clearly this was impossible. I was not appearing as a drag artist, and the audience must not discover the truth about my gender. The doctor came up with a solution. He furnished me with a letter confirming that I was undergoing treatment prior to a sex-change operation. He then suggested that I change my name by deed poll. I was called Caroline on my contract, and I would need to make it legal to safeguard my position.

The process was simpler than I had imagined. By merely paying a fee and instructing a solicitor, I legally became Caroline Cossey. I was never to introduce myself as Barry again.

Rehearsals were gruelling. We had three weeks to get the show into shape. For me it was the first few days that were the hardest. I was paralysed with nerves and certain that I must seem ridiculous. There was one other showgirl – a woman called Diana. The rest were trained dancers, all old friends, and dressed in leotards and tights. I had turned up in a pair of shorts and a T-shirt. For most of that morning I sat alone in a corner watching them glide effortlessly through their routines.

Then came the dreaded moment; it was my turn. As I stood up I felt all eyes on me. The dancers, taking a break, were ranged around the room chatting in small groups, drinking coffee and eating chocolate. David took me slowly through my first steps. He had it all written down on a piece of paper – turn, count, stepball, change – but I couldn't concentrate. Every so often one of the dancers would burst out in a peal of laughter at some private joke. I was certain they were laughing at me. 'They know about my past,' I thought, shaking with nerves. 'They know I'm still a boy.' David tried to reassure me. 'Don't worry,' he said. 'You'll be just fine. You'll look marvellous.'

And my costume *was* extraordinary. Red, with sequins, it had a huge three-foot headdress, tail feathers, and a silky shawl to drape across my shoulders. Diana performed topless, but my breasts were nowhere near large enough to impress an audience. I wore a padded bra to boost the little I had, and, by dint of Sellotape and inspiration, created a cleavage for myself.

That was the least of my problems. Wearing minuscule red bikini pants, how was I to conceal my penis? It wasn't exactly large, but it would still leave a rather disconcerting bump. This was a problem I was to learn to live with in the next three years, and I tried a variety of solutions. One of the most successful strategies involved sticking plaster. I would tuck my penis back between my legs and tape it flat. Effective but excruciating! The sticking plaster would leave sores on my skin, and every night I would have to lie in the bath soaking it off. It also made urination an impossibility during the show. If I drank too much before curtain up I was in big trouble!

Eventually I found a kinder solution. All the girls wore G-strings under their costumes, and I constructed my own personal G-string from an extra-strong elastic material. I could keep this valuable garment on throughout the show, thus saving Diana and the other girls any unnecessary embarrassment.

After the ordeal of opening night, I soon settled into the show. I acquired the skill of smiling and moving at the same time, and soon didn't even need to watch my feet as they found their way around the stage. The atmosphere backstage was good, and soon I felt relaxed enough to open up a little and talk to some of the girls about my transsexuality. I made a firm friend of the other showgirl, Diana. She had known about me from the beginning. She wasn't bothered in the slightest. Before the show a few of us would get together in one of the dressing rooms and split a bottle of wine. I loved the backstage life, with its laughter and camaraderie. After we finished the second show, we went to eat breakfast in one of the all-night clubs. The Cavendish Hotel in Jermyn Street was a real favourite. It was open until six in the morning, and we would pile in there at about 2.30 a.m. to join London's night creatures: the bunnies, clubbers and party animals. It was a strange and heady atmosphere. I remained very shy, but I began to relish the adrenalin of performance.

Diana and I spent much of our time together, visiting each other's flats at the weekend, and cooking meals for each other. I was still lonely, and felt grateful for her company and her easy acceptance of my transsexuality. Diana had been a model, and one of her boyfriends was a photographer. She had confided in him that I was, in fact, a boy, and he'd come to see the show. If he was expecting some kind of freak, then he was clearly surprised. He asked Diana if I would be willing to pose for some photographs. 'I'm interested,' I told her. But, as she explained more, my enthusiasm dissolved.

It was a scam to make money from the gutter press. His idea was to sell the photographs to a tabloid and then take another set of me as a boy and offer them to a rival newspaper. I rejected the idea outright, and refused to meet with him. Diana was in no way to blame, but her connection with that photographer was ultimately to prove fateful.

I was still so innocent. Privately I was mortally ashamed of my sexuality. It was a secret that I wished to conceal for the sake of my family. As yet I had no idea that my gender might

41

become the object of morbid curiosity, or that my personal history might bring the tabloids flocking.

Until I began the hormone therapy, I had returned to Norfolk every three months or so to spend the weekend at home in Brooke. I looked forward to those visits, but on the journey from London to Norwich I had to transform my personality. I tried to dress more to my father's taste, and, although I could do nothing about my hair, I assumed what I thought was a manly air. I was unable to talk about whole sections of my life and had to invent suitable anecdotes to amuse them. Now I was a showgirl and living entirely as a woman, I agonized over how to bridge the gulf between us. How could I tell them about my life in London and my hopes for the future?

Once again it was my brother who came to the rescue. He rang me up to say he had a few days' holiday and could he come and stay with me in London? After I had put the phone down, I went back upstairs to my bedsit and looked around the room at the dresses, shoes and make-up. I began to pack them away. But this time I stopped myself. Why should I pretend? Why should I have to live this double life? I had trusted Terry before and now I was about to trust him again. I decided to let him see me as I was.

Terry realized by now that I hadn't 'grown out' of the feelings we had discussed. He never questioned me about my life, but I sensed that he accepted me as I was. How would he feel when I told him about the hormone tablets and my plans to have gender-reassignment surgery?

That evening I made myself look as feminine as I possibly could, taking extra care with my hair and make-up. Then I sat down in a chair, lit a cigarette, and waited for him to arrive.

As he walked through the door I stood up to give him a hug. He stopped dead and just stared. We both stood frozen, then, after a long pause, he spoke: 'My God, that's amazing! Is it really you?'

We began to smile.

We talked all evening. I told him about my job at the Latin Quarter and the money I was now earning. I referred back to our earlier conversations.

'I don't feel hopeless any more, Terry. This doctor has given me so much support. I feel I can look forward to true long-term happiness. I know this operation is right for me.'

'Are you really, *really* sure?' he questioned.

'Positive,' I replied. 'But Terry, I'm scared of telling Mum and Dad. What do you think I should do?'

His reply was music to my ears: 'I'll tell them for you.'

As I said goodbye to him at the end of his visit I felt overwhelmed with gratitude and love. He could have rejected me, been appalled or mocking. Instead he had listened with patience and understanding as I explained my feelings.

As I watched him walk away down the road, I knew he would soon be back in Brooke, and my only thought was, 'Will my dad feel the same way? Or am I about to lose my family?'

The call came early the next morning. It was Dad, and he sounded angry.

'What the hell are you doing with your life, Barry? What are you getting yourself into?'

Immediately I was on the defensive. 'Dad, you don't understand,' I protested. But he didn't want to hear. He ordered me to cut my hair, put on a suit, and get my life in order. He made light of my new career.

'I hear you've got yourself a Danny La Rue job,' he said. 'Is that right?' I stayed silent. He knew he had hurt me, but he was still too damaged himself to be able to rescue the conversation. 'I want you to come home to Brooke. This nonsense has got to stop.'

Those were his parting words, and we both put down the phone in anger.

If I had been just a little older, I would have been able to understand his reaction. He was in shock and anxious for me. But I was young and headstrong and we were both very stubborn. I had expected rejection. 'And now,' I thought,' I've got it.'

All my father needed was time. But it was too late for me. I decided to cut myself off from him. I didn't go home, and would ring only when I knew he wouldn't be there. Even with Mum I was careful never to stray on to the subject of my operation. I would tell her I was OK and working hard, but no mention was made of my new life. 'Send my love to Dad,' I said, and left it at that. I was determined to show him I was right. I fantasized about becoming rich and successful and turning up at the house dressed immaculately.

In truth, the estrangement made be deeply unhappy. I missed my family and longed for their love. Pam and I talked often on the phone, but she was still at school and our lives seemed miles apart. In the light of the extraordinary support my family have since shown me, I feel sorry that I underestimated their love. But I was terrified that if I went home my parents would try to change my mind. The love I had for my family was the strongest thing in my life, but nothing could have stood in my way. I was fighting not only for the right to make my own choices, but for my very sanity. If the hope of surgery was snatched from me I knew I would deteriorate mentally.

I threw myself into my work. On David's advice I took dance classes with Molly Malloy at the Dance Centre. I started to loosen up on stage. One night, as a joke, someone hung a coat hanger from my tail feathers. As I turned my back to the audience and wiggled for all I was worth I could hear giggling. I couldn't work it out. Why were they laughing? When I got off the stage I realized what had happened. Such was my new-found confidence that I was able to enjoy the joke.

The Latin Quarter was considered a prestigious place to work, and David Toguri was very much the man of the moment. His shows received rave reviews. The club, in Wardour Street, seated about 300. Inside, it was decorated in plush red velvet and gold. The stage was reasonably large, with a small revolve at the back, and the music was provided by a twelve-piece band. In the cast there were ten dancers, four singers, two showgirls, and a star name topping the bill. David was a great perfectionist, and drilled the dancers until they were exhausted.

The rules at the Latin Quarter were strict. Members of the cast were not allowed into the restaurant and bars, and fraternizing with the customers was forbidden. Working in Soho in the early 1970s, it was important to the management to retain an ultra-respectable image. So we came and went through a special stage door. But there were always one or two 'stage-door Johnnies' hanging around after the second show.

I lacked the confidence to make a relationship with a man.

I was lonely, but just living as a woman provided enough challenges for the moment. After the show, if I didn't go for a meal with some of the girls, I would go home in a taxi. Wardour Street was a regular pull-in for taxis, and there were usually a number parked there, the drivers drinking coffee at a stall and reading the early editions of the papers. I struck up a friendship with one of them, and his cab would be waiting to take me home at the end of the evening.

Dark and well groomed, he was a London lad in his late twenties with a broad cockney accent. He treated me with respect, and though he made it clear that he found me very attractive, there was no sexual pressure in the relationship. I felt safe in his company, and after a few months I invited him in for coffee.

We sat on the sofa and chatted. Nervous lest he make a pass, I froze when he slipped his arm around my shoulder. But it seemed he was as cautious as I was. After one tentative kiss he said goodnight and left. The relationship developed from there. I knew that I ought to tell him the truth, but I was happy. 'Perhaps I can keep it this way,' I thought.

A few times he tried to take it further. But I always put him off with an excuse. One evening he said he was terribly tired, and asked if he could spend the night. I didn't know what to do. I told him he could get some sleep – but nothing more. Swaddled in a dressing gown and a blanket, I lay down beside him on my single bed. He put his arms around me and we drifted off to sleep. When I woke in the morning he was gone. The blanket was on the floor and my dressing gown lay open. I realized immediately what had happened – he had undone it in the night and discovered the truth. I lay there sick with panic. 'What if he tells someone?' I thought. I suppose I was lucky that he hadn't become violent. That evening I looked for him at the stage door, but there was no sign of him. I never saw him again.

We began rehearsals for a new show. I knew that if, like Diana, I could appear topless I would earn another £5. It seems ridiculous today – the price of three packets of cigarettes – but at the time it was a fortune. I exceeded my prescribed dose of hormone tablets in the hope that my bust might grow faster.

John, the production manager, remained unconvinced. 'Wait and see how they are in six months,' he said.

But I was impatient. I knew that it was possible for breasts to be surgically enlarged, and I was determined to have the operation. I soon discovered that it was prohibitively expensive – it cost several hundred pounds – and with the money I was putting aside for my sex change, there was no way I could afford it.

The Cavendish Hotel remained a favourite haunt, and Polly would sometimes meet me there for breakfast. One evening a large entourage of people swept in. They created a stir. In the centre of the party, surrounded by bodyguards and glamour girls, was a tall, distinguished Arab. Two men, rather obviously Special Branch, were checking out the room. Polly and I were fascinated. 'Who is he?' we asked the *maître d'hôtel*. 'An Arab prince,' he replied. 'And he's been asking about you.' I was well known by the staff at the Cavendish. If the prince had been making inquiries, they were sure to have told him about my past. I caught his eye several times as I ate my meal. His curiosity was apparent.

I was to see him a number of times before we spoke. One night he came to the show, and was waiting in the Cavendish Hotel when I arrived. He introduced himself. 'I have a proposal for you,' he said. 'My uncle, the king, is most anxious to meet you. I have told him all about your situation, and he is fascinated. He may be able to help you.' He invited me to a party a few days hence. 'Bring a friend,' he said, 'if that will make you feel more comfortable.'

I was intrigued. I'd grown up in the tiny community of Brooke. Here was a world I knew nothing of, a world of kings and princes, bodyguards and food-tasters. In those days I was impetuous and eager for all new experience. I accepted his invitation and asked Polly to accompany me.

We were to meet at the Cavendish. I was still in my stage make-up – false eyelashes, lacquered hair.

When I see photographs of myself from that time, I can't help but laugh. With all that eye make-up and the bouffant hairstyle, I look more like a drag queen than I ever did when I dressed up for a night on the town! But that was the style of the time. Women *wanted* to look like Raquel Welch and, of course, make-up for the stage had to be that much more obvious.

So we arrived at the club with me peering through a forest of false eyelashes. The prince was holding court with the now familiar crowd of heavies, cuties and toadies. He was tremendously courteous and invited us to sit beside him and drink a glass of champagne. Our presence created a certain atmosphere; the security men glowered from under their shades, and the glamour girls stiffened with hostility. I felt a laugh gathering somewhere in my stomach – the situation was so bizarre.

'We are going to Grosvenor House for a party,' announced the prince. 'Would you like to accompany us?'

I glanced at Polly. She was grinning like a Cheshire cat. 'Yes please', I replied. 'We'd be delighted.'

'Thank God you're with me,' I muttered, as we climbed into a huge, black limousine.

'Ooh. This car's got tinted windows!' said Polly.

As the fleet of cars drew up at the Grosvenor House, there was quite a reception committee waiting. We were led through a maze of corridors to a huge suite of rooms. I had never seen such opulence. The party was in full swing and, still grinning, Polly and I each downed a glass of champagne.

'Who *are* all these people?' she asked.

'Haven't a clue,' I said.

'But where, oh where,' I thought, 'is the king?'

My question was answered when the prince came up, took my glass, and asked me to follow him. Having done two shows, I was feeling relaxed, and the champagne had rather gone to my head. We walked for what seemed like miles, along more corridors and up more stairs. Eventually we came to the back of the building and to the king's private apartment. It was vast, and I remember being dazzled by the sparkling light from a massive chandelier. I had been given strict instructions. 'You are not to ask his highness any questions. You are merely to respond to the questions that he asks you.'

I was shown into a bathroom and asked to undress and put on a bathrobe. 'If you feel comfortable enough, the king would like to see your body.' I was feeling more and more like part of a freak show. 'What does he expect?' I thought. 'Horns?'

47

His highness was seated on a large gilt chair at the far end of the room. A bearded old man dressed in white robes, he ordered the prince, his son, to leave, and gestured for me to approach. The first thing I noticed about him were his eyes. They were dark and piercing and the dominating feature in his face. Frail as he was, he still radiated authority. On one rather thin wrist he wore an enormous gold Rolex watch. Studded with diamonds, it glittered in the light. He motioned for me to sit in a chair that had been placed next to his. Feeling awkward and shy, I was relieved when he reached down to a bottle of champagne at his side and poured me a glass.

We talked for about half an hour. Or rather, he asked the questions and I answered. He spoke in broken English, but I had little trouble understanding him. His questions lacked subtlety.

'Do you get erections? Do you have sex with women? . . . '

To him I was an object of morbid fascination, a curiosity, a toy. I began to feel irritated and determined to speak out. When he asked me to open my robe and show him my body, I did so out of a kind of defiance. I almost wanted to shock him. There was a silence as he looked me up and down. Finally he spoke: 'Do you have sex with *anyone?*'

My reply was blunt. 'No,' I told him. 'Until I have surgery it will be impossible for me to function as a woman. I regard my penis with distaste. It gives me no pleasure at all.'

He seemed to be struck by my honesty. I explained the details of the operation and told him I was saving up for breast surgery.

'Why?' he asked.

'I'll be able to earn £5 more in the show if I can go topless. But more important, it will make me feel more of a woman.'

He asked how much the operation would cost and I told him. The conversation drew to a close, but before I left he produced a sealed envelope.

'Here's a little something,' he said.

I didn't open it. I put it in my bag and returned to the party.

By now dawn was glimmering on the London skyline. I woke Polly, who had fallen asleep on the sofa, and we were escorted to the limousine that was to take us home. As we drove through the deserted street, both yawning and heavy

48

with exhaustion, I remembered the envelope. I tore it open. Inside was £500 in notes. I gasped and Polly began to laugh. Neither of us had ever seen that much money before. To a girl who earned £30 a week, it was a fortune.

'Looks like you just got your breasts,' said Polly.

I was so excited I couldn't sleep. As soon as the surgery opened, I rang my doctor. 'I want to have my breasts done,' I gabbled down the phone. 'I've got the money. Who should I go to?'

'Slow down,' he said. 'Come and see me this afternoon and we'll talk about it then.'

I came away from the surgery later that day with the names of three plastic surgeons who might be willing to perform the operation. The doctor had asked me where I had got the money from, but I had deflected the question. If I had told him the truth – 'Oh, a philanthropic Arabian monarch gave it to me' – I don't suppose he would have believed me.

All three surgeons had practices in Harley Street. Looking my most glamorous, and taking Polly for moral support, I went to see them. The first surgeon on the list had moved address, and the second was unwilling to operate on a transsexual for reasons of 'reputation'. I was beginning to feel despondent when we knocked on the door of the third. He was, and still is, one of the best plastic surgeons in London. We shook hands and I handed him my doctor's letter. When he read it he looked startled. He had assumed I was a woman. But he was courteous and informative. He explained what the operation would entail.

'We make a small incision beneath the breast and place a bag of silicon underneath the pectoral muscle. Initially the skin will seem rather taut and stretched, but it will loosen up in time. It will be possible to cover the scar with a little body make-up if it should bother you.' He was very keen to know why I was so desperate to have the operation. I explained that I intended to have a complete sex-change operation. 'But why are breasts so important?' he asked. 'You already have a small bust. Many women would be happy with that.' I told him that I needed a larger bust for my career. 'If I can go topless,' I said, 'I'll be able to afford the operation that much sooner.' He seemed satisfied that my reasons were well thought out and

49

balanced. He gave me a time and date for the operation. But he was a very busy man and couldn't operate for another six weeks. I was impatient. I would have had the operation that day!

That evening I went to see John, the manager of the show, and told him the good news. He looked a little alarmed.

'Don't worry,' I laughed. 'Nobody will be able to tell the difference.' I think he had imagined huge scars and lumps of silicon! Once I had explained he became enthusiastic. Two topless showgirls were better than one.

The six weeks dragged by. I had stopped taking the hormone tablets, so at least I no longer felt nauseous in the mornings. I'd had surgery once as a child with appendicitis, but I had no fear of pain. To me, having this operation seemed the most natural thing in the world. I was to be in hospital for just over five days. It was a private clinic off Harley Street, run by nuns. They were kind and gentle. An hour before the operation I was given a pre-med. As I drifted in and out of sleep, I remembered these quiet, dignified women lifting me out of bed and wheeling me down the corridors. They made me comfortable and reassured me all would be well.

When I came to, I was back in bed and Polly was sitting beside me, holding my hand. I struggled to raise my head.

'They look incredible,' said Polly.

She exaggerated. In fact, they were almost entirely covered with bandages. But with the swelling and the dressings they did seem large, and I think Polly was more affected by the size than anything else! The only area of skin I could see was around the nipples, which were stretched and very, very shiny.

'Wish they were mine,' said Polly, wistfully.

Feeling as I did, I would happily have given them away. Not only was I parched with thirst and dizzy with nausea, but the pain in my breasts was excruciating.

'This isn't a bundle of laughs,' I groaned. 'I feel as though someone is holding me off the ground by my nipples.'

Poor old Polly winced sympathetically and fell silent. I *was* uncomfortable; there was a little bottle of blood between my breasts with tubes disappearing into bandages, and I could hardly move my arms for the bruising around my chest. But in truth I was enormously excited. Gingerly I touched the side of my breasts to see if they felt either hard or unnatural. Because of the padding it was impossible to tell.

The blood bottle was removed the next day, and after four days I was discharged from hospital. The bandages were to stay on for a further ten days, and the doctor told me I was to stay in bed and rest. Polly became nursemaid. She was wonderful, doing all the cooking and cleaning. She was as anxious as I was that the operation should prove a success, and at the end of the ten days she came with me to Harley Street, where I was to have the stitches removed.

'Good, very good. I'm very pleased with you.'

The doctor stood over me smiling and nodding with approval. My eyes were streaming – he had pulled off the plasters with four sharp tugs. 'I didn't hurt you, did I?' he asked, noticing a tear trickling down the side of my face.

'No,' I lied. 'Can I see them?'

He helped me up off the table and led me to a mirror. I stood there silent with wonder. In the reflection I saw the woman I had always believed myself to be. My breasts were perfect – soft and gently rounded, they seemed in no way artificial. I turned to the surgeon and, beaming, kissed him on the cheek.

'Thank you so much,' I said. 'I couldn't have imagined anything better.'

Polly was as stunned as I was. When she got me home she poked and prodded them and declared them to be perfect.

'Now we must buy you some new clothes,' she announced.

We went a bit mad. For women who have seen their breasts develop from puberty and become accustomed to their shape, my behaviour must seem peculiar. But I was so proud of my new body, I wanted the world to notice. I bought tops with plunging necklines, silk bras, see-through blouses. It took me a while to calm down!

My costume was altered for the show, and was now identical to Diana's outfit. Now, instead of a padded bra, I wore nipple caps stuck on with Copydex and hid my scars with body make-up. My salary was raised accordingly. And the extra money joined the funds I had already saved towards the main operation.

I was full of optimism. My life had purpose; I knew what I wanted and I knew how I could get it. There was only one thing holding me back – my relationship with my family.

5

The Truth Torments

I was desperate for my family's support and acceptance. I needed to explain myself to them before I could go forward. I had to know that I was clear enough in my thinking and strong enough emotionally to deal with their reaction – good or bad. I expected the worst, but had come to the point where it was no longer possible to compromise. The time for hiding was over. My parents had brought me up and given me life, but I had to follow my own course. Without the operation I knew that the conflict in my body and my mind would destroy me. But I still lacked the courage to break the silence.

Pam spoke to me on the phone.

'They miss you so much,' she said. 'And so do I.'

Pam had left school and was working in the bridal department of a large Norwich store. But she hated our being so far apart and dreamt of coming to London. She'd visited a few times, but not since I had got my new job and had the breast operation. She asked me if she could come and stay, and I said, 'Yes.'

People often ask Pam and me if my transformation from 'brother' to 'sister' didn't affect our relationship adversely. But I never had a moment's doubt about Pam's support and understanding. I think in her head she had always thought of me as her sister, and being close to me as a child, she understood the pain and unhappiness I had gone through. So as I stood on the platform at Liverpool Street Station waiting for her train to arrive, I felt no anxiety, only excitement.

She threw her arms around me and we hugged and kissed each other. Then, standing back, she stood and stared.

'Where did you get *those* from?' she said. 'You're bigger than me.' We burst out laughing, and hugged each other once more.

'I'll tell you all about it when we get back to the flat,' I promised.

That night we talked and talked. I told her all about my new job, the operation, and my plans for the future. And Pam talked about Mum and Dad.

'They're worried about you, Caroline. I think Mum will understand. Dad is just hurt and confused. Neither of them has any idea how beautiful and how *normal* you look. Dad's got this picture of wigs, false eyelashes and sequins. But when he sees what you're really like . . . '

Her words echoed my own thoughts. It was time to go home.

I told no one I was coming. That weekend I got on a train to Norwich and took a taxi from the station to Brooke. It was dark, and I asked the taxi driver to drop me at the end of the lane. As I walked towards the house, a light was switched on in one of the bedrooms, and I saw the figure of my mother pass in front of the window. She seemed so near and yet so far away. I stood for a long while in the darkness, feeling the wind on my face. I needed to look at the house and remember . . . At that moment it seemed a very real possibility that I might be seeing it for the last time. My heart was thudding. I smoothed down my hair, straightened my skirt, and walked up the path to the back door.

In those days the doors were always left unlocked, and I let myself in. I heard Dad shout, 'Who's that?'

Pausing before I answered, I said, 'It's Barry.' The name sounded strange on my lips.

He came down the stairs but stopped half-way as he caught sight of me.

'Hello Dad,' I said softly.

He was silent, his face pale with shock. All he could do was stare. Then he moved towards me. He held out his arms, and I began to cry. Mum had been standing at the top of the stairs, and as we embraced each other she followed him down. Without missing a beat she asked, 'Are you hungry or thirsty, love?'

I laughed through my tears and turned to give her a kiss. Then we sat down to talk. We talked all through that night. And it was not an easy conversation. I broke down at least three times, and Mum and Dad wept with me. But I was determined to speak the truth. I wanted them to know it all.

I told them about my homosexual experiences and how unhappy they had made me. I spoke about Cathy and my attempt at heterosexual intercourse, and I gave an account of my visits to the psychiatrist. It wasn't all plain sailing. At times my dad, his head in his hands, seemed unable to understand.

'Well, what do you call yourself now?' he demanded.

My mum knew how hard this was for me. She was terrified that he might reject me. 'Oh, Bob,' she said gently and laid one hand on his shoulder.We drank cup after cup of tea as Dad struggled to come to terms with all this information. He'd never heard of transsexuality, and the thought of my having to undergo surgery greatly concerned him. He was amazed by my breasts and kept asking, 'Are they yours? Are they really yours?' Both he and Mum were staggered by my appearance. 'You look so feminine,' he said. 'It's not at all what I expected. You really do look like a beautiful girl.'

As I talked about my unhappiness as a child I could see that so many things were becoming clear to him. He knew that I had been isolated and often depressed. As a father he felt he had failed me. Now as I sat with him and felt free at last to speak from my heart, he could come to terms with his own feelings of frustration and sadness. 'So much makes sense now,' he said.

It was nearly light when we finally went to bed. 'This is going to take some time to understand,' said Dad, 'but I want you to know that we will support you in any way we can. We must think about what we should say to relatives and friends in the village. I don't want you being given a hard time.'

My eyes filled with tears again. I had expected rejection and instead was being offered unconditional love. I went up to my bedroom, and as I lay in that familiar bed staring up at the ceiling, I remembered all the sadness I had experienced as a young child, and felt it dissolve. For the first time in my life I was at peace with myself.

The next day we continued to talk. Both Mum and Dad made an immediate effort to call me Caroline. I was over-whelmed with gratitude. We decided that only our immediate family should know the truth. 'Wait until you have had the operation,' said Mum. 'Then, when you feel stronger and more confident, you can talk to the rest of them.' For the time being I would arrive and leave under cover of darkness. When friends asked after me, Mum and Dad would play the long-suffering parents of a heartless child who never thought to visit. This was all fine by me – I was just relieved to have the support of my family.

Dad drove me to the station that Sunday night. We hugged. 'This is your home,' he said. 'We will always want to see you here.'

'Thanks, Dad. I'm sorry I stayed away so long,' I said, wiping the tears from my eyes.

The next nine months were among the happiest of my life. The new show was a great success, and I was earning good money. Whenever I found the time, I would return to Brooke to spend the weekend with my family. I'd stay indoors for the two days, and if anyone came to call I would dash up the stairs and hide in the bedroom. Over the next three years this was to become a real routine. One Christmas, an uncle came to call and I sat upstairs waiting for him to leave. He was there for four hours! We had no central heating in the house at that time and I began to freeze. Mum came up twice with hot-water bottles. And I lay shivering under the covers, a prisoner in my own home!

Dad had begun reading everything he could find on the subject of transsexuality. He wanted to know exactly what I was going through. 'I'm only sorry we didn't understand earlier,' he said. 'I would have behaved so differently.'

'Dad,' I protested, 'you're not to blame. No one is to blame.'

One weekend he moved me to tears. 'I know this operation is very important to you. And I know it's going to cost a lot of money. I've got some savings that should just about cover the fee. Your mum and I would like you to have the money.'

I was stunned by their generosity. My dad was not a rich man, and he was offering me money he had managed to save out of years of hard work. I couldn't accept it.

'This is something I have to do for myself,' I explained gently. 'In any case, I must prove to the psychiatrist and the surgeon that I can live and work as a woman for three years before they will even consider operating.'

My relationship with my dad blossomed over the next few months. We could show each other affection. He gave me great confidence about my appearance, and would compliment me on my dress sense. But he did think I wore too much make-up. 'You've overdone the lipstick,' he would say. 'You've got lovely looks, Caroline. You don't need to cover them up.' Mum, on the other hand, would ask for my advice. 'Do you think this colour suits me?' she'd ask. She slipped into a mother/daughter relationship as though things had never been any different. Years later she was to tell a reporter, 'I had a beautiful son and now I have a beautiful daughter.' I was her child. She loved me no matter what.

I now had the confidence to go forward in my career. The Latin Quarter was the best club of its kind in London, but the height of every showgirl's ambition was to join the Bluebells. I was tall enough: at six feet I wouldn't be the tallest, but I was well above the minimum – five feet nine. And so, when I saw an advert in the *Stage* announcing an open audition for the troupe, I went along.

The casting director's name was Peter. He set me a simple routine to learn and seemed impressed with my performance. After the audition he came up to speak to me.

'I think there is a place for you in the Bluebell Revue,' he said. 'But I'd like to see you on stage first.'

I told him that I was appearing at the Latin Quarter, and the following evening he came to see the show. He waited to speak to me afterwards, and offered me the job. I was fantastically excited.

'Normally we send new girls to Paris, where they can gain some experience. But I feel so confident about your abilities that I want to send you straight into the show that is touring Spain at the moment. How do you feel about Barcelona?'

'Great!' I replied.

I didn't tell him I had never been abroad before! I handed in my notice at the Latin Quarter and began winding up my affairs in England.

First, though, I had to get a passport. I went to see my doctor to ask his advice. He gave me a letter for the passport office, stating that I intended to have a sex-change operation.

'Take that and your documents concerning your name

change down to Petty France. There shouldn't be any problem in issuing you a passport as a woman,' he told me.

At the passport office I was interviewed by a sympathetic lady. She asked me when I intended to have my operation, and I told her I was saving up for it and had got about a quarter of the money.

'Until you have undergone full surgery,' she explained, 'I can only give you a temporary passport. It's valid for one year. Keep me in touch with your progress and eventually we should be able to issue you with a ten-year passport.'

'Will it be possible for anyone to discover the reason for the one-year restriction?' I asked. She assured me that any information about me would remain confidential.

I took the document straight round to Peter so that he could make my travel arrangements for me. I let my flat, said farewell to my friends, and prepared for Europe.

But a few days before I was due to leave I received a phone call. It was Peter. 'Can you come into the office?' he asked. 'I want to ask you about something.'

I had already signed a contract and assumed it must be some minor detail that he had to discuss. But as I walked into his office I could tell from his expression that all was not well. He sighed.

'Why didn't you tell me, Caroline?' he said.

My heart missed a beat.

'Tell you what?'

'That you are not a woman.'

His reply stung me. 'I *am* a woman,' I protested. To me it was no lie; I felt like a woman, thought of myself as a woman, and looked like a woman. What more did he want?

'I know how you feel,' he said kindly. 'But you must understand my position. You haven't had surgery, and if the truth about your sexuality were ever discovered, the reputation of the Bluebells would be destroyed and I would lose my job.'

My eyes filled with tears. 'How did you find out?' I asked.

'The Spanish authorities made inquiries about the restriction on your passport, and our legal department had to check it out.'

He was very diplomatic. Obviously he didn't want to name his source. To this day I don't know whether it was the pass-

58

port office or one of the dancers at the Latin Quarter who tipped him off.

'Well, what happens now?' I asked, still hoping that all might not be lost.

'I'm truly sorry, Caroline, but while you are technically still a man I cannot offer you a job with the company. The moment you've had surgery you would be more than welcome to reapply.'

I was shattered. I had given up my home and my job and now I was left with nothing. Peter offered one ray of hope. He told me of a club in Paris where he thought they would take me on, and he gave me the name and number of a friend of his, a German girl called Helga.

'She's an ex-Bluebell, and she should be able to help you make a start in Paris.'

As I walked away from his office, my mind was in turmoil. I had no friends in Paris, and no certain prospect of work. But the idea of going back to the Latin Quarter and begging for my old job was unthinkable. I had too much pride.

'What the hell,' I thought. 'I've got nothing to lose.'

I left for Paris three days later.

6

Paris – Loneliness and Love

It was my first time abroad and my first time in the air. I felt as though the ground had literally been pulled away from under my feet! But I was desperate that no one should know that I was new to flying, and I sat there looking as nonchalant as possible. In truth, I was petrified! I kept my mouth open throughout take-off – I was convinced my ear drums would burst!

As soon as I arrived in Paris I rang Peter's friend Helga. She welcomed me to the city and gave me the addresses of several cheap hotels.

'Give me a ring when you are settled in and I'll come on over and take you out for a meal,' she said.

I took a cab to the first hotel on her list. It was in Montparnasse, and only five minutes from the club Peter had mentioned, the Alcazar. I was given a room on the first floor. It had wooden shutters and overlooked a courtyard paved in cobblestones. The furniture was basic: a wardrobe, chair, table, bed and wash-basin. But it was clean, and the proprietor offered special rates if you took the room for more than two weeks. I put my bag down on the bed and looked around. It wasn't home, but it would do.

That night Helga and I ate together in a little bistro around the corner. I liked her immediately. She was a tall, striking blonde, with short, cropped hair, and her manner was warm and friendly. She ran a small nightclub in Montparnasse, but had been a showgirl for several years.

'The Alcazar is one of the best,' she told me. 'I'll take you to the show and you can see for yourself.'

Helga knew from the beginning about my transsexuality. Since the club she ran was largely gay, she had no prejudices, but I did explain that I would rather no one else knew.

'I understand,' she said.

The next evening we went together to the Alcazar. It was nice walking down the street with Helga. So often I felt that I towered over people, but she was as tall as I was.

Helga talked as we walked.

'The show at the Alcazar is artistically better than the one at the Lido,' she said. 'There's more variety – singing, dance, comedy, drag. It's not just glamour. The Lido attracts more tourists because of the Bluebell legend. But the Alcazar pays better money.'

I was prepared to be impressed, but I could not have imagined the spectacle of the three-hour performance at the Alcazar. The stage was about ten times larger than the one at the Latin Quarter, and the club must have held a thousand people. They were ranged on three different levels. The show was technically sophisticated – the stage opening up to reveal a fountain during a stunning Busby Berkeley number, and then closing again for a skating scene set on ice. There was a moving staircase and an extraordinary cancan routine. I remember an animal act, a war scene with cannons that shot out clouds of glitter and coloured smoke, and the most accomplished drag artist I had ever seen, doing a perfect impression of Marlene Dietrich.

I was dazzled by it all, but I was also dismayed. I turned to Helga during the curtain call. 'The standard here is so high,' I said. 'They'll never even look at me.'

'Nonsense,' came Helga's reply. 'I know you're good. Peter told me all about you. All you need is a touch of Parisian hauteur.'

'Do you really think they might give me a job?' I asked.

'I'm certain of it. I'll find out when they are next auditioning.'

She rang me the next day. 'They are holding auditions in two days time. You'll need a routine to show them, but don't worry about the costume – they'll provide that. Be confident. A friend of mine tells me they are short of showgirls. I think you're in with a real chance.'

I passed the next few days alone and in a state of great tension. If I didn't get the job I would have to find something to keep me going. I was determined not to dig into the money I had saved from my time at the Latin Quarter. I remembered

Helga's words and tried to stay confident. I took myself off sight-seeing. It was dispiriting being alone in a foreign city. I found Paris very beautiful, but I had no one to share it with. And at that stage my French was not up to more than 'Bonjour', 'Au revoir', and 'Où est la toilette?' I had a terrible experience in a taxi, trying to explain to the driver that I wished to be taken to the Eiffel Tower. I guess my mime skills can't have been up to much!

Helga came with me to the audition. First we stopped at a café and shared a carafe of red wine. I needed to steady my nerves. The director of the show interviewed me, and since he spoke very little English and my French was non-existent, Helga acted as interpreter. After I'd told him about my experience as a showgirl, he sent me off to see the wardrobe mistress backstage, to slip on one of the girls' costumes. I put on a G-string, a towering headdress and nipple caps. Then I stepped out on to the vast stage.

The lights were blazing, and the auditorium was swallowed up in darkness! Hearing the first beats of the music, I launched into my routine. I had nowhere near enough material to cover that vast space – I was used to the modest little stage at the Latin Quarter, and after a while I began to run out of ideas. I could hear the director shouting from the auditorium.

'Plus sexy, plus sexy!' he yelled.

'That needs no translating,' I thought, as I threw myself into my routine with renewed vigour.

'Belle, belle. C'est bon, c'est très bon. OK, OK.'

The house lights came up and I slipped into the wings. Changing back into my clothes, I went out front to face the verdict.

'When can you start?' the director said.

'Tomorrow,' I replied.

I practically danced down the street. 'I've got a job. I've got a job!' I shouted. Helga laughed and gave me a hug.

'There, you see. What did I tell you?'

I went for costume fittings the next day. I was given a number of different outfits. No two showgirls had the same costume, but we all wore body make-up – multicoloured glitter dust that looked amazing under the lights. I was given a mass of feathers to wear, and a beautiful diamante G-string with three strips of diamonds fanning out across my hips. I had long, silky gloves that were also decorated with stones and sequins. The money spent on my costume alone must have been almost as much as the entire Latin Quarter wardrobe budget.

The director explained that he planned to bring me into the show in slow stages, and I spent the first week watching every performance. Then, at last, I was given a small part. Covered in body make-up, I had to stand on the moving staircase as part of the fountain tableau in the Busby Berkeley number. From that rather humble beginning, I was gradually integrated into the whole show, and eventually performed on an equal basis with the other showgirls.

Backstage the atmosphere was very relaxed. All the girls helped each other with their body make-up, and the two French girls I shared with would walk about the dressing room in the nude. I felt awkward and anxious. Obviously I couldn't take my G-string off. I faced further embarrassment when I realized that the backstage shower was communal; men and women were washing their body make-up off together. I went back to the dressing room and waited until everyone had gone, and then had my shower. Obviously I couldn't do this every night. But nor could I go home covered in body make-up. There was no other way – I would have to face the sniggers of the cast and shower in my G-string. They could put it down to my being an inhibited English girl.

Without Helga my life in Paris would have been very lonely. The cast were not unfriendly, but they were, for the most part, French, and I felt excluded from their conversations. The girls in my dressing room were both dancers, not showgirls, and there is a traditional rivalry between the two. Showgirls are paid more, and yet it is often the dancers who work the hardest. I put my head down and got on with the job, but I made no real friends. I spent the days alone, wandering around Paris. The little time I had free in the evenings I passed in the company of Helga.

One night she took me to a small club near Montmartre where they had cabaret. We were seated at the bar, sipping drinks, when Helga met a man she knew. She introduced me. He was good-looking, with a moustache, and despite the language barrier we got on well. At the end of the evening he asked, in broken English, if he could see me again. I agreed, puzzled by the mischievous gleam in Helga's eye.

The following week we went for a meal in a small bistro. It was a pleasant evening, and we communicated with sign language, pidgin English, and goodwill. I gave him a kiss as I was leaving. I liked him, but didn't expect the relationship to develop. Helga was desperately curious about the evening.

'How did you get on?' she asked.

'Well enough,' I replied. 'Why are you so keen to know?'

Then she told me. The 'man' I had had dinner with was actually a woman. She, like me, was waiting for her operation.

'Why didn't you tell me?' I said.

'Her sexuality, like yours, is a private matter. I have no right to go around telling people,' she replied.

I forgave her. But I felt very foolish. And I also felt sorry for the 'man'. Male-to-female transsexuality was hard enough, but for women wishing to become men, the surgery was terribly complex and often unsuccessful.

The whole episode left me feeling depressed and a little paranoid. How was I to form a successful relationship with a man, caught as I was between two sexes? I was terrified that my secret would be discovered. There were many men who would have become violent if they knew I was, technically, male. But of course, as a showgirl I attracted a great deal of attention. The Alcazar was a haunt of playboys and media personalities. There would often be a famous face or two in the audience. And after the show they would send champagne backstage for the cast. We would come front of house to meet them. I received many dinner invitations, and even accepted a couple.

But these experiences left me feeling dispirited. After a few dates, the man in question would become amorous, and I would have to start fighting off his advances. I could never relax. My standard line was, 'I am English, and I wish to be a virgin when I marry.' This was the 1970s, but even then I must have seemed a prude. I started to think that men were interested in one thing only, and that one thing was something I would never be able to provide.

I concentrated on the thought of the money I was earning,

and started drinking to keep cheerful. Opposite my hotel there was a little bar-restaurant where I used to eat, and down a glass or two of wine before going to the Alcazar. One evening, drowning my sorrows, I rather overdid it, and arrived at the club unsteady on my feet and grinning like a Cheshire cat. I struggled through the first half of the show, getting my steps all wrong but managing to arrive in the right place at the right time. But things fell apart in the second half, and disaster struck during the grand finale.

At the end of the show the stage opened up, and from out of the middle rose an enormous fountain gushing water. At the same moment girls throwing streamers and confetti were flown in on rockets. The showgirls moved to the front of the stage for the last song, throwing streamers into the audience, and then we were supposed to step back, to the side of the fountain, so that the dancers could come forward and take our place. I missed my footing, lurched backwards, and fell flat on my back in the fountain. The cold water hit me like a slap. I lay there, shivering, and scared witless. If I stood up the audience would see me, but if I stayed in the water any longer the dancers would have moved back upstage, and I would be exposed crouching in the fountain like a drowned parrot. I could see the stage manager signalling from the wings. He looked furious.

'Get out of the water!' he hissed.

I climbed out of the fountain and took my place with the other showgirls. The finale lasted an eternity. The girls around me were shaking with laughter as my flattened tail feathers dripped disconsolately on to the stage. My body make-up had run, and patches of my natural skin were showing through. I longed for the ground to swallow me up. As the lights went down I scuttled off the stage towards the safety of my dressing room. The stage manager beat me to it. He stopped me just as I reached the door.

'You were drunk!' he yelled. 'You were drunk throughout the whole show!'

I denied the accusation. My drenching had done much to sober me up. But, nevertheless, he gave me an official warning. If it ever happened again I would be out of a job. It never did. Once was quite enough!

After the show it took a while to wind down from the adrenalin, and the cast would often go out to eat or drink. A favourite late-night haunt was the Calvados, a small piano bar just off the Champs-Elysées. Being near the Lido, it was a popular spot with the Bluebells. There were one or two British girls in the troupe, and it was a relief for me to talk in English. One night as I was leaving to go home, a very tall, handsome man on his way into the club held the door open for me. As I walked away, I turned to look back over my shoulder. Our eyes met in the briefest of glances. The image of his face stayed in my mind all the next day. The following evening, during the show, I spotted him in the audience. It was in the Brazilian scene – the showgirls were moving through the auditorium and, as the music started up, we would begin singing and dancing our way up the aisles and on to the stage. It was carnival time! As I passed this rather intriguing stranger he looked up at me and smiled. He had a beautiful face with large, dark eyes, and I assumed from his appearance that he was Middle Eastern.

He was waiting for me after the show. 'Congratulations on your performance. I thought you were stunning. Would you consider having dinner with me?'

I laughed. His manners were so perfect and his smile so engaging I couldn't refuse.

He took me to a wonderful restaurant, and at the end of the evening drove me back to my hotel.

'Will you have dinner with me tomorrow?' he asked. I looked at his face – his warm eyes and his frank smile. I knew that the relationship couldn't possibly work. 'It's bound to fizzle out like all the others,' I thought. But somehow I hadn't the heart to refuse his invitation.

I lay awake that night, thinking about this man, my loneliness in Paris, and my need for a stable relationship. If he were to become seriously involved with me I would have to tell him the truth. The idea appalled me. I was so frightened of rejection.

'Perhaps he'll get bored,' I thought.

But he didn't. And, in the end, telling the truth was simpler than I could ever have imagined. After that first evening we spent every day together. We went sight-seeing, climbed the

Eiffel Tower, ate lunch in Montmartre, shopped in the Rue de Rivoli, and dined in some of the best restaurants in Paris. He showered me with flowers, gifts and affection. I was nineteen and falling in love. He told me he came from Kuwait, and was living in a suite at the Georges Cinq. He was clearly very wealthy. He spoilt me and cared for me in a way that I had never experienced, and the idea of losing him seemed more difficult with every day that passed. But he had to know the truth and, finally, one evening over dinner, I plucked up the courage to tell him. The physical attraction between us was strong, and he had been getting steadily more and more amorous. So, clearing my throat, I began with 'I've got something to tell you . . . '

But it was I who was surprised. He didn't bat an eyelid.

'It makes no difference,' he said. 'You are a very beautiful person, and I am in love with you.'

And there began a summer of great happiness. He asked me to move into the Georges Cinq with him, and I agreed. I was nervous at the thought of a sexual relationship, but I was also starved of physical affection. I needed to be touched, to be loved and accepted. He made me feel relaxed about my body.

'You are beautiful,' he told me. 'You have nothing to be ashamed of.'

But it wasn't long before the differences between us became apparent. He didn't want me to work at the Alcazar. He only had a few more weeks in Paris, and wanted me to spend all my time with him.

'I can't give up work,' I told him. 'I need the money for my operation.'

'You don't need an operation,' he argued. 'You're perfect as you are. You've got the best of both worlds. You are a boy and a girl – unique. Don't change.'

Anyone could have predicted that those differences would become more pronounced as time passed. But I was wilfully blind. I had struggled alone for so long that I needed the comfort and security of a relationship. And so, when H asked me to come back with him to Kuwait, I agreed. For the first time since leaving home and coming to London, I was allowing myself to be deflected from my goal. Later I was to see this episode in my life as a very important one. Subconsciously, I was setting myself a final test. Could I be happy as I was? He may have had homosexual tendencies, but he was primarily interested in me as a unique human being. He loved both the male and female in me. This man loved me for what I was. He was offering to support me and care for me. If, after all that, I was left feeling lonely and dissatisfied, I would know for certain that surgery was the only option.

I broke the news to the production manager at the Alcazar.

'I'll be sorry to see you go, Caroline,' he said. 'You're good at your job, and we were hoping to offer you a bigger part in the next show. If things don't work out for you with this man, remember, you can always come back.'

Some of the girls were anxious for me. 'You must be careful. The men in these Middle Eastern countries have a very different view of women. You may find H very changed when he is in his own country.'

I didn't entirely ignore their warnings. If things didn't work out I was prepared to contact the producer of a show at the Casino de Lebanon. I had met him in the Alcazar, and he had told me he was always looking for experienced showgirls.

H had flown home ahead of me, but he rang every day. He had promised to find me an apartment.

'I want to create a beautiful home for you,' he told me on the phone. At last a letter arrived with a first-class ticket inside. I said goodbye to everyone at the Alcazar, packed my bags, and flew out of Paris. Ahead of me was Kuwait, the desert, and one of the strangest episodes in the story of my life.

7

Kuwait – a Gilded Cage

The desert. I stared down at the unfamiliar landscape stretched out before me. I had expected white sand, palm trees, herds of camels. But the reality was infinitely more mysterious. An endless plain of brown and ochre, sculpted by the wind, with no people or houses to be seen. Every so often a tongue of fire would appear burning on the horizon. I squinted, trying to make out the source of the flame. Grouped around these huge columns of fire were clusters of tiny buildings. Later I was to learn that these were oil wells burning off the excess oil.

As I stepped off the plane the heat rose up from the tarmac to greet me. It was like walking into an oven. I stood still for a moment, breathing in the thick air with its strange scents. My hair, which had been freshly curled that morning, wilted along with my courage. Suddenly I felt nervous. This was a very foreign land, and I had only one friend in it.

The terminal building was a huge corrugated-iron shack. I was standing in the queue, waiting to clear immigration, when a man in uniform came up and asked me if I was Caroline.

'Please follow me,' he said, and, waving a document at the official on the desk, led me past the queue and into the baggage area. Again, no checks were made, and my luggage was chalked with a white cross. I was ushered outside, and towards a huge, gleaming, black Cadillac with tinted windows. The chauffeur opened the back door, and there was H, dressed in white Arab robes and wearing dark glasses. I was so pleased to see him, I didn't think to ask 'Why all the secrecy?' But later, when I knew more about him, I realized that he was desperate not to be seen.

We drove out of the city to a place called Salamia. Salamia was a small resort perched on the edge of the ocean, and rather naively I asked if we could go for a swim.

'It is forbidden for women to wear bikinis in public. Besides, I do not wish you to sunbathe. The sun is very fierce in Kuwait, and you will damage your skin. It is better if you stay covered.'

I pulled a face. But at that moment the car drew up outside a huge block of flats and the subject was dropped.

'Here is your new home,' said H.

The building towered above us.

'There is no one else living here,' he explained. 'I bought the whole block and have had people working day and night to furnish and decorate the penthouse. The other apartments are shells. From your window you can see the sea.'

We took the lift up to the top flooor, and H picked me up and carried me over the threshold. I stood there gaping. The flat was vast. A huge living room led on to a palatial balcony. I ran out to look at the view. The sun was setting and, seated on a great sand dune, staring out at the sea and the sunset, were a group of Arabs, motionless apart from the gentle flapping of their robes. I stood hypnotized. H came out to join me. He took my hand. 'Come. I have more surprises for you,' he said.

He showed me the main bedroom, all decorated in a cool blue that reminded me of the sea, and the adjoining bathroom with a sunken bath and a mirror that covered one entire wall. In the lounge there was a stereo that piped music to all the rooms, a television, and a film projector.

'Have you looked inside the wardrobe?' he asked, smiling.

I ran back into the bedroom and threw open the wardrobe doors. They were filled with beautiful clothes – designer dresses, silk lingerie, impossibly glamorous negligees. On the dressing table stood two jewellery boxes crammed with exquisite gems. I had no idea that such opulence was possible.

So began a new episode in my life. I lived in complete luxury. I had every material comfort that money could buy. The fridge was kept stocked with every delicacy imaginable. I had only to ask for something and it was brought. The flat was kept spotless by a small team of domestics, and I had a personal bodyguard who lived on the ground floor opposite the lift. If I wanted to go out, or needed anything fetching, I had only to call him on the phone. I had my own car – a black Cadillac with tinted windows – driven by my own chauffeur.

After the noise and excitement of Paris, this was a very quiet and secluded life. I saw no one but H. He would visit me three times a day: in the morning around eight o'clock, at lunchtime, and in the evening.

'Why can't you stay the night?' I asked. But he told me that would be impossible.

'I live with my family, and they would disapprove of my being involved with a European girl. Please do not be offended. They are very old-fashioned.'

I told him I understood. But instinctively I knew this could not be the only explanation. H was a handsome and wealthy man in his late thirties. One day, after I had been in Kuwait for about three weeks, I challenged him.

'Are you married?' I asked.

He told me that not only did he have a young Kuwaiti bride, he was also married to a Japanese woman. I was horrified.

'Why didn't you tell me this in Paris?' I demanded.

'I was so scared you wouldn't come to Kuwait. Please, please don't be angry, Caroline. I love you. That is all that matters.'

I was a fool for soft words and forgave his duplicity. H explained that in his country marriages were arranged.

'It's all a matter of family, money and property,' he said. 'And men here can have as many as eight wives.'

We made our peace, but with every passing day I became more and more unhappy with my life in this gilded cage. I spent my days watching films, visiting the beauty salon, and preparing for H's visits. He loved my hair, and demanded that I washed and styled it every day, and he liked me to be immaculately dressed and perfumed. I had wanted to experience a settled relationship, but here I was beginning to feel more like a favourite pet than an adored partner.

I tried to stave off the growing boredom. I learnt to cook, and H bought me a library full of cookery books. At first I was hopeless, but through practice I improved. One day I decided to cook H a traditional English meal – stew and dumplings. I rang my mum and she gave me the recipe. With the bodyguard and chauffeur I went to the supermarket. It was a strange experience. Everywhere I went people stopped to stare at me. I had tried to dress as modestly as I could: I wore a blouse with a high neck and a pair of linen trousers. I had pulled my

71

hair back into a ponytail and left my face bare of make-up. But still I created a sensation. The men were not used to seeing women with their heads uncovered, especially not women as tall as I was. I tried to outstare them. They turned their faces away. The women, hidden behind their black veils, hissed with disapproval. I felt like a freak and left as quickly as possible.

'Why don't you ask your family to visit you?' suggested H. 'I will pay for their tickets.'

But he wasn't the only one who had been telling a few lies. I had told Mum and Dad that I was on tour in the Middle East. Desperate as I was for affection, I was able at first to ignore the more perverse elements of this relationship, but I didn't expect for a moment that either of my parents would feel the same way. They were bound to tell me that I was being exploited. And I knew it would disturb my father terribly if he were to learn that I was engaged in a sexual relationship with a man. I spoke to them often, but managed to stay vague about life on tour. Sitting in splendid isolation in my penthouse, the sound of my mum's voice on the telephone would make me ache with loneliness. I was homesick.

I was also feeling claustrophobic. I could never leave the flat on my own, and I would stare enviously at the people wandering along the beach in the cool of the early morning or the shade of evening. One day I decided to break the rules. 'I'll go exploring on my own,' I thought.

At the far end of the top floor there was a service lift that was seldom used. I went down to the ground floor and sneaked out of a side door without the security guard spotting me. It was glorious to be outside! I crossed the road and walked towards the beach. The traffic ground to a halt. Everyone was staring at me, and a few of the men were waving and whistling. I gritted my teeth and strode on.

The beach was deserted apart from a group of three or four women, their black robes rustling in the wind. They were standing at the water's edge, feeling the waves lap at their bare toes. I walked towards them. But the moment they spotted me they covered their faces and turned away. I shrugged my shoulders and walked on. Behind me I heard the now familiar hiss.

I walked for about two miles. But the further I went, the

more alarmed I became. Heads would pop up from behind the sand dunes, and soon it became obvious that there was a group of men following me. I passed three fishermen who dropped their rods in amazement and stared. I no longer felt safe, and turned back in the direction of the flat. The watchers-in-the-sand followed me and I quickened my pace. By the time I reached the apartment block, I was nearly running.

Safely back in my apartment, I slammed the door and stood with my back pressed against it, panting. I was hot and tearful. When I had caught my breath, I walked out on to the balcony. The big sand dune in front of the apartment building was covered with groups of men, all staring up at the flat. I ducked behind the curtains. 'Oh my God,' I thought. 'They know where I live.' It felt like I was under siege. I spent the rest of that day sitting inside and praying that H would not discover I had gone out alone. When he arrived that evening, he said nothing. But that was the last time I ventured out unaccompanied. I felt like a prisoner in my own home!

Very occasionally H would visit me at weekends, and once or twice he took me away. We would go for long drives into the desert. I saw the oil wells with the fountains of flame I had spotted from the plane. H owned a villa ten miles down the coast and one Saturday he drove me there. We travelled across miles of barren land, and then, all of a sudden, an oasis of green materialized from among the dunes. It was like some absurd Hollywood film set. The villa was magnificent, a small palace surrounded by water and trees. It was protected by high walls that ran right into the ocean, and at night the sea was lit up by powerful searchlights to frighten away the sharks.

These outings were a great treat for me, but they happened only rarely. For most of the time I was left alone. I would sit in front of my mirror staring blankly at my reflection, or empty the jewel box on to the table and run my fingers through the cool, smooth gems. I had been used to working since the age of fifteen, so this enforced idleness was enervating. My fondness for H diminished with every day. Sex became the battleground.

From the beginning, H had rejoiced in my body *as it was*. Initially this brought an extraordinary sense of relief. I hadn't been able to stand naked in front of anyone for so long that there was a kind of luxurious abandon about the sensation. He was in no way effeminate, and treated me privately and publicly as a woman. To be adored and worshipped by such a good-looking man gave me an enormous confidence boost. I'd never experienced that kind of attention before. But the sexual side of our relationship afforded me little satisfaction. I loved to be kissed and held, and I was happy to give him pleasure. But I hated him to touch my penis. To begin with I didn't complain. It seemed to give him such happiness that I kept quiet. But as time went by, it was more and more difficult to bear. I found that part of my body so repulsive that his desire for me began to sicken and repel me.

'How can you possibly love me as I am when I find myself so hideous?' I asked.

But H was essentially a selfish lover. It didn't much concern him that I was getting little or no sexual satisfaction from our relationship. I was pretty much incapable of having an orgasm or maintaining an erection. All those months of taping myself had almost certainly damaged me. The excitement for me had been largely generated in my head. I was happiest when he lay on top of me and simulated heterosexual intercourse. Then I could imagine that I was the woman of his dreams. I was hooked on romance, but the reality was rather different. He wanted anal intercourse, I refused, and we began to have fierce rows.

'What you want is a boy, not me,' I told him.

'I've never slept with a boy in my life,' he retorted.

He would lecture me for hours on the beauty of my body. 'Stay as you are,' he would beg. 'You are so desirable.'

But I wanted to talk about a date for my surgery. I knew Casablanca was not so very far away. I begged H to let me go there and have the operation. He refused.

'If you stay as you are, I will give you whatever you want. But if you have surgery you must pay for it yourself.'

The discussions would end in tears and shouting. Then, to punish me, H would stay away for a few days, and I would be left totally alone. I would retaliate my letting my appearance go. I would leave my hair unwashed and not put on make-up. H felt very hurt and upset. He could see that he was losing me. He made one last effort.

'Marry me,' he declared one day after dinner. 'I can take another wife. Nobody need know about your past, and you and I can live together.'

But it was too late. That night, after he had left, I stood before the mirror and gazed at my naked body. H's words were ringing in my ears. 'You will *never* be a woman, Caroline. No matter what the surgeons do.'

Perhaps he was right. But at least surgery would give me the chance to experience a sexual relationship that didn't leave me feeling nauseated and abused. I couldn't relate to the image I saw in the mirror, and this liaison with H was only adding to my mental torment. I had been deflected from my goal long enough. It was time to go back to the real world.

I told H that I wanted to leave. He broke down and sobbed.

'At least wait until winter. Then we can return to Europe together. I will be there for three months. We can live together in Paris. It will be better, I promise. You'll be free to visit all your friends.'

But I knew it was over. I couldn't wait a further two months in the luxurious home that had become my prison, and I was beginning to feel alarmed lest he should not let me go at all.

Finally he handed me my air ticket and some money for travel expenses. I rang Pam and told her I was coming back. I took the clothes I had arrived in and nothing else. There were thousands of pounds worth of jewellery in that flat, but I left it untouched. I had been brought up knowing that it was wrong to steal. If H had offered, I would have wanted to take something to help with the cost of the operation. But relations between us were not good, and I was just anxious to get away.

As the plane took off for London, I looked down at the buildings as they got smaller and smaller. Life in Kuwait had been an experience, but I was relieved to be going. I had been offered everything by a man who wanted me as I was, and it had not been anywhere near enough. I was still young and naive, but I now knew one thing for certain: I had to have gender-reassignment surgery or reconcile myself to living alone. The other thing I had learnt was that men were not always to be trusted. They told lies. I decided that when I found a man to love he would have to be honest and faithful. Second-best would never do for me.

8

Variations on a G-string

After the desert, the green Norfolk fields were a joy to behold. I sat on the train grinning like a happy idiot. I was home at last and on my way to see my parents. I had never felt so pleased to see the Broads. They lay damp and lush under a heavy sky. Even the rain seemed exotic.

I hadn't told Mum and Dad that I was coming home; I wanted to surprise them. I took a taxi out to the village, taking care not to be seen by any of the neighbours, and crept into the house through the back door. Mum was upstairs ironing in the spare room. I called up to her and then bounded up the stairs and threw myself into her arms. She was overwhelmed.

'But I thought you were still in the Middle East! You only phoned two days ago. Are you all right, sweetheart? Nothing bad has happened, has it?'

I laughed. 'Slow down, Mum,' I said. 'Everything is fine. Things just didn't work out with the job. And besides, I was homesick.'

'Your dad'll be home in a minute,' she said. 'I'll go and put the kettle on. And when he gets in you must tell us all about it.'

My dad was fascinated by my stories of the Middle East and the Muslim culture. He had travelled a good deal himself during the war and loved to hear about other people's adventures. It was hard not telling them both about H and my lonely life in the penthouse. We talked for hours.

'So, what next?' asked Dad.

'I don't know,' I replied. 'I've nowhere near enough money to pay for the surgery, so I'll need to find a job that pays well. I don't think I can bear to wait much longer.'

Dad could see that, despite my cheerful demeanour, I was

anxious and becoming increasingly desperate. He repeated the offer he had made to me before I went to Paris.

'Let me pay for the operation, Caroline,' he begged.

But I had to refuse. 'I really can't, Dad. It's something that I have to do for myself. Besides, these operations do not have a guarantee of success, and I couldn't stand it if I thought it was your money that had been wasted.'

He put his arm around me and gave me a hug. 'I understand,' he said.

But the question remained. What *was* I to do? The experience with H had left me deeply unhappy. I needed the operation in order to be able to live an open and fulfilled life. But where was I going to find a job that would pay enough money? I didn't want to have to wait another two years while I saved. I thought about returning to the Alcazar but winced at the idea. I had said my farewells and headed off to a new life of domestic bliss with H. I couldn't bear the thought of those people knowing that the Kuwait trip had been a failure. I was heavy enough with my sense of shame and inadequacy. Any more humiliation and I felt I would crumble.

I bought a copy of the *Stage* and scoured the pages for job advertisements. But it was the wrong time of the year: none of the troupes were taking on new girls. In London, the Latin Quarter still offered the best pay. The Talk of the Town were reasonably generous to their dancers, but they didn't employ showgirls. There was nothing else for it. I would have to summon up all my courage and pay a visit to my old friends in Wardour Street.

Walking in through the stage door, I bumped into one of the dancers, a man named Adrian, who I had always liked and got on well with. He was pleased to see me.

'How are you?' he asked. 'You look amazing. Are you still with the Bluebells?'

I told him the whole story over a cup of coffee, and asked him whether there were any jobs going at the club. But he had a better idea.

'If you want to make money fast, Caroline, don't come back here. Go abroad and work in striptease. That's where the money is.'

I burst out laughing. Adrian knew that I was still waiting for my operation. I may have convinced audiences as a showgirl – but striptease! He explained. 'In many European countries striptease acts stop, by law, at the G-string. You wore a G-string as a showgirl and nobody could tell the difference. Your breasts look wonderful. You move well. Why shouldn't you be able to strip? It may not appeal to you much but I assure you it's the way to make money.'

I went away and gave the idea some thought. Being a stripper would not be something I could feel proud of, and I wouldn't want to tell my family. It would mean more anxiety about exposure. I would be putting myself and my sexuality in the brightest of lights, and I knew that, given my overwhelming fear of rejection, that was a rather perverse thing to be doing. But . . . I was used to appearing topless, and I had been living as a woman for so long now that I felt confident that people saw me as a female without question. What was between my legs was my business and no one else's. The biggest incentive was the money. Flying to Paris without the security of either work or friends had proved to me the strength of my own willpower. If I had done it before, I could do it again.

The next day I rang Adrian.

'I think your idea is a good one, and I have a favour to ask. Would you help me put together an act?'

He agreed, and I was delighted. Adrian was a talented dancer who worked both at the Latin Quarter and the Talk of the Town. He was a natural choreographer. We started work at once. I was keen to avoid anything tacky. I knew that my looks and my height gave me a certain sophistication, and I wanted to market that quality. Adrian agreed.

'You should play it very cool and slightly severe,' he advised.

I had very little money to spend on costume, but I worked with that basic idea, and adapted a black halter-necked dress that I had. It was split up the sides, and Adrian suggested I get it sequinned.

'That way it'll catch the light,' he said. 'Then, with your hair piled up on top of your head and a feather boa draped round your shoulders, you have the basis for an act.'

I added a tight-fitting corselet and a G-string made from the faithful old extra-strength elastic that I had relied on as a showgirl. We chose 'Baby Blues' by Barry White for the music. It was slow and sultry with a heavy drum beat. We worked out a basic routine, and then I ran it again and again until it was as smooth and controlled as I could make it. Adrian was pleased with the end result.

'It looks good, Caroline. I think you'll be a real hit.'

We discussed various places where I might try for work. I decided on Italy. It was as good a place as any, and I had got on well with the Italians I had met in London. And so I packed my little black dress, my G-string, my feather boa and my cassette tape, and bought a ticket for Rome. Once again I was heading into the unknown.

9

A Stranger in Rome

I fell in love with Rome at first sight. The terracotta roofs, the noisy streets, the sense of history, and the physical beauty of the people all overwhelmed me. This seemed a city dedicated to the pleasures of life.

I found a small hotel near the Piazza Barberini. It was central and not prohibitively expensive. I booked in and then found a trattoria where I had my evening meal. As I ate I planned my next move. I had about £200 with me, but most of that I considered an emergency fund. I needed to buy a guide of the city's nightlife, a map, and a guidebook. Then I could begin doing the rounds of those clubs that offered striptease acts. I spoke almost no Italian, and so persuading prospective employers would not be easy. I would have to take Barry White with me and be prepared to do an on-the-spot hard sell.

I woke early the next morning and began my search. Working on the notion 'the bigger the ad, the bigger the club', I picked out the Astoria – a club that offered dinner, cabaret and striptease. It opened at ten in the evening. So that night I grabbed the black dress, stuffed the boa into a bag, and, mustering all my courage, went to call.

The club was a great deal smaller than I had imagined, but it was well designed and cleverly lit. There was a tiny dance floor that could be raised up to form a stage for the cabaret and striptease. I asked if any of the staff spoke English, and one of the cocktail waiters came out to talk to me. I told him I was a dancer, had danced in France and England, and was looking for a job.

'How old are you?' he asked.

Not knowing what the law in Italy was about dancers, I lied and told him I was twenty-one. I was in fact only just twenty.

'It's possible you might be able to find work here,' he said.

'But you will have to come back tomorrow and speak to the manager.'

The next day I went through the whole ordeal again. This time the manager came out to speak to me. He spoke little English and was very abrupt.

'You have photographs to show me?' he asked.

Of course, I had none. I tried to distract him by describing my costume and parts of my act. He watched impassively as I gabbled away. Finally he interrupted: 'OK. I see how good you are. You go on tonight. Do the show. If I like you, I give you the job.'

I froze in horror. It had taken all my nerve to get this far. But to have to perform right then and there . . . The manager was staring at me, waiting for my answer.

'Fine. OK. Right,' I stuttered, and headed for the bar and a stiff drink.

As I sat there holding panic at bay the show started. All the performers seemed remarkably accomplished. A Chinese girl performed small miracles with fans, a flamenco dancer set the place alight with rhythm, and a belly dancer wiggled her way into everyone's heart.

'You're next,' hissed the stage manager. 'Go and get changed.' With a sinking heart I handed him the tape and headed for the dressing room.

Somewhat anaesthetized by alcohol, I gave that performance everything I had. From the very first beat of the music, I smouldered with all the sex appeal I could muster. Even I was surprised by what I managed. With one deft move I loosed my hair and, as it tumbled down around my shoulders, I glowered at the audience. 'Well, that should scorch them,' I thought. 'Let's just hope my G-string doesn't snap!' Each time I did something suggestive I would chuck a 'you can look but you can't touch' stare at the men in the audience. 'I hope they don't think I'm just bad-tempered,' I thought, and felt a giggle coming on. I reached the end of the routine without mishap and was amazed to hear the audience burst into spontaneous applause. I smiled, bowed rather awkwardly, and ran for the dressing rooms. The manager was waiting for me. He had a grin the size of his face.

'When can you start?' he asked.

My mother in her late teens

My dad in his army uniform

As a young boy with a horrendous short-back-and-sides that did me no favours

Even at four I fantasized about having boobs!

Getting cuddles from Mum, aged two

One of our regular weekend picnics at the coast

Posing in Pam's swimsuit, which I much preferred to shorts

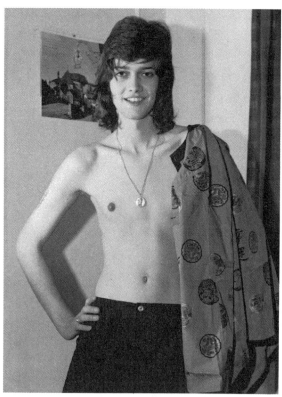

In London at
sixteen

At the Latin Quarter: before my breast operation

Able to work topless

With the cast from the Latin Quarter
backstage

Top My first modelling card

Page three shot: one of my first topless photographic assignments

The famous Smirnoff shot

Taken by Greg Barratt in Australia for Jane
Cattlin in Australian *Vogue*

Publicity shot for the Bond film *For Your Eyes Only* taken in Greece

Above Modelling in
Italy for
photographer
Bruno Oliveiro

Beauty shot taken
by Sanders
Nicholson

'As soon as you want,' I replied.

'You can have a contract in the morning and start work tomorrow night.'

'Fine,' I said, playing it cool. Secretly I was thrilled. It may not have been the job of my dreams, but the money would be great. 'I'll see you tomorrow,' I said, and headed for the door.

And so I began my life as Caroline – the English Rose, striptease star of the Astoria. And what a strange life it was. No one knew my secret and I had no close friends in Rome to confide in. I became quite schizophrenic – I was attracting a lot of sexual attention from men in my job, but in my private life I was discouraging all advances. The Astoria had women employed as hostesses whose job it was to encourage the clientele to consume vast quantities of champagne. I could get commission on sales if I wished to join the table of any member of the audience who sent an invitation. But it was entirely at my discretion. I wasn't obliged to drink with anyone. Of course, in time I realized that this was the way to make money. But I had to make it clear that I was not available for any kind of relationship. I told everyone that I lived with my boyfriend and couldn't see people after work.

Initially the hostesses were wary of me. I was a new face in town and, as such, in demand. I was making a small fortune in champagne commissions. But with time they got to know and like me, and even shared a few tricks of the trade.

'If you don't want to end each evening smashed out of your mind,' they told me, 'you have to get rid of your drink. That way you stay sober and the customer buys more champagne.'

There were a number of ways of emptying your glass. You could tip the wink to a waiter and he would arrange to 'spill' the glass while you and the gentleman were on the dance floor. Alternatively, you could tip the full glass into the ice bucket when your escort's attention was elsewhere. The favoured method was to simply pour the stuff straight on to the floor. The first time I gave that a whirl it ended in disaster. The champagne hit the deck and proceeded to froth noisily on the carpet.

'Never mind,' said my drinking companion. 'Have another glass.'

Later the girls explained where I had gone wrong. 'You have to get the bubbles out first!' they exclaimed.

I had no idea that it was possible to get the bubbles out of champagne, but apparently, if you 'twizzled' a swizzle stick round and round your glass *before* chucking it on the carpet, the bubbles would all be released and your escort, having missed this extraordinary sleight of hand, would simply assume that you were a truly enthusiastic drinker. It didn't take me long to become an expert, and soon I was 'selling' up to ten bottles of champagne a night. I stayed sober, but the carpet was pickled.

I didn't particularly like the champagne 'scam' but, at the end of the day, if I felt awkward I could always get up from the table and walk away. The hostesses didn't have that choice. It was their job to keep the customers drinking. And there was a sleazy side to the club. A number of the hostesses were making extra money by prostitution. It was all done very carefully, but it certainly went on. I got to know two of the girls, and was shocked to learn just how hard their lives were. Both of them were single mothers, and both had been deserted by the fathers of their children. They struggled to survive. I admired their guts, but I didn't envy them their jobs.

I remained isolated and anxious. For me, life before surgery could not be anything but a waiting game, but Rome did begin to work its magic, and I started to relax. I found it easier to learn Italian than French, and I was soon able to hold basic conversations with people. I was somewhat ashamed to be a stripper, and I certainly didn't tell anyone outside the club about my work, but I cannot deny that there were aspects of the job that I enjoyed. It certainly beat the hell out of hairdressing, and I got quite addicted to the adrenalin of performance. I was hungry for male reassurance. Not able to validate myself in a one-to-one sexual relationship with a man, I needed to prove my femininity in a public arena.

It may be hard for women who were born female to understand how I felt. Most women who have grown up accustomed to feeling secure about their identity would have been irritated or even angered by the catcalls and wolf whistles that followed almost every foreign girl in Rome. But I lapped it up. To be getting the sexual recognition that for years I felt I had been denied was amazing. I was so vulnerable. I needed to see myself reflected back in those men's eyes as an attractive woman. Only then could I truly believe I was desirable. Now I am older and wiser I find it hard to believe I was so hungry for attention and so very naive. I was in my twenties, but emotionally I was still a teenager, trying to find first love. The formative years that a woman spends learning about her sexuality in order to be free of it were lost to me.

So when men in the audience cheered and whistled, I basked in the light of their attention. I particularly remember Friday nights. That was when the soldiers came in – it was their pay-day I suppose. There were only four or so strip clubs in Rome, and the soldier boys headed straight for one or another of them. The place would be packed with these remarkably handsome young men, all pressed up close to the stage. They never had much money, but I would sit with them anyway, and forget the champagne commissions. They were high-spirited, witty and surprisingly courteous. On those nights I would make a special effort to put on a good show.

One evening my dedication nearly brought disaster. I was half-way through my routine, and things were going really rather well. I had reached that ever-popular moment when, lying on the floor with one leg above my head, I ran my hand slowly and seductively down the back of my thigh. Suddenly there was a loud 'ping'. It was my worst nightmare come true – the elastic on one side of my G-string had snapped. My whole life passed before my eyes. 'Well, this is it,' I thought. 'I'm about to be lynched by fifty enraged Italian servicemen.' But never one to give up the struggle, I grabbed at the loose threads of elastic and, heart thudding, attempted to tie the two pieces back together again. This delicate operation was performed to the cheers, laughter and general delight of the audience. I achieved the impossible and, with my secret still under wraps, carried on with the act. Afterwards, seated in my dressing room with a large vodka for comfort, I reflected on my lucky escape. If I had been standing up at the point the G-string gave way I wouldn't have had a chance. The prospect was so terrifying that I began to shake with nervous laughter. From that day on I ran some very intensive tests on the elastic before every show. I was taking no chances.

After I had been in Italy for several weeks, I had moved from the hotel to a private house owned by a couple who let rooms to students. I told them I was a dancer, and they were happy to let me rent. It was a nice place, and I had a small room of my own, with a wash-basin. I shared a bathroom and a kitchen. Best of all, I was given my own key so I could come and go as I pleased.

As the weather got warmer, I spent more and more time on the beach perfecting my tan. After coming back from Kuwait whiter than the driven snow, I was determined this time to impress my family with my bronzed skin. The beach was thirty minutes away by train, and I would go most days. Anxious as I was to avoid trouble, I refused all invitations from men to join them, and spent my time in splendid isolation. The last thing I needed to do was get involved with a man. All I wanted was to work hard, save as much money as I could, then go home to have surgery. If I couldn't get it done in England, I would go to Casablanca. It was all very clear-cut, and I thought I had the situation settled. Then, one day, Claudio came padding along the sand.

He was tall, with blond, sun-bleached hair, and big blue eyes. He smiled and said, 'Hello.' I smiled back, and soon he was sitting on the sand beside me telling me about his job as a pilot for Alitalia.

'What do you do?' he asked.

'I'm a dancer,' I lied. I should have told the truth, but I didn't expect to see him again and I wanted this lovely man to go on talking and smiling for as long as possible.

'Where do you dance?' he asked. 'I'd love to come and watch you.'

'Oh, I'm not going to tell you that,' I said coyly, hoping he wouldn't press. He asked no more questions, but as the sun sank lower in the sky and I got up to leave, he was unwilling to let me go.

'Please, at least let me take you out to dinner,' he pleaded.

'I'm busy every night.'

'Oh, come on, you must have a night off. You'd drop with exhaustion otherwise!'

I laughed. 'OK. It's true I do have one night off a week.'

'Say you'll spend it with me,' he said.

I agreed, and the following week we went out to eat.

It was a blissful evening, with all the romance that Italy can offer – a candlelit restaurant, a balmy evening, spectacular scenery, and even a red rose. After dinner we went dancing. He wrapped his arms around me and I put my head on his shoulder. I could have stayed there for ever. But with physical closeness came sexual desire and that for me signalled disaster. I gently pulled away, told him I was tired, and asked him to take me home.

'When can I see you again?' he asked.

Much as I liked him, I couldn't afford to encourage this relationship. Another experience like Kuwait would have shattered me.

'I really am busy every night,' I said. 'And I don't get home until very late.'

I gave him a swift peck on the cheek and slipped into the house before he had time to argue. But he wasn't about to give up. When I returned home the following evening, he was waiting for me outside the door.

'Hello,' he grinned.

'I'm afraid I'm just on my way out,' I lied.

'Oh yes? Where are you going?'

'To eat.'

'Well, I'll come with you.'

This wasn't working.

I tried another tack. 'I'm a stripper at the Astoria!' I blurted it out, turned on my heels and fled inside.

But still he was undeterred. The next night he was waiting for me outside the club. We went out for a meal and after that evening he waited for me after every show. He wouldn't come into the club – he said it disturbed him to see all those men staring at my body. 'It doesn't seem like you at all,' he said.

The relationship developed, and I could feel myself once again caught up in a web of deceit. As we saw more and more of each other, Claudio became increasingly amorous. He was never overbearing but naturally when we got close he would want to express his desire for me. I felt like a goalkeeper fending off the shots.

'I can't,' I'd say. 'It's . . . difficult.'

I tried to stop seeing him. But he would become upset and

bewildered, and I missed him terribly. Finally I told him that I was waiting for an operation, and was unable for the time being to make love. It was as close to the truth as I dared get. There was no possibility of telling this man the whole truth. He was rather 'macho', and I knew he would have been horrified. I was playing a dangerous game. 'If I can just buy a little time,' I thought, 'I can get to Casablanca, have the operation, and then he need never know.' If the relationship moved towards marriage, then obviously I would have to tell him. But it might never come to that.

I worked like a demon, and the champagne sales rocketed! At the end of every week I put my pay cheque straight into the bank and rushed home to my pocket calculator. The weeks turned into months and finally I had sufficient money. I wasted no time. I gave in my notice at the Astoria, packed my bags, and said my farewells to Claudio.

'I'm going home to see my doctor,' I explained. 'I'll phone you whenever I can. But don't worry if you don't hear from me for a while. I'll be back just as soon as I am well enough.' He drove me to the airport and we hugged and kissed. 'O God,' I prayed, as he held me close, 'please let this operation work out. I want to be free of all this fear.'

Back in London, I moved into the Chelsea Cloisters. The Cloisters were serviced apartments that you could rent for twenty-one days at a time. I rang Polly to tell her I was back.

'I think I'm going to Casablanca,' I told her. 'I can't wait any longer.'

She came straight round to see me. She had heard several worrying stories about the quality of the surgery in Morocco. Two recent operations that she knew of had gone disastrously wrong, and the surgeon there was charging exorbitant rates.

'Why don't you go and see your old doctor in the Edgware Road. You may find that you can get a referral from him.'

I took her advice. The doctor told me that there was a surgeon in London who had had tremendous results with gender reassignment surgery.

'But before you can see him you will have to go to another psychiatrist, a Dr R. He specializes in gender dysphoria, and if he considers you to be mentally stable he will provide you with a letter of referral. From there the rest is really straightforward and, since you'll be a paying patient, there shouldn't be a long delay before you receive surgery.'

'But what about Casablanca? Do you not think it would be quicker and easier?'

'No. You've come this far, Caroline. What's another few months? In Morocco you would be far from your family and friends. This is a long and complicated operation. You're going to need a lot of support. Take my advice. Stay in this country.'

Dr R had a surgery in Harley Street. (I would have liked to be able to use both his and the surgeon's real names in the hope that the information would help other transsexuals, but they have asked to remain anonymous and I must respect their wishes.) His reputation had preceded him. Polly had told me he was extremely thorough. If he thought you showed any sign of mental instability or immaturity, he would delay things for anything up to three years. Every transsexual has to go through this psychiatric procedure in order to get their letter of referral. Without it no surgeon in this country can operate. Consequently the possibility of establishing any atmosphere of trust within which serious counselling can take place is very limited. To me at the age of twenty this meeting with Dr R was just another hurdle I had to jump. I needed to convince him of my suitability for surgery. All the areas in my life that had caused me pain or bewilderment had to be suppressed. Any fears that I might have for my future were left unspoken. Dr R might be able to impress upon me that I could never become 100 per cent female. But what he couldn't do was prepare me for my life as a transsexual.

Polly was right: he was tough. But he was also thorough. He took blood and saliva tests. The blood tests allowed him to examine my hormone levels; the saliva test, which is called a bucle smear, gave him vital information about my chromosomes. He made an extraordinary discovery. Most women have two X chromosomes and men have one X and one Y. Transsexuals very often (although not always) have two X chromosomes to one Y. Dr R discovered that I had three Xs to my one Y. Chromosomally, my body appeared to be at war with itself.

This in no way deterred him from the gruelling session of questions and answers that was to follow. He covered all the same ground that my earlier doctor had gone over: my childhood, my relationship with both my parents, my homosexual experiences. He was tough on me and on several occasions brought me very near to tears. It was his job to be certain that I was a true candidate for surgery. Any error on his part could have had disastrous consequences. But sitting there in his office battling with all these questions, it was hard for me to see it that way.

'You do understand, don't you?' he said over and over. 'You'll *never* be a true woman.'

I began to feel irritated. What was a *real* woman in any case? Of course I understood that surgery could never make right the great confusion I had experienced as a child, but it could help me to function in the world I lived in, it could help me to live the life I wanted for myself, it could enable me to express my sexuality. I felt then, and still feel now, that it is all too easy for people to hand out advice. But unless you have known what it is to live with your body and mind at war, I don't think it is possible *really* to understand the sense of torment that I was experiencing.

'No matter what surgery we perform,' he continued, 'we can never transform your sex.'

I was determined not to get rattled. This was a gate that I had to pass through and here was the man who could open that gate.

'I understand what you are saying,' I replied. 'And I accept it. I still feel, however, that surgery would be of great value to me.'

He asked me whether my family knew of my intentions.

'Yes, they do,' I replied. 'And they are firmly behind me.'

He was impressed. Sadly, many transsexuals are rejected by their families. I was blessed with having the love and support of my mum, dad, sister and brother.

'I should also warn you of the legal implications,' he continued. 'Although you will be able to change your passport, you cannot alter the gender on your birth certificate. In the eyes of the law you will remain legally a man. You cannot marry. Or at least if you do, you will never be able to defend that marriage in a court of law. In the event of a divorce you will have no legal rights.'

This harsh fact was to be brought home to me forcibly later, but at that moment the legal niceties of my position as a transsexual couldn't have been further from my mind. Evidently, Dr R thought it necessary to try to dissuade me from surgery. But once he had proved to himself that I was both determined and mentally strong, he began to soften. I had to see him on several more occasions. At the last meeting, he handed me a letter to give to the surgeon, Mr P.

'I'd like to see you after the operation,' he said. 'I would suggest that you come to see me on a regular basis. I can't demand that of you, but I do feel that it might be beneficial.'

I did go back just once, after the operation. But in common with many transsexuals, I didn't feel that therapy could offer me anything. It was my body that needed attending to, not my mind.

I took the letter, thanked him for his time, and walked out of the surgery. It was addressed to Mr P and marked 'private and confidential'. I was fairly confident that Dr R had given me a positive letter of recommendation – but I had to be sure. Besides, after all those questions, I was eaten up with curiosity. As soon as I got home I boiled a kettle of water and held the letter over the steam. The news was good, if a little difficult to translate, being couched in technical jargon. I had to pore over it for some time before I felt I had grasped the meaning of its message: Dr R considered me to be mentally stable at present, but in order to prevent mental deterioration, I should undergo gender-reassignment surgery as soon as possible. This was the diagnosis I had wanted to hear. I carefully re-sealed the letter and phoned Mr P's secretary to make an appointment.

After the psychiatrist, Mr P was sweetness and light. He was polite, straightforward, and reassuring. He had to cover the same ground as Dr R, asking questions about my childhood and so forth. But he was brief, and after a short conversation in which I told him about the disappointments of my sexual life, he asked to examine me. I undressed and lay down on the examination couch.

'Well, you appear to have healthy tissue and plenty of penile and scrotal skin. I see no reason why your surgery should not be completely successful.'

He must have noticed my worried face. 'I've done 750 operations like this one,' he added, 'so I should know what I am talking about.'

He told me to get dressed and come back into his office. Then, having sat me down on the other side of his desk, he started to explain the surgical procedure. First, he told me how sexual identity in the embryo is determined at quite a late stage of development. Until the forty-second day of life the male and female are indistinguishable. The reproductive glands, or gonads, differentiate into testes at seven to eight weeks and into ovaries at about eleven to twelve weeks. The external genitalia of both sexes are identical until the end of the eighth week of embryonic life, and have the potential to develop into the organs of either sex.

'Men and women are more similar than you might think,' he said. 'It won't be too difficult, visually, to make you a woman.'

He explained that the penis could be viewed as a version of the clitoris. 'There is no reason why anyone having this operation should not be able to function fully in their new gender. The tissue will remain as sensitive and as capable of sexual arousal.'

At the time, I was more than a little bewildered by all this information.

Later I was able to understand the process more clearly. The surgeon removes both the penis and the testicles, and at the same time constructs a vulva (the external female genital organ) and a vagina. This transformation involves, first, the removal of the skin surrounding the penis and the scrotal sac. The tube of penile skin is then used to line a 'vaginal' canal situated in front of the anal canal. The testicles, spermatic cords, and the shaft of the penis are all amputated, and a new urethral opening made on the body surface to enable urination. Finally, labia (the vulval lips) are created from the scrotal skin.

There is a vast amount of ignorance and mythology surrounding gender-reassignment surgery. Most people, for example, are convinced that the result must be either freakish, painful or unsightly. But in truth, 75 per cent of male-to-female sex-change operations are entirely satisfactory, resulting in a vagina that is perfectly adequate for normal sexual intercourse, and external genitalia that are indistinguishable from any other woman's. The greatest challenge for the surgeon is the creation of a vaginal canal. This canal has to be able to accommodate an erect penis during intercourse. Some transsexuals experience difficulty with intercourse because the 'vagina' is either too short or too narrow. There is also a slight risk of prolapse, and special care has to be taken immediately after the operation to ensure that this does not happen.

The thing that most surprises people learning about gender-reassignment is the fact that approximately 80 per cent of male-to-female transsexuals are capable of reaching orgasm. When I have explained this to friends or journalists, I am invariably met with the same look of disbelief that I encounter when I inform people that visually it is impossible to tell the difference between me and a woman who was born fully female. The tissue that is refashioned to form a clitoris is every bit as sensitive as a normal clitoris. The removal of the testicles does not prevent orgasm – sperm may be the sign of male climax, but it is not the cause.

Mr P explained it all carefully, but I was too excited and too anxious to be able to digest fully all the medical details.

'How soon could I have surgery?' I asked.

His reply dismayed me. I had hoped that I would be given a date for surgery that week, but he was very booked up and couldn't fit me in until just after Christmas. We agreed on 29 December.

'You won't make it to any New Year's Eve parties, I'm afraid,' he said.

'Oh, I expect I can manage without,' I replied.

I went home for Christmas. It was a strange few weeks. I veered between feelings of great excitement and terrible appre-hension. I was there in secret, as usual. On Boxing Day the relatives came to call and I was banished to the back bedroom. Peering out of an upstairs window, I made Pam laugh by pressing my face up against the glass and mouthing, 'Let me out! Let me out!' We giggled over the presents they left for me: aftershave, socks, big white handkerchiefs. Mum and Dad felt awkward. 'It doesn't matter,' I told them. 'They are show-ing they care. How could they know their gifts are unsuitable?' But both my parents were fiercely protective of me. I imagine they thought I would be offended.

Underneath the laughter and the good humour lurked real anxiety. 'What if the whole thing is a failure?' I thought. 'What if I have to spend the whole of my life hiding?' Sitting in the gloom in that back bedroom, hearing the voices chatting and laughing downstairs in the warm sitting room, I felt very alone. I had always loved Christmas, but I couldn't wait for this one to come to an end.

Finally the time had come. I was on the train as it pulled out of Norwich station and began the journey to London. I had dreamt about this moment for nearly four years. I had saved and planned and prayed to make that dream come true. Now at last I was on my way, and about to face an experience I hoped would change my life.

10

Charing Cross Hospital

I was admitted to the Charing Cross Hospital on 29 December 1974. The Charing Cross is situated in Hammersmith and specializes in gender reassignment. In 1974 it was a brand-new and rather impressive building. I was in the private wing on the fifteenth floor, and my room reminded me rather more of a hotel than a hospital. It had an enormous double-glazed window with a small balcony and great views over London, a private bathroom, television, intercom system, and an amazing bed that could be raised and lowered at the push of a button. Pam stood on the balcony staring out at the view.

'This is great!' she called. 'What a shame you don't like heights.'

My operation was not due until 31 December, and during those two days I was allowed nothing to eat and very little to drink. The anaesthetist came to see me to check my blood pressure and heart rate, and I was given an enema. But apart from those routine procedures, I was left very much on my own. Time dragged and my mind became prey to fears and worries. 'What if it doesn't work?' I kept turning that thought over and over in my mind.

In the afternoon Mr P came to see me. 'I have some forms that you will need to sign, Caroline. Look through them and I'll be back in a short while to check that everything is OK.'

He left the room, and I stared down at the papers he had put on my bed. They were formal documents that, in the bluntest of language, set out the procedure for the surgery. I had to sign authorization for 'the removal of the penis and testes' and, 'if it should prove necessary', a skin graft. There it was in black and white, impersonal and brutal. But there was worse to follow. The document went on to state that should the operation fail to provide an adequate and viable 'vagina', I would have no recourse to the law. I would, in effect, have to accept whatever the surgeon could do for me. Without my signature on this document, he would not operate. I began to panic. The entire procedure seemed like an ill-considered gamble. In the preceding weeks, I had contemplated the idea of failure, but not until I saw it laid out before me in clear legalistic terms did I realize what effect that eventuality would have on me. 'If this operation doesn't work,' I thought, 'I'm not sure I will be able to cope.'

I reached for the phone and called Mum. The moment I heard her voice on the line, I began to cry. She tried to comfort me, but the more sympathy she showed, the worse I felt. She called my father to speak to me.

'Calm down,' he said. 'You're overreacting. This document is a formality. If the surgeon didn't have complete confidence in his ability to do the operation successfully he would never have taken you on as a patient, and if he didn't have a high success rate he wouldn't be in business at all. He has to cover his back, that's all. With something like this there is always the chance that someone will sue him. It's a safeguard, sweetheart. Don't worry about it.'

His sense and his calm manner were reassuring. But the thought that it might all go wrong continued to haunt me. When Mr P came back to collect the forms I told him of my fears.

'I can assure you that everything will be all right, Miss Cossey,' he said. 'This is just a formality. After your operation tomorrow you will feel delighted with what we have been able to do for you. Now all you have to think about is getting a good night's sleep. Since you are clearly more than a little anxious, I'll prescribe a couple of sleeping tablets for you.'

After he had left, a nurse came in with two Mogadons, a bowl and disposable razor.

'What's that for?' I asked.

'You'll have to shave your pubic hair,' she explained. 'Would you like me to help you?'

I blushed. 'No, thank you,' I muttered. 'I think I can do it for myself.'

Despite the sleeping tablets, I slept badly that night, drifting in and out of an anxious slumber. I remember my mouth was dry with thirst and my stomach grumbled with hunger. When the nurse came in to open the curtains in the morning, I was wide awake.

'Did you sleep well?' she asked.

'Afraid not,' I said. 'I worried my way through the night.'

'That's normal,' she told me. 'Most people are frightened of surgery.'

She ran a bath for me. I locked the door and climbed into the warm water. I sat there, my knees pulled up against my chest, and began to cry. Tears dripped off the end of my nose and joined the water in the bath tub. I felt so vulnerable and alone that I began to pray. 'Please God, make this operation a success,' I whispered. 'I've worked so hard for this.' I began to feel like a little child. 'I've never done anything really bad. Please look after me.'

I climbed out of the bath, wrapped myself in my dressing gown, and sat on my bed waiting for the nurse to return. 'Perhaps the pre-med will make me feel better,' I thought.

It didn't. If anything, it made me feel worse. As the nurse helped me into my white gown and fixed an identity bracelet to my wrist, my thoughts became steadily more irrational. 'What if they muddle me up with someone else,' I thought, 'and someone has my operation by mistake?' Normally a thought like that would have made me roar with laughter. Now, the tears dripped down my face like rain.

The pre-med began to take effect, and two porters dressed in white jackets came in and lifted me on to a trolley. 'Cheer up,' one of them said, noticing my tear-stained face. 'It won't be that bad, you know.'

I was unconvinced, and as they wheeled me down the endless corridors there was only one thought going through my mind: 'What if it goes wrong? What if it goes wrong?'

In the operating theatre I was surrounded by masked figures in long gowns. I stared at the bright light above me and felt my tears well up again. A nurse stroked my forehead and spoke soothingly into my ear: 'Don't worry, everything will be just fine.'

The anaesthetist came over and stood beside me. 'Hello, Caroline,' he said. 'I'm going to give you an injection. You won't feel much . . . ' He pricked my skin with a needle. 'Now I would like you to start counting.'

I stared up at the masked figure. Behind his head was a circle of lights. They softened as I looked at them. 'One,' I said, and fell asleep.

When I woke it was dark. There was a dim nightlight by my bed, and I could just make out the figure of a nurse.

When she saw that I was awake she came over to speak to me. 'Hello, Caroline. You just missed Big Ben. Happy New Year!'

I managed a wan smile and fell back into a morphine-induced sleep. Over the next few hours I drifted in and out of consciousness. I was still so anaesthetized I felt no real pain, just a heavy dragging sensation in my crotch. My legs were stiff and bruised where they had been held apart during the operation, and I noticed I had drips in both my arms.

The whole of the next day passed in a haze. Pam sat with me for much of the time, but it wasn't until the evening that I was able to talk to her.

'You were in the operating room for five hours,' she said, 'so you've had a pretty hefty dose of anaesthetic. But I've spoken to Mr P and he says that the surgery was an unqualified success. Isn't that wonderful?'

'The best Christmas present a girl could have,' I replied. 'Happy New Year!'

We talked for a while, but I soon felt tired and drifted back to sleep. It may have been 1 January 1975, the first day of the rest of my life, but I was hardly in a state to celebrate.

When I next awoke, the pain began. I had been warned that the operation would cause discomfort, but I was unprepared for this gnawing agony. I called the nurse and she gave me a pain-relieving injection.

'The worst of it will last about six or seven days. We can give you injections at regular intervals, but we can't exceed the stated dose. The pain-killers are narcotic, and we have to be careful not to let you get addicted.'

I tried to be brave, but at times the pain got the better of me. It felt as though someone was tearing my flesh out. To add to the discomfort, I had a catheter draining my urine and a mould holding my 'vaginal' canal open. By tea time the injection had begun to wear off, and I was sweating with the agony. I rang for the nurse.

'I need an injection,' I said.

She told me that I was not due to have another shot for a couple of hours. From where I was lying that seemed an eternity.

'I can't wait that long,' I replied. 'This is unbearable.'

'Well, I'll check with matron – but I'm pretty sure that she will say no.'

Matron did say no. I swore violently and burst into tears.

'Look, I'm a private patient,' I sobbed. 'I'm paying. Sod the addiction. Just give me the fucking injection!'

The nurse handed me a couple of aspirin and left. She was used to situations like these.

The days passed in a muddle of pain. At the weekend my mum and dad came down from Norfolk bearing flowers, grapes and magazines. I lay on the bed like a beached whale, unable to move.

'I'm so uncomfortable, Mum,' I complained. 'I was expecting to feel excited but instead I cry all the time.'

'That's perfectly normal, darling. You're full of drugs. It'll take your system a while to recover.'

She was right, and as time went by I felt more and more optimistic. My room was full of cards and bouquets from friends and family. And I had different visitors every day.

The surgeon came to see me each afternoon. He seemed pleased with the progress I was making. 'We should be able to take the mould out soon,' he said. 'After that we wait a few days before we remove the catheter and you can start a salt-bath regime.'

I had been told the operation was a great success, but I still had no idea what my new genitalia looked like. When he and the sister had left, I decided to take a peek. Hauling myself up into a sitting position, I winced with the pain. I propped myself up on the pillows, reached for my cosmetic mirror and angled it between my legs where it would catch the light. I was startled by what I saw. Not only was I very swollen and bruised, but the mould holding my vagina open had created a cavern. It seemed vast. 'My God!' I thought. 'If anyone tries to make love to me, they'll fall in!'

I was so disturbed by what I had seen I called a nurse. Plumping my pillows she explained: 'You can't possibly tell how successful the surgery has been until we remove the mould and the stitches. When the swelling goes down I assure you you'll look beautiful.'

After six days, Mr P decided that the time had come to take the mould out. I had been dreading this moment. I was still so sore that the thought of being touched made me shudder. Also I knew that this would be a very telling moment. Not until the mould was removed would I know for sure that the operation had been the success everyone said it had. Mr P came to see me early one morning. He told me that he had two student doctors with him, and would I mind their being in the room when the thing was removed? In the end it was only my pride and the presence of those two men that kept me from screaming.

It was unimaginably painful. First Mr P removed the bandages and gauze that had been packed around my crotch. Then, producing a sinister instrument that reminded me of two shoehorns stuck together, he pushed it right up inside me, gripped the mould and pulled. I clung on to the bedframe and shut my eyes. One of the students held my arm. The sensation was hideous. It felt as though my insides were being wrenched out from my throat downwards.

'There,' said Mr P cheerfully. 'All done.'

As he swabbed away the blood and cleaned me up with surgical spirit, he chattered enthusiastically, pointing out to the students the success of his surgery. I lay there weak and shaking. The tears were pouring down my face, and I longed for everyone to go. 'Nothing can be worth this much pain,' I thought.

The next ordeal I had to face was the removal of the catheter. As Mr P pulled the tube out I felt as though I was being cut by a thousand tiny blades, and my stomach lurched like a deflating balloon. I gasped and bit the knuckle of my hand.

'Well,' said the ever-cheerful Mr P, 'you're on your own now. Just let the nurse know when you want to urinate and she'll help you go to the toilet.'

'But how will I know when I want to go?' I asked.

'Oh,' he replied airily, 'it'll be pretty much the same as before.'

I wasn't convinced. I knew that they had made an opening for the urethra just by my vagina, but I couldn't quite believe that it would work or that I would recognize the sensations.

When I finally did feel the need to urinate, the experience was alarming. My urethra had been twisted by the catheter and was still swollen. Consequently the stream wasn't directed down but rose in a vertical jet and hit the wall. I began to sob. 'I can't even piss properly!' I cried.

The nurse told me to put my head between my knees. 'That way the flow will hit the bowl,' she said.

'But I can't do a bloody headstand every time I need a pee!' I wailed.

'It'll be fine as soon as the swelling goes down. Just relax.'

Easier said than done.

On my last day in hospital I had a party in my room. I invited the surgeon, the nurses and a few of my friends. I was allowed a small glass of champagne and someone made a toast.

'To Caroline!'

I sipped my drink and grinned with happiness. I knew it would take me some time to recuperate, and the doctor had warned that I would have to keep to a strict diet.

'You need lots of fibre,' he said. 'Whatever happens, we must avoid constipation. Any straining could damage you internally.'

He told me that I would be able to have sex after about three months. But he added a word of warning: 'Don't expect too much at first. It will take you a while to be able to relax.'

I listened to his advice, but the thought of home and family had made me light-headed with happiness. I was in no mood for serious talk.

Before I left Mr P paid me one last visit. He produced a curious phallic object with a handle. 'This is to keep your vagina dilated. I know it seems rather unnatural, but you need to insert it a few times every day. It may cause you discomfort at first, but if you persist with it and keep up the salt baths, you will heal a great deal faster.'

Pam came to pick me up from hospital. I felt very weak and

shaky. That evening she drove me to the station and put me on the Norwich train.

'Dad'll be there to meet you at the other end,' she said. 'Do you think you'll be OK?'

I told her I was fine and we kissed goodbye.

It was a strange journey. My legs felt like cotton wool, and my brain was still misty from all the drugs. Every sight and sound assaulted my nerves. It was as though I had no skin. I was sitting on a packed commuter train, surrounded by businessmen in suits and, curiously, my first feeling was one of fear. I was hit by the full realization of my vulnerability. 'What if I were to be raped?' I thought. This must seem a perverse thought to have had. I suppose I was hallucinating slightly from the drugs, and after the pain I had undergone the idea of being touched was a hideous one. I tried to bury myself in a magazine, but I was convinced all eyes were on me. 'They all *know*,' I thought. One man, dressed in a white shirt and a dark-blue suit, seemed to be paying me particular attention. I prayed for him to look the other way. For the first time in my life the attention of men was something I wished to avoid. 'This is one aspect of feeling female that I hadn't expected,' I thought to myself.

As I stepped carefully down from the train I saw Dad walking towards me. I was very moved to see him there. Normally he would park in the car park and wait for me in case anyone from the village recognized us. This time he had thrown caution to the winds. He put his arms around me and gave me a hug.

'Welcome home, sweetheart,' he said. 'You look great. I'm a lucky man to have such a beautiful daughter. Your mum and I are going to look after you and get you well. She's waiting back at home, so let's get in the car.'

I cried with relief and happiness. Now the operation was behind me I felt that finally things were going to work out. I would be able to live a normal life as a woman, an unremarkable and perfectly average life. 'No more dramas,' I thought.

I spent two weeks convalescing in Brooke. My parents spoilt me rotten, anticipating my every need, and helping me to keep my spirits high. There were times when I grew weary of all the discomfort. I had to take salt baths every day, and I still bled heavily. I couldn't close my legs properly because of the swelling.

Mum reassured me: 'I was just as swollen when I gave birth to you,' she said. 'You'll be amazed how quickly it'll return to normal.'

Those two weeks also gave me time to come to terms with my experiences. I had been shocked by the trauma of surgery, but I had no sense of loss. I was tremendously relieved to be free of a part of my body that had caused me such anguish. But I didn't feel that much more 'female' because I'd had a 'vagina' created for me. It wasn't purely the ability to have heterosexual intercourse that made me feel a woman. I had always felt myself to be female and I still did. The operation gave me the chance to function in a sexual relationship. It gave me the choice. And it gave me a chance to live a more normal life with a man.

As I began to heal I realized just how impressive a job Mr P had done. I studied myself in a mirror. I looked like any other woman, give or take a bit of residual swelling. I had slightly more labial skin than I would have liked. I had that neatened by a plastic surgeon a few months later.

With each day I grew stronger, and soon I was ready to return to life in the 'real world'. I had spoken to Claudio a few times on the phone, and he was missing me.

'When are you coming back?' he asked.

I talked to Mum and Dad. 'It's time to get on with my life,' I told them. 'I feel great. The bad times are truly behind me now.'

I told them I was going back to Italy. I still had money from the sum I'd saved, and I felt I needed a holiday. Pam wanted to come with me. She was unhappy with her boyfriend and tired of London life. We loved being in each other's company, and the idea of living together in Rome was irresistible. After so much sadness I needed sun and laughter. So Pam and I packed our bags, waved goodbye to the grey English skies and caught the first available flight to Rome.

11

Tula – International Model

It was wonderful to be back in Italy. In my memories of those months spent with Pam in Rome the sun is always shining. I took my little sister on a tour of the sights – we ate pistachio ice cream by the Trevi Fountain, heard the Pope address the crowd in St Peter's Square, and consumed more pasta than can have been good for us. Surgery had relieved me of my greatest worry and I felt as happy as a lark. It was such a pleasure to be abroad with someone I cared for. Discovering Rome with Pam filled me with a kind of wild energy.

And there was Claudio. He had met us at the airport, and I had flung myself into his arms. Just knowing that I no longer had to conceal myself physically gave me a profound sense of legitimacy. He was obviously delighted with my high spirits.

'How did the operation go?' he asked.

'Couldn't have been better!' I replied, kissing the side of his face. He picked up our bags and headed out to the car.

'He's very handsome,' whispered Pam.

He drove us to my old bedsit, where I was welcomed back like one of the family.

'I'll leave you to settle in,' said Claudio. 'But I'll be back in an hour or so to take you both out to dinner.'

I spent that evening and every other evening for the next two weeks in Claudio's company. I knew he wanted me to spend a night with him and he had even asked me if I would consider moving in with him. 'One thing at a time,' I thought. It was obvious that I desired him but the idea of sex was daunting. I spoke to Pam.

'What if it hurts?' I said. 'He might damage me.'

Pam told me not to worry. 'I'm sure if you ask him to take it easy he'll understand,' she said.

'Do you suppose he realizes I'm a virgin?' I asked. We both fell off the bed laughing.

But virginal was how I felt, and I suppose Claudio must have recognized my fear. For when we did finally sleep together, he was very gentle, leaving me plenty of time to respond to his touch. I can't pretend that the earth moved. But then most women experiencing their first man are more likely to feel relief than ecstasy. I felt a small amount of discomfort and I was anxious lest he should 'rupture' me in some way. I certainly wasn't ready for orgasm. But these were small matters compared to the great wave of tender eroticism I did experience. Here was a whole book of love written in a language I could read. I knew that it could only get better.

And once Claudio and I had started there was no stopping us. It took me about a year before I could reach orgasm – I still found it hard to relax completely – but I was a fast and determined student with a lot to learn.

It was this curiosity about sex that was the downfall of my relationship with Claudio. As the weeks turned into months he became ever more enamoured. I was terribly fond of him, but I had years of catching up to do. I wasn't ready to settle down, and certainly not as an Italian housewife. He had bought a place by the beach and spent hours trying to persuade me to live there with him. But it was all too predictable. I had just escaped from one prison and wasn't about to lock myself up in another. I was twenty-one years old and I wanted to see the world before I settled down.

I broke off the relationship with Claudio. He was upset, but I felt I had to move on. Pam and I were running short of money and we began to think about getting a job. Claudio had suggested on several occasions that we think about becoming Go-Go dancers. We were good dancers, and an evening job would leave us free to enjoy the sun, sea and sand during the day.

Go-Go dancers were a real thing of the 1970s. Wearing hot pants or bikinis, they would dance in cages above the heads of the audience. We found a club that hired dancers and went along to see the manager. He was happy to take us on provided we promised not to let him down.

'The girls I've hired in the past have proved to be very unreliable.'

We undertook to stay at the club for at least six months. The money wasn't great, but if we carried on sharing a room and cut down on meals in restaurants we thought we could manage. It was hot work – we took turns to dance for twenty minutes at a stretch – and we would end the evening drenched in sweat. But we enjoyed it. It kept us fit and we made a lot of new friends. During the day and at weekends we would take trips up the coast, exploring the rest of Italy.

We attracted a lot of attention from Italian males, and although I was immensely protective of Pam and kept her out of the clutches of any number of lascivious men, I went a little wild myself. I felt I needed to experiment and experience a number of relationships. I wasn't exactly promiscuous but I did feel tremendously liberated. Now, if a man's hands started to wander, I wasn't gripped by panic. I could afford to make a few mistakes. I suppose I was lucky to have been living in a time when such experimentation was possible.

None of the men I slept with had any idea about my past. They certainly couldn't have noticed any physical difference. But, perfectionist that I am, there was one thing that continued to bother me. Although no one ever commented on it, I felt that my Adam's apple was the last visible reminder of my life as a male. When I wore my hair up I felt acutely self-conscious of the small bump on my throat. I knew that it was possible to have it removed, but that the surgery was fraught with potential complications. I had been through so much pain, was this further operation really necessary? I felt it was, if only because I suspected I would continue making money from my natural good looks. Many people had asked me if I was a model – my height and bone structure seemed to make me a perfect candidate for catwalk work. I was having too much fun in Rome to think seriously about the future, but I knew that winter was coming on and soon I would have to return to England and find work. I decided to use my remaining time in Italy to save as much money as I could. There was a little capital left from the sum I had saved for my gender-reassignment surgery, and by late autumn I had all the money I needed.

Pam and I were both missing home and wanted to see Mum, Dad and Terry, so we packed our bags and left Rome. Back in London I contacted the surgeon who had performed my breast operation (augmentation mammoplasty) and asked his advice. He referred me to an ear, nose and throat specialist who he thought would be able to help me.

The specialist was very helpful, but he was anxious to point out the risks involved in surgery of this kind.

'It involves a complete reconstruction of your voice box. I must warn you that there is a very real possibility that you could lose your voice permanently.'

He did his best to deter me, but I was young and headstrong and determined to finish the job I had started.

'If I don't actually lose it,' I asked, 'will there be a change in my voice in any case?'

'Yes,' he replied. 'You will find your voice is a lot softer. You will have less ability to project, and you may lose much of the range of tone.'

I felt that the risk was worth taking and I asked him to give me an appointment for surgery.

'While you're there,' I quipped, 'you might as well fix my nose and eyes. Make me look like Sophia Loren.'

He didn't find the joke funny. 'You people are never satisfied with your lot,' he complained. 'The throat operation is risky enough. Don't push your luck.'

He looked up from his notes and noticed my grin.

'We'll leave it at the throat surgery, then,' I said, still smiling, and he began to laugh.

The operation to remove my Adam's apple was nowhere near as painful as my main operation, but even so it caused me a great deal of discomfort. It left me feeling as though I had gone down with an acute case of tonsilitis. For several weeks after the operation, I was not allowed to smoke or to talk above a whisper. Even now, it causes me trouble. I frequently lose my voice and suffer from repeated bouts of laryngitis. Externally, the surgery left virtually no scar. There was one tiny incision mark, but that was hidden in a crease of skin on my throat.

Once I had recuperated I had to think seriously about making my living. I didn't want to go back to working in clubs.

Being a showgirl had been fun, but those days of feathers, G-strings and body paint were over. I wanted an altogether quieter and more dignified life. Besides, I needed to disassociate myself from those people who had known me before surgery. I still kept in touch with Polly and Diana – my secret was safe with them – but I had no desire to be known to people as anything other than an ordinary woman.

I was flicking through the *Stage* one day, wondering whether I should try for some promotional work, when I noticed an advertisement for a modelling agency called New Faces. They were looking for new girls. I had no real experience as a model, but I did have a small portfolio of photographs. They were mostly publicity shots for the shows in London and Paris, but there were also one or two amateur snaps that were well lit and flattering. I rang the number and was told I could go along any time between five and six. I decided to give it a go. I wasn't desperately excited at the idea of working as a model, but I felt that with no qualifications, no training and very little experience of the world, I had few options. I wanted to be able to earn my living, and if there was a chance I might be able to do that as a model, then that was what I was going to do.

The head of the agency was a woman called Yvonne Paul. I was shown into her office and she stood up to greet me. She was an impressive woman, brisk and professional, with a determined manner. An ex-model herself – she had been one of the Benny Hill girls – she appeared to be highly organized. I handed her my portfolio. She perused it carefully, saying little, and when she had finished she looked up at me. She was about to speak when I interrupted:

'Please give me your honest opinion,' I said. 'I don't want to waste either your time or mine.'

'I'll give you an honest opinion in any case,' she replied, 'but you certainly aren't wasting anybody's time. These photographs are not great. They are mostly too theatrical. But it is clear that you are very photogenic. You have the height and figure of a model and I suspect you have the ability to be a real professional. You need to get rid of most of your make-up – you wear far too much. With your bone structure you should be aiming for a more natural look. I'll get our in-house photographer, Steven Yass, to take some shots of you. We'll look at the results and if they are any good we'll get a publicity card together.'

It was clear that she was a fast worker. I was delighted.

'You want to take me on, then?' I asked, smiling.

'Yes, I do,' she replied.

And there began my modelling career. Yvonne was a highly motivated agent. She organized a test shoot and brought out a publicity card within two weeks.

'We have to decide on a name for you. I already have a number of Carolines in the agency. How about trying to find something more striking?'

We talked it over while she flicked through her books.

'I've got it!' she said, stopping at the picture of a striking blonde. 'Tula!'

'Who's Tula?' I asked.

'She was a Swedish girl we had on our books a few years ago. She was about as tall as you.'

'What does the name mean?'

'Well, apparently it means "pure gold" in Hindi.'

'What does it mean in Swedish?'

'I think she told me it meant "tree".'

'That sounds like me,' I said. From then on my working name was Tula. It was short and memorable.

I had some immediate success as a model. Photographers seemed to like working with me. My years as a showgirl had taught me discipline and patience. I was still a very private person and didn't chat much, but I did get on with the work. I felt so delighted to be working successfully in my chosen sex that I had no time for temperament or tantrums. I did what I was asked to do and I did it well. Looking back, I realize that, paradoxically, my very success was my downfall.

If I had stayed out of the public eye and worked in Boots or Sainsbury's as a check-out girl, I don't suppose the newspapers would have ever taken an interest in me. Many transsexuals recognize that professional success brings with it the risk of exposure, and they deliberately limit themselves in their chosen career in order not to arouse public interest. 'Why become a model if you've had a sex-change operation?' is the cry of so many ignorant people who believe that transsexuality carries with it the penalty of humble obscurity. They seem to feel that transsexauls who become successful are courting publicity and deserve the treatment they get. That wasn't how I saw it then, and it certainly isn't how I see it now. I had lived and worked as a woman for six years when I began to make it as a model. For all that time I had been treated by everyone who met me as a woman. I was foolish enough to believe that my past was my business and no one else's. It had ceased to matter to me that I had been born a boy, and I couldn't imagine it would matter to anyone else.

This was where a different kind of therapy might have helped me. Perhaps if I hadn't spent so much time thinking and talking about being a woman, and perhaps if the psychiatrist who examined me had spent less time focusing on those aspects of my life which could never be changed by surgery, I would have had more opportunity to think about myself as a transsexual. It was exposure by the press that forced me to talk about my transsexuality, and it was a painful way to have to learn to do so.

But back in my days as a model, I had no desire to think of myself as anything other than a woman. I was naïve and blind to the possibility of disaster.

The first hint of trouble came straight after I had done a page-three picture for the *Sun*. I had appeared in the paper during a 'new faces' week, and the phone hadn't stopped ringing with offers of work. Yvonne was an agent who specialized in glamour work, so much of the stuff I was being offered was pin-up or calendar assignments. Two weeks after I appeared, the *Sun*'s photographer rang me again. He had heard that I had a sister and that she was also a model. The paper was planning a sisters week and he asked if Pam and I would be interested in appearing. I knew that a photo in the *Sun* would do a lot for Pam's career; she had only just started modelling and she needed a lucky break. We agreed to do it and were photographed together topless. Naturally no one suspected that we had ever been anything but sisters.

One day, soon after the *Sun* feature, a photographer calling himself Brian rang Yvonne and asked if he could book me. She rang to tell me he had called, leaving his full name and address. When I received the message, a cold shiver ran down my spine. This was the same photographer who had been interested in me when I was working at the Latin Quarter; it was Diana's old boyfriend, the man who had wanted to make a quick buck out of my transsexuality. If we were to meet I was certain he'd recognize me. I was determined to avoid such a confrontation and had to think up an excuse for Yvonne. I rang her up.

'A very close friend of mine was once treated very badly by this man,' I explained. 'I really don't want to have anything to do with him.' Yvonne accepted my explanation without further question. Life went on, more jobs appeared, and I forgot all about the incident. Little did I know that fate was catching up with me.

The next few months were some of the busiest of my life. I worked constantly and, as my career broadened and I was given more overseas work, I became used to living out of a suitcase. I had assignments in Tobago, Portugal, Kenya, the Maldives, Hawaii. There wasn't time for a serious relationship because I was never home long enough to form an attachment.

I began to pull in the reins on the glamour work. I was in danger of being typecast as a topless model, and I wanted to get out of the swimwear and lingerie work. It was giving me too much of the wrong sort of publicity, and I disliked the fact that I had little or no control over the pictures that were taken of me. Photographers would often sell their work overseas, and with the reappearance of Brian I couldn't afford to take any chances. I spoke to Yvonne about my growing reluctance to do glamour work. She was very understanding and it was not long before I landed my first contract job. I became Miss Air Monitor and appeared in their ads for the rest of that year. The contract also obliged me to promote their products at major exhibitions. As I became more successful I was asked to attend all sorts of functions. I would open clubs, cut ribbons, smash champagne bottles, and smile, smile, smile.

That was fine by me. I was earning as much as £300 a day and saving to buy a place of my own. Pam and I had moved out of the Chelsea Cloisters and into rented accommodation in Kensington. It was nice enough, but I longed to have a place of my own. As the Air Monitor contract came to a close, I was offered a similar contract with a company who made crash helmets and other accessories for motorbikes. The advertising company who held their account had the idea of imitating something the famous model Verouschka had done ten years previously: they decided that rather than dressing me in real leathers, they would hire artists to paint the clothes on my body. The campaign became known as the Painted Lady Campaign, and it gave me a lot of publicity – which was just as well, for the actual shoots were unbelievably tedious. I spent hours frozen in a certain position while three artists painstakingly painted on every detail of the clothing, right down to the individual teeth on a zipper. Thank God the photographer shot only one section at a time, so I never had to be painted from head to toe at one sitting! I developed an incredible sympathy for artists' models. How ever do they stay still that long, I wondered.

When I finished the publicity tour as the Painted Lady, I returned to London and concentrated on getting as much TV work as possible. I had walk-on parts in 'The Two Ronnies', 'Robin's Nest', a Max Bygraves show, 'The Other One', and even graduated to a kissing scene with John Alderton in 'The Upchat Line'. No one ever questioned my sexuality; I was accepted as a woman without hesitation.

I'd deliberately stayed away from the world of pin-ups, page three and calendar girls. But when Yvonne received an offer from the French magazine *Lui* for a centrespread, I was reluctant to turn it down. They were offering me the chance to work with a world-famous photographer, Francis Giacobetti, and the money was extremely tempting. They promised that it would all be done in 'the best possible taste'. It was an old cliché, but the magazine was elegant and restrained – women were never photographed with their legs open, and pubic hair was seen only from the tactful side view. This was glamour photography at its best. I agreed. I didn't expect the pictures to receive much attention in this country, and I badly wanted the opportunity to work with a really top-class photographer.

Everything was going well for me. I was in regular work and beginning to be able to pick and choose assignments. Then the opportunity to audition for a new TV show called '3-2-1', hosted by Ted Rogers, came up. I didn't have any serious hopes of landing the job. There were hundreds of girls trying for it, and my only advantage was the possession of a full

Equity card. I was amazed when they rang up and asked me to attend a recall. Compared to '3-2-1', the tiny bits of TV I had done before were insignificant. This job could turn me into a recognized TV personality. I knew they would want to know about my background and experience, so I had worked out a story. I saw no reason to lie about my acting work, and told them I had done practically nothing. 'I'm primarily a model and dancer,' I said. 'I've never had a speaking part on film or television.'

As for my past, I told them that I was from Italy and had arrived in London at the age of sixteen. (My Italian was fluent by that time and I knew Rome well, so I was confident that I could make the story sound credible).

'We like you a great deal,' said the director of the show. 'I realize that you haven't had much experience in camera work, but I'm sure you'll learn fast. You'll certainly look beautiful on screen.'

'Do you mean I've got the job?' I asked.

'Yes, I do,' he replied.

That night I lay in bed thinking. I knew I should have rung Yvonne straight away and told her the good news, but there was a part of me that wanted to hold back. I needed time to think this one over. I was nervous of appearing on television in a show as unpredictable as this one was clearly going to be, and I was also anxious about the effect that the publicity would have on my life. Now that the operation was behind me I had sworn that I would no longer be a prisoner of my own fear and paranoia, and my life had never been happier. Did I want to risk that happiness for the sake of an opportunity to further my career? After much thought I came to a decision. I couldn't spend the rest of my life cowering. I had to trust and hope that I was not important enough to grab the newspapers' interest.

The next morning Yvonne called me. She had spoken to the casting director and was delighted with the news.

'Well done,' she said. 'You did brilliantly to land that job.'

I confided a few of my worries. 'You don't think I'll look stupid? I've never done anything like this before.'

Of course I couldn't divulge the real source of my fear. 'It's all going so fast,' was the most I could say.

Yvonne reassured me: 'All the other girls are in exactly the same position as you. Don't worry so much. You'll have a ball.'

Rehearsals were great, and I got on with the five other women. They were a real racial mix: English, American, French, West Indian and Asian Indian. Right up to the opening show things were going well. Then disaster struck.

12

The Price of Privacy

The show was to be recorded in Yorkshire in front of a live audience, and we travelled up to Leeds together. Everyone was excited and in high spirits, and even I was beginning to enjoy the adrenalin. The rehearsals had given me a lot of confidence. 'Perhaps I could get really good at this,' I thought.

We were given a large dressing room to share and I sat with a cup of coffee, waiting to be called in to make-up. One of the girls came over to join me and we were chatting about the show when, out of the blue, she asked: 'Why is it that you've never worked with Brian?'

I felt the blood drain from my face and I reached down into my bag for my cigarettes.

'Brian who?' I said lightly, struggling to keep the tremor from my voice. My hair was shielding my face and she couldn't see my pallor.

'Brian—'

I fought to stay calm. 'Oh,' I said. 'Has he tried to book me? I've been so busy lately, and my agent doesn't always keep me up to date with work offers.'

But the girl persisted. 'Well, he's tried to book you on a number of occasions. He seems to have got the idea that you don't want to work with him. Is that right?'

'I don't even know him,' I replied. 'Is he a friend of yours?'

'He's my boyfriend,' she said. 'You'll meet him this evening. He's coming to see the show.'

I changed the subject as naturally as possible, but I felt as though I had been punched in the stomach. As soon as the girl left, I fled to the loo and locked myself in. Leaning against the door, shaking uncontrollably, and with tears coursing down my face, I felt as though my world had broken into a thousand pieces. If there were money to be made out of it, this man would lose no sleep over exposing me.

The idea of my privacy being shattered in that way was too terrible to contemplate. I had been living and working as a woman for so long, how could I possibly bear to be turned into a freak show, a creature to be stared at and talked about? I would sooner die.

I tried to get out of the show and went to see the casting director, pleading ill-health. But she didn't buy it.

'You're just having an attack of first-night nerves,' she said. 'As soon as the show is over you'll feel a lot better.'

By the end of that dreadful day I felt suicidal. With two left feet and a mouth as dry as sawdust, I had stumbled through the show. Under the bright studio lights the world took on a surreal aspect. I knew that Brian was there watching from the wings, and, judging by the expression on his girlfriend's face every time she looked at me, he had shared my little secret with at least one other person. 'It's only a matter of time before they all know,' I thought to myself, feeling a trickle of sweat run down my spine.

That night I travelled by train back to London. Looking out at the pin-points of light in an otherwise black landscape, I felt more alone than ever. Other people's houses, other people's lives – it seemed as though everyone had a place in the world except me. I was afraid.

Back in London, I knew what I had to do. If I stayed in the show, the pressure could only get worse; I was on a thirteen-week contract and I had to find a way to get out of it. I knew it wouldn't be easy, but I was determined not to make another TV appearance. I went to see my local doctor and begged her to write a letter for me, stating that I was suffering from mental exhaustion and needed a complete break. I was in such a distressed state that she didn't need much convincing. Then I called on Yvonne.

'I don't want to do this show,' I told her. 'It's not my type of thing at all, and I don't think I can do a good job.'

I had hoped it wouldn't be necessary to tell the whole truth, but she wasn't persuaded by my arguments. 'Caroline, you are contracted,' she said. 'Not only would it be nearly imposs-ible to get the TV company to agree to release you, it would also put a severe blight on your career. Jobs like this don't come along every day. Look at all the publicity you are getting.'

As I left her office I realized I was going to have to come clean. I went back to my doctor and this time gave her the whole story.

'If I am exposed as a transsexual, I think it will break me. I have to get out of this contract.'

In full possession of the facts, she could appreciate the gravity of my situation. 'Don't worry,' she reassured me. 'I'll write a very strongly worded letter to the TV company. I'm sure if your agent sends that along with her own plea, they will feel obliged to release you.'

In her letter she stated that she believed me to be in the middle of a severe nervous breakdown. Screwing up my courage, I took the letter to Yvonne. It was time to tell her the truth.

I fully expected her to throw me out on my ear. But she reacted magnificently, with kindness and understanding. She had always been protective and now, with motherly zeal, she went into battle on my behalf. She rang the producer and spent over an hour on the phone persuading him to grant me an unconditional release.

'Caroline is under the most dreadful personal pressure,' she told him. 'I'm sorry that this has happened, but if you force her to continue I cannot answer for the consequences.'

Her determination won the day. He agreed to release me, and we both sighed with relief.

But the reprieve came too late. The next day the phone began to ring, and the press pressure started in earnest. All they had to go on were rumours, but they had smelt blood. I had the *People*, the *News of the World*, and the *Sunday Mirror* knocking on my door. And it wasn't just me they harassed. Soon I received calls from my friends and family saying that they too had been approached by journalists. 'Say nothing,' was my only advice. I thought that perhaps if they couldn't prove anything they would drop the story. But I had seriously underestimated the gutter press. They weren't about to call it a day. In all it took them a good three years to gather the information they needed. They were prepared to wait.

One morning there was a ring at the door and I opened it

to find a man from one of the Sunday papers. He told me he was keen to do a story on me.

'Why did you drop out of the show?' he asked.

I told him that I had been unwell, and he appeared to accept my explanation.

'I'd still very much like to do a profile of you,' he said. 'You are remarkably beautiful, and a lot of people would like to know a little more about your life.'

I was befuddled by all the telephone calls I had received, and I hadn't yet learnt to distrust tabloid journalists. Stupidly, I imagined that by inviting him in and giving him an interview I could control the situation. But, of course, under close questioning the Italian story soon began to crumble, and I felt increasingly cornered. Finally he came clean.

'Look,' he said, 'there are a lot of rumours flying about that say you are a sex change. Would you like to comment on that?'

I was getting out of my depth, and decided to call Yvonne.

'Excuse me,' I said, and left the room.

'Don't say anything,' Yvonne told me. 'Just ask him to leave.'

'But what if I showed him my passport?' I suggested. 'That says I am female.'

'Please, please, listen to me, Caroline! Don't tell him anything. If you show him your passport that's a story in itself – "Model has to prove she's a woman" – I can imagine it now. You've got to realize these people are vultures.'

I put the phone down and returned to the journalist.

'These are nothing more than malicious rumours,' I told him. 'There's nothing more I can say. And now, if you don't mind, I've got another appointment.'

He left, clearly disappointed. Yvonne advised me to go and talk to a solicitor.

'If we find someone really good,' she said, 'he may be able to protect you.'

I went to see someone the very next day. He asked me point blank: 'Is it true?'

'Yes,' I said.

He thanked me for being honest. 'And now I must be straight with you,' he said. 'If the papers come out with the story, there's absolutely nothing we can do. After all, it is the truth. But until they feel confident that they do have an accurate story, they will be wary of being sued for libel. If I issue a really stern and threatening letter, it may dissuade them from taking the matter any further. What are the chances of their being able to prove the story?'

'Well, they've already been snooping around my home village, Brooke. But no one apart from my family and one or two very close friends knows the truth. My family will never talk to the papers.'

'What about other people in the village?' he asked. 'Where do they think you are?'

'Mum and Dad have told everyone that I'm living in Australia. They've portrayed me as the reprobate son who hasn't bothered to stay in touch. Whenever I go home, I always do so under cover of darkness, so there's no chance I would have been spotted.'

'In that case,' he said, 'all they have to go on is supposition and rumour. This is going to be a war of nerves.'

And war it certainly was. The chief aggressor was one Bill Rankine, a journalist with the *News of the World*. He travelled up to Brooke and began harassing my family for information. He tried my brother first and wrote him a letter suggesting that his story could be worth a lot of money. My brother ignored the letter, so, having failed there, Rankine approached my father at work. He went to the bus depot one lunch hour and caught Dad eating his sandwiches and reading the paper. Terry had spoken to Dad about the letter he had received, so the visit came as no shock.

'How's your daughter's modelling career these days?' asked Rankine, producing a selection of my photographs, including the 'Two Sisters' shot I'd done for the *Sun*. Dad played it very cool.

'Pam's doing very well,' he replied. 'Why do you want to know?'

'It's not Pam I'm interested in. I want to hear all about Tula.'

Later Dad told me how, keeping his face perfectly straight, he hit the ball back into Rankine's court.

'Who's Tula?' he asked.

Rankine held up the 'Two Sisters' picture. 'Isn't this your other daughter, then?'

Dad laughed. 'I only have one daughter. Tula was a girl

who shared a flat with Pam, and that photograph is just a publicity stunt.'

But Rankine persisted. 'Where's your son Barry these days?' he asked.

'He's in Australia, not that it's any of your business,' said Dad, beginning to lose his cool. Rankine then produced several photographs of me in which my hair had been touched out.

'Could that be your son?' he asked.

'No.'

'What would you say if you heard that your son had had a sex change?'

'Don't be ridiculous,' snapped Dad. 'Now if you'll excuse me, I'd like to eat my lunch in peace.'

Rankine left Brooke empty-handed. The next day the *News of the World* received a letter from my solicitor. It had the desired effect. The telephone stopped ringing, and it looked as though the story had gone cold. I felt that I could breathe again.

Yvonne and I devised a plan of action. Although the publicity from '3-2-1' had brought in a lot of offers, including one from the 'Benny Hill Show', we both felt that I should lie low for a while and concentrate on catalogue work and assignments that took me abroad. I needed to stay well away from the British press.

Things quietened down, and I immersed myself once again in work. Through a friend I had met the sports presenter Desmond Lynam. We got on well and began a friendship. We never had a chance to spend a lot of time together, but what time we did have was happy. Then, one evening over dinner, when we had known each other for about six months, he turned to me and said something that left me feeling profoundly shocked: 'I know all about you. So don't think you've had the last laugh.'

I stared at him over the table, horrified. It wasn't so much his knowing that upset me, it was the idea that he thought I'd been laughing up my sleeve at him. I asked him how he knew, and he told me that he had learnt about it a few weeks previously from a theatrical agent. I suppose he felt he'd been cheated and that had made him anxious and aggressive.

'It's not easy confiding in people,' I explained. 'But I can tell

120

you one thing. I get no pleasure from deception. Knowing that I'm a sex change doesn't belittle *you* in any way, but it will change your attitude to *me*. I don't want to be an object of sexual curiosity. I want to be with a man who desires me as a woman.'

He apologized for being insensitive, and in some ways the friendship was stronger as a result of that conversation. A few months later he asked me to marry him.

Sexually my confidence was dented. What I had taken to be spontaneous passion now seemed like curiosity. I was probably paranoid, but in bed I felt deeply self-conscious. All this had also fuelled another fear – that men would really believe that my transsexuality was some kind of homosexual trick, that I was conning them and laughing at their ignorance. These anxieties, coupled with the press hounding, convinced me that I needed to get away from England.

I had considered New York. A high-powered agent from the States had approached me with an offer and some good advice. Her name was Wilhelmina, and she had been a hugely successful model in the 1960s. She was in London recruiting girls who were at least five feet nine to do three to six months' high-fashion and catwalk work in New York. We met in the Ritz for lunch and I showed her my portfolio.

'You've got the height, the looks, and the grace,' she told me, 'but you're doing far too much glamour work. Long term, there's no future in it. If you come to the States with pictures like these, you'll find that after an initial burst, the glamour work will dry up. High fashion and advertising are more lucrative and they offer you long-term prospects.'

I told her that I was tired of pin-up and would be happy to move on to other things.

'Well, let's start work straight away, she said. 'Before you come to the States you'll need a new portfolio. I'll set up some sessions for you in London, we'll give it about three months, then I suggest you fly to New York.'

I was very excited. Not only was this a considerable career boost, it would also get me out of the country.

But then tragedy struck. Wilhelmina died of a cancer that had been growing undetected in her lungs. She was only forty, and left behind a husband and children. It was a terrible shock.

Obviously the trip was cancelled, and the agency closed. Yvonne suggested that I should go to New York anyway and hustle for work. But I knew from other models that it was a tough city. I lacked the confidence to launch myself without the security of a contract.

It was my hairdresser, Pencil, who suggested that I try Australia. (His real name was Stewart, but he was nicknamed Pencil because he was so tall and skinny.)

'I've got a friend in Sydney who you could stay with until you got settled. You'd have no trouble finding work, and you'd love the country. Why not give it a try?'

'Why not indeed?' I thought. I rang Yvonne.

She was surprised at my choice. 'You do realize that I've got no contacts over there, Caroline? You really would be on your own as far as work goes.'

'Yes, I'm aware of that,' I said. 'But you know how desperately I need to get away. This seems like the only solution.'

She agreed, but made me promise to keep in touch. 'The press won't be on your tail for ever. Give it a few months and then come home.'

As the plane took off for the long-haul flight to Australia and the English countryside drifted away, pushed into an ocean of blue, I felt nothing but relief. 'Down under' no one knew me and I knew no one. It was a chance to start again.

13

Spiders and Monsters

For the first two weeks I stayed with Pencil's friend. She was a wealthy woman with connections in the modelling world, and she suggested that once I had recovered from jet lag, I take my portfolio to an agent named Vivien.

'She's the best,' she told me. 'And she'll love the way you look.'

Vivien was impressed with my portfolio. 'How long do you intend to stay?' she asked me.

'About three to six months, depending on the work situation.'

'Well, I can tell you now, you'll have no trouble finding work. But you may find it a little tough to begin with, as we don't have a card-mailing system in Australia, and you'll have to take yourself round to each photographer in person.'

It was a hard slog, but it paid off. I saw an average of ten photographers a day, and soon the offers of work came piling in. Because so many of Australia's top-class models packed their bags and headed for Europe, there was a real need for professionals. I was asked to do all kinds of work: Australian *Vogue*, *Cosmopolitan*, advertising, catwalk and promotional assignments for David Jones, the Australian equivalent of Harrods. I wasn't the ideal candidate for some of these jobs and I would often be pinned and clipped into clothes that were either too short in the sleeve or simply not my style. But with the money they were paying, I didn't complain.

Rents were surprisingly cheap in Sydney, and I had found a house of my own in Elizabeth Bay. It had four bedrooms, a garden and garage, and a view of the ocean. It was only two minutes from the city centre, and ideal in every way. Well, almost every way . . .

Creepy crawlies love Australia. I had been there less than

two weeks when I was introduced to the antipodean version of the cockroach. It was running around my bedroom, the size of a large and frantic mouse. I persuaded a friend to catch and kill it while I stood on the other side of the door squeaking with horror. When the beast was finally dead, I decided to send it home in a matchbox to show my family just what I was up against. But it defied the dimensions of the matchbox – no amount of squashing could get it in in one piece.

Spiders were the other major menace. I heard spine-chilling stories of species called redbacks and funnel-webs.

'The redbacks are really quite pretty,' one friend told me, as I sat rooted to the spot with horror. 'But they have a nasty bite. Their toxin can kill a child and leave an adult seriously ill. They hang out in fruit and vegetables, so be careful when you unpack your shopping bag.' But there was worse to come.

'The real bastards are the funnel-webs,' he continued. 'There's an antidote to the redback's bite, but none for the funnel-web. One bite and you're dead.'

'Wh-where do they live?' I asked, stuttering with fear.

'Oh, usually outside, in the garden.'

My romance with horticulture ended there, and from then on I wore rubber gloves when handling bunches of bananas – I wasn't taking any chances.

Wildlife apart, I enjoyed my time in Australia. It gave me a chance to relax and live something approaching a normal life again. I spoke to Yvonne regularly on the phone, and she told me that if I was ready to come home, there was plenty of work waiting. The Australian winter was approaching, and things were getting quiet, so I decided to go back to London.

I went straight into a catalogue contract, and then was booked for the Smirnoff 'Well, they said anything could happen' campaign. I was photographed water-skiing behind the Loch Ness monster. The poster was blown up and pasted all over London, but that didn't alarm me. My name was not used, and it would have been hard to recognize me. I was proud of that piece of work – it was witty and original.

And then I was asked to audition for the new Bond film, *For Your Eyes Only*. The first interview was a formality, but once they had whittled it down to twenty girls, they invited us to a meeting with the producer, Cubby Broccoli, the director, John Glenn, and half a dozen executives. Bond girls often have very little to do in the film itself, but they are a vital part of the promotional work. They are asked to take part in a world tour, attending all the premières, and being photographed with the star. I was still so surprised at being considered that I hardly stopped to think what all the publicity might mean for me.

The casting was a trial by fire. I had to sit at a table opposite a row of unfamiliar faces and 'put my personality across'. That old chestnut – 'So, tell us all about yourself' – usually causes me to stammer, blush and fall silent. This time I had prepared myself with two large, swift drinks, and I blathered cheerfully on about my career, my travels, and even my family. I was just about to launch into a description of the insect world of Australia when I was interrupted.

'Thank you very much, Tula. I think we have learnt all we need to know.' One of the men in a perfectly tailored suit was smiling at me.

'Oh shit, I've blown it,' I thought.

'So,' he said, 'do you think you might want the job?'

That silenced me!

'You'll automatically be offered a *Playboy* spread,' he went on. 'And the promotional tour attracts an extraordinary amount of publicity.'

That night I grew more and more apprehensive. Far from making me, being a Bond girl could actually break me. What chance would I have of fending off press interest? I phoned Yvonne the next morning.

'I don't think I can take the job,' I told her.

She listened carefully while I confided my fears, and when she spoke her advice was calm and well considered.

'I think you have a clear choice, Caroline. If you are going to turn down an opportunity like this, then you may as well give up modelling altogether. There is no point in putting yourself through all this fear and frustration. But if you feel that you want this career, a scummy newspaper should not be allowed to stand in your way. You should go ahead.'

We agreed that if they had been going to print the story they would have done so by now. Perhaps they had given up on me. Since the solicitor's letter had gone out, I had heard nothing from any of those journalists. I decided to risk it.

'Tell the casting director that I would like to accept the offer,' I said.

14

News of the World Nightmare

The shoot was in Corfu, and we were given a great press send-off. There were eight 'Bond girls' of all nationalities, colours, shapes and sizes. I knew several of them from previous modelling assignments, so it was not as if I were joining a group of complete strangers. Despite the fact that we were really nothing more than glorified extras employed to decorate the set, we were given star treatment on the plane and were put up in a comfortable family hotel.

We were there for two weeks only, and much of that time was spent waiting for the right light. Filming is a slow, laborious process, and each shot takes for ever to set up. But the sun shone and the company was good.

I was in two scenes, but my performance was hardly memorable. It was a case of 'don't blink or you'll miss me'! I remember being asked to walk round a swimming pool, dressed in a bikini, and then scream. So I walked and I screamed and everyone seemed more than happy.

I got on well with Roger Moore. Three other girls, the producer, the director and I all had dinner with him one evening. We ate great Greek food, drank retsina and ouzo, and even tried a little ethnic dancing. He is a very easy man to like – unaffected, humorous and friendly.

While I was in Corfu, I was introduced to a representative of *Playboy*, who asked me if I would be interested in doing some shots. I told her that it would very much depend on what sort of shots.

'I want to get away from nude modelling. But I'd happily do swimwear or even topless, if it's tastefully done.'

She assured me that that would be possible, and I instructed her to get in touch with my agent to negotiate a fee.

When I returned to London, Yvonne told me that *Playboy*

had rung. They were doing a fashion spread in Guadaloupe, and were short of a model. They thought that if they used me for the spread, they could combine that with the publicity shots for the Bond picture. It was a smart idea, and I agreed.

Guadaloupe was everyone's idea of the perfect West Indian island. With its white beaches, palm trees and blue, blue ocean, it seemed like paradise on earth. Unfortunately the shoot was nowhere near as idyllic. The photographer wanted to shock the eye with contrast, so he positioned me dressed in finely sculpted, elegant clothes against the backdrop of a stinking, tumbledown market. I stood staring enigmatically into the lens whilst chickens struggled in hessian sacks and fish flapped around in buckets of filthy water. A group of locals gathered around us and stared open-mouthed in disbelief.

Two days later we travelled up into the forest for the Bond pictures. There, surrounded by huge green plants, I was photographed perched on a rock in the middle of a fast-flowing and icy river. Up above in the sunlight flocks of exotic birds were calling to each other as they flew from tree to tree. It could have been the Garden of Eden were it not for the mosquitoes. When I returned to the hotel that night I counted a total of eighty-seven bites on my body.

I arrived back in London full of travellers' tales and longing to speak to my parents. But when I phoned home I got a nasty shock. Dad came on the line: 'You won't believe what I'm going to tell you,' he said.

I guessed it could only be bad news. Things had been going so well, and I had had the feeling my luck couldn't last.

'What is it?' I asked.

'That bastard, Rankine, from the *News of the World* has been snooping round the village again, asking questions.'

I listened in silence while he told me what had happened. This time they hadn't stopped at my family, but had been questioning neighbours, my old schoolteachers, and even the boys I'd been at school with.

'They've got some photos of you, shots with the hair touched out, and they've been showing them to all sorts of people, asking them if they recognize you.'

'Has anyone said anything?' I asked, feeling my heart pounding with terror.

'I don't think so,' he said. 'One bloke told him that you were effeminate as a kid, but most have kept quiet.'

'Have they been asking you and Mum what all the fuss is about?'

'We've had a few letters from neighbours saying that they're sorry we're being given such a hard time. But most people don't know what to think. I suppose they feel awkward about it.'

'Oh, Dad,' I said, beginning to cry. 'I'm sorry to have caused you all this trouble.'

'Don't you worry about it,' he reassured me. 'All that matters to me is your happiness.'

Later Mum told me that Rankine had been back to the garage, asking to talk to Mr Cossey, but his boss had told him that Dad wasn't there. 'But then he thought that Rankine might come to the house and question me,' she said. 'Your dad didn't want that, so he went out and caught him just as he was getting into his car. He gave him a piece of his mind, and now he's worried that he's done the wrong thing and shouldn't have got angry.'

'Tell him he did what was right, and he's not to give it another moment's thought.'

I felt terrible for my family. These journalists were placing them in an impossible position. Terry rang. He had been approached again and had been offered money for 'an inside story'.

'I feel like killing the bastards,' he told me.

'Try to forget all about it,' I said.

It was good advice I gave, but I couldn't follow it myself. I had been looking forward to going to the première of *For Your Eyes Only* at Leicester Square, but with the *News of the World* back on the trail, I knew I couldn't risk it. I accepted a job in Rome, and told the publicity people that I would be out of the country.

The Rome job shifted to Sardinia. The photographer chose some fantastic locations and I should have enjoyed the work. But I was sick with worry, and rang Pam every day to see if the story had been printed. Everything stayed quiet. It seemed that once again they had lost interest.

Two months passed, and I returned to Rome on another

assignment. Late one afternoon, walking back to my hotel and enjoying the warm sunshine, I felt more relaxed than I had done in a long time. 'Perhaps things really will work out for me,' I thought.

As I walked through the foyer, the receptionist called: 'There's an urgent message for you. You must call home immediately.'

'The news isn't good, I'm afraid,' Pam said when I rang.

'What's happened?'

'Yvonne has had a call from the *News of the World*. They say that they are going to print a story on you, and they asked her if she would like to comment.'

Pam said that Yvonne had denied everything, told them I was out of the country, and then disappeared herself for the weekend.

I caught the next available flight to London, arriving at Heathrow on Sunday morning, the day the article was due to appear. I rushed to the first newsstand I saw and bought a copy of the paper. There was nothing in it about me.

I spent the rest of that week in a state of nervous terror. On Friday the *News of the World* contacted Yvonne again. They sent her a copy of the article with an accompanying letter asking for her comments. She rang them straight back: 'If it's taken you three years to come up with something as ludicrous as this, you're in the wrong job. That article is laughable.'

She was convinced they were bluffing, and when another Sunday came and went and there was still nothing in print, I began to hope that she was right. Then, in the middle of the third week, Rankine himself called and asked to speak to Caroline Cossey. As I took the phone I was shaking from head to toe, but I was determined to keep any tremor out of my voice.

'Have you read the draft of the article?' he asked.

I told him I had and found it utterly ridiculous.

'Caroline,' he said. 'Be sensible. The piece *will* appear. If you give us an exclusive, or even just a quote or two, you'll be able to exert some control over how your story is told.'

I fought to keep my temper. 'You go right ahead and print. Your story is garbage and so are you. I have nothing whatsoever to say to you. But if that article appears you'll be hearing

Towering above the local men in the Maldives

On location in Kenya I was befriended by this little boy

Getting away from it all with my Mum in
Calabria, Italy

Right Getting love and support from my
Mum and Dad for a photo session for
Woman magazine by John Paul after my
story first broke in the press

A relaxing meal at a Greek taverna on holiday in Rhodes with (left
to right) Paulo, Glauco and Pam

Above Being serenaded in
Venice with Glauco

Taken by a friend of Glauco's
before a cocktail party

Visiting Pam with my mother in Rome

With Dad, Mum and Pam on New Year's Eve 1986/7 – the last
before he died

Photo by John Hedgecoe for one of his books

Modelling for Victor Hromin
in Italy

Cover shot for *Osrati*, an Arab fashion
magazine.

Cutting our wedding cake in the beautiful Lancaster Room at the
Savoy Hotel

Kissing and thanking my bridesmaids and pageboys for handling
my train so well

Above Looking happy and relaxed with my little helpers after the ceremony

Posing for friends in front of the old Rolls-Royce that was to take us to the ball

On honeymoon in Acapulco: a photo taken by me of Elias with
my hairdresser Owen and his boyfriend Jonathan

A happy honeymooning couple sightseeing in Acapulco

from my solicitor first thing on Monday morning. I hope you can afford it.' I put the phone down.

On the next two Saturday nights I took a taxi down to Leicester Square to pick up the early editions of the tabloids. I sat in the back of the taxi leafing through the papers, my heart in my mouth, searching for the headline. It was over a month since the first threat of publication, and still nothing had appeared.

'They haven't got enough evidence to go to print,' my friends reassured me. 'The story isn't coming from you, and without you there isn't a story.'

I began to relax. And then, the next Sunday, it happened.

JAMES BOND GIRL WAS A BOY

The headline hit me like a slap across the face. There beside the article was a picture of me wearing a £1,500 chinchilla bikini that I had modelled three years previously. They had done it. Despite what they must have known it would do to me and my family, they had printed their article. And in the name of what? Surely not news. How could my very personal and private struggle merit coverage in a national paper? 'The people have a right to know,' one journalist told me. 'What right?' I thought as I stared at that paper. 'What right does anyone have to hound another human being, to harass their family, to ruin their career, to take away a dignity that was so hard won?' That story wasn't news. It didn't help people to live better lives, it didn't enable them to understand current affairs, or make sense of British politics. I wasn't even a criminal whose misdemeanours should be held up for all to see. I had hurt no one, and now felt that my life was in tatters. Everywhere I went I would be known as 'Tula – the transsexual'. How could I hope to establish a relationship with any man?

I needed to talk to my mum. As soon as I heard her voice I began to sob. All I could say was, 'Mum, it's in.' I didn't need to elaborate. She began to cry as well, and I heard her calling, 'Bob!' My dad came to the phone and, speaking calmly and slowly, asked me to tell him what had happened. Between sobs I explained. 'They've done it, Dad. They've printed the article.'

'Where's Pam?' he asked. 'Is she with you?'

But Pam was still asleep. 'Go and wake her up,' said Dad. 'I need to speak to her.'

By now I was incoherent with grief. I could say no more and I put the phone down. Stumbling into the bathroom, I locked the door behind me and then sank down on to the floor, my head in my hands. At that moment I felt I couldn't possibly go on. The thought of having to face all those people, of having to answer questions, of being laughed at, despised, misunderstood, made me frantic with grief. An overdose seemed the only answer. In the distance I heard the phone ringing and Pam answering. I knew she would be talking to Dad. I looked at the bottle of sleeping pills on the shelf above me. It would be an easy solution. But it was a solution that would cause my mum and dad untold suffering. They had stood by me through all this and I couldn't let them down now.

No one who hasn't been in that situation can imagine how ashamed and frightened I felt sitting on the bathroom floor that Sunday morning. As time has gone by and I have become accustomed to interviews, articles, and public curiosity, I have grown to accept the idea that my transsexuality does fascinate people. But at that time I was in no way prepared for exposure. It should have been my choice to discuss my sexuality when and if I felt ready to do so. The *News of the World* had taken that choice away from me. I felt raped, and was overwhelmed by fears and feelings I hadn't experienced in years – an awareness that I was different, a freak, someone who could never hope to lead any kind of normal life. My long struggle to achieve normality and acceptability seemed to have been for nothing. The *News of the World* had sent me right back to the nightmare of my teenage years.

The sound of Pam tapping at the door pulled me from my thoughts.

'Caroline, are you OK? Come out, sweetheart. Dad's on the phone and he wants to speak to you.'

I got up slowly, went to the sink and threw some cold water

on my face. Then I unlocked the door and walked to the phone.

'Now listen to me,' said Dad. 'I want you to come home.'

'I can't, Dad. I have to sort this out for myself.'

There was a silence before he spoke. 'Well, OK. But I've told Pam that she and her boyfriend are to stay with you. We'll face this out together. As a family. Don't crumble. You have to fight. Remember, you're not a criminal and you've done nothing wrong. Find your anger. That'll help you through.'

As time went by and the hurt turned to fury, I was better able to follow his advice. But on that Sunday I felt too devastated.

In the afternoon Pam persuaded me to go out with her. 'You can't stay inside for ever,' she said. 'There's a heat wave, so grab your bikini. We're going to Regent's Park to soak up some sun.'

I remember walking to the park in a haze of tears. I couldn't stop crying. Pam and her boyfriend struggled to keep me distracted, but every time a passer-by looked at me my eyes would fill.

'They're all staring at me,' I muttered to Pam.

'Don't be paranoid,' she said. 'People always look at you. You're beautiful and that's reason enough.'

In the park we lay on the grass. My head had begun to throb and I closed my eyes for a moment, trying to relax. When I opened them again there was a man standing a few feet away. He was focusing a camera on Pam and me, and was about to snap.

'They're after me,' I hissed.

Pam sat up. 'Don't be daft. He's not a journalist. Look at his camera. He's just a tourist taking shots of London.'

'I want to go home,' I said.

She could see that I was in a bad way, and we walked back to the flat. I had a small supply of Valium and as soon as I got in I took two and fell into an uneasy sleep. The following day all the other tabloid journalists would be on my case, and I expected to be under siege. I was booked for a calendar job at the end of the week – a press launch in Leeds. Would they still want me to do the job? And, more importantly, would I feel able to face the cameras?

Yvonne called me first thing on Monday morning.

'The agency want to know if you're still prepared to do the assignment. I've told them that the *News of the World* article was untrue, and they don't seem at all worried about it. What do you want to do?'

I paused for a moment, then, remembering my dad's advice, I answered: 'Tell them of course I'll do it.'

'Good girl. How are you feeling?'

'Not too great. I'm going to see my doctor later today.'

The doctor prescribed more tranquillizers and a complete rest. 'Go on holiday for a week or so,' she advised.

That seemed like a good suggestion, and Mum and I arranged to go to Italy for a week as soon as I returned from the Leeds job.

By Thursday I still hadn't left the flat, even though I needed to buy things for my holiday. Finally I plucked up enough courage to wander down to the local supermarket. The place was crowded and I didn't notice any reactions. My confidence began to return – until I made the mistake of calling in at the local greengrocer's.

The shop was run by a couple of London lads who had got to know me, and would smile and wolf whistle whenever I walked by. This morning I was met by a cold silence. Neither of them would look me in the eye, and the one who served me asked abruptly: 'What do you want?'

Not a word was said as he went through my list, but as I was leaving he made a strange remark: 'Try to have a nice day.' And then he laughed.

He wasn't the only one to treat me like a social leper. A neighbour of mine, a man called Gregor, had always made a point of looking up at my flat whenever he passed. It was obvious that he fancied me – both our flats had balconies, and if I went out to water the plants or sit in the sun, Gregor would always find some excuse to wander out on to his balcony. But it was also apparent that he was very shy and I had doubted if he would ever summon up the courage to talk to me. In the end we met over a taxi – we both hailed the same cab, discovered that we were heading in the same direction, and shared the journey. I learnt that he was in show business too, and we found we knew some of the same people. When he dropped me off he asked me if I'd like to have a drink with him one evening. I said I'd love to and he promised to phone me. That had been a few days before the *News of the World* article appeared. The Thursday morning when I had returned despondent from my shopping expedition, I looked out of the window and saw Gregor walking by, his shoulders hunched and his eyes firmly fixed on the ground. It was obvious that he had read the exposé and would never phone. It wasn't a major blow, but it was yet another disappointment. 'Oh God,' I thought. 'Is this how life is going to be from now on?'

I was dreading the Leeds job. What if there were journalists there? How would I cope if anyone were abusive? I travelled up on the train with a man from the agency. We had a couple of drinks together, and then I broached the subject of the press. I told him that the matter was in the hands of my solicitors, and that I didn't want to discuss it at the launch. He was very understanding and promised me that I would not be given any trouble.

But I was so nervous when I got to the hotel that my hands shook as I tried to apply a fresh coat of lipstick. I decided to phone Mum – she would give me the moral courage I needed.

'You've got nothing to be ashamed of, darling. You're a beautiful girl and a successful model, so hold your head up high. And if you start to panic, just think of me. Do it for me. I love you very much.' I went down to the reception with a new resolve. No one mentioned the *News of the World* and I calmed my nerves with alcohol. None the less, I was relieved when the whole thing was over and I was sitting on the plane bound for Italy.

That week I spent in Rome with my mum gave me a chance to think about the future. It was only a matter of time before newspapers all over the world picked up on my story. It was obvious that my life would never be the same again. The exposure would have an immediate effect on my modelling career. The catalogue assignments, corsetry, swimwear, which provide the staple of a model's income, were likely to dry up. I had had regular work modelling things like maternity bras and pregnancy fashion; those companies would not want to use me again. Any big campaign that brought too much publicity would also be out of the question. The moment my face was recognized, the journalists were bound to come sniffing around. Besides, the fashion world is a very gossipy one – it wouldn't take long for the story of my past to circulate.

But if I didn't stay in modelling, how was I to earn my living? I had a mortgage to pay and no other qualifications. I talked it over with Mum and she agreed that it would be best if I restricted myself to low-key work in future.

'Perhaps if you told your side of the story,' she said, 'it would stop all the speculation. Then at least the agencies wouldn't feel that they had been deceived in any way.'

Her suggestion made a lot of sense to me. The inaccuracies that had been printed about my life were adding to my growing sense of outrage. One magazine in Italy claimed that a boyfriend had paid for my operation, another had printed a photograph of me beside a shot of a group of schoolboys, one of whom was supposed to be Barry Cossey. In fact the boy they'd picked out had been at the school five years before I had gone there. Most damaging of all was the constant misuse of the terms 'transsexual' and 'transvestite'. Journalists genuinely didn't know the difference and they seemed to feel that my transsexuality was some vast joke made at the expense of an unsuspecting public. As the days went by I felt a growing need to set the record straight. It might be too late for me, but an honest account of what it means to be born transsexual might be of tremendous value to all those people who were going through a similar experience.

I put the idea to Yvonne when I returned to England. She was very much in favour.

'I've already been approached by a number of journalists,' she said. 'But instead of writing a newspaper exclusive, why don't you write a book?' She told me that she had spoken to several publishers and a great deal of interest had been shown.

And so I wrote my paperback, *Tula – I am a Woman*. It was written with the help of John Goldsmith, who provided invaluable advice, and was tireless in his efforts. The book was put together at great speed, and was fuelled by my sense of anger and hurt. I felt that I needed to make a statement, to help right some of the wrong that Rankine and his kind had caused. I had never wanted to stand up and be counted as a transsexual, but now that everyone knew the truth, I felt I had to put in my own plea for tolerance and understanding.

'Perhaps when people read my story and look at the photographs of me, they will see that transsexual women are not freaks with stubbly faces and hairy chests,' I thought. And I do think that that book and my subsequent interviews did go some way to changing public opinion.

The book went a long way to putting me back on my feet; I was ready to speak out. But I was in no way prepared for the publicity and the promotional tour that accompanied publication. I was still remarkably naïve about the kind of rough questioning the media can come up with in pursuit of a good interview or story. The idea that everyone knew about my past had not had time to sink in. Now, when I do television shows or radio phone-ins, I can take whatever insults anyone likes to throw at me – I'm a seasoned campaigner. But at that stage I felt as though I were being fed to the lions. They were ready to make money out of me, and all I wanted to do was hide away. I decided I couldn't take it any more and told Yvonne that I wouldn't do any more promotional work for the book. My behaviour put everyone in an awkward position. But I did what I felt I had to.

I left the country and went to Italy by myself for a week, spending the days wandering along the beach. I needed time alone to do some serious thinking. I decided that now I had made a public statement, in the shape of a book, I wasn't prepared to talk any more about my transsexuality. I had done my bit and I was ready to return to anonymity. I would only accept those assignments that would safeguard my privacy.

I resolved to change agents. Yvonne had been as kind, as lovely and as helpful as she possibly could have been. She was excellent at her job. But I felt that by turning down so many offers of work, I was proving to be a real disappointment. I wanted to make a complete break with the past. When I returned to England I explained how I felt. She was very understanding: 'I wish you all the luck in the world, Caroline. If you ever want to come back, I'd be more than happy to represent you again.'

I found myself a new agency, Take Two. I established with them from the very beginning that I wanted to pick and choose: no glamour, nothing with major publicity, and as much high fashion as possible. It is possible for models to work in very low-profile jobs and still make a living, and Take Two were prepared to find me the right assignments.

There was only one thing left that I had to do, and that was to return to Brooke and face the neighbours. Brooke was still my home and I was determined that the *News of the World* wouldn't rob me of that security. Mum and Dad had already broken the news of my operation to the rest of the family. When the press harassment was at its worst, they had decided that they must protect the relatives from any determined journalists.

'Don't worry about what they think,' Dad had said. 'They're all 100 per cent behind you.'

It wasn't easy going back, and I did feel apprehensive. But I had my family's support and with that I felt I could face anything. In the end everybody was incredibly nice. I was never made to feel awkward, but was welcomed back as though nothing had changed. Even the lads who had teased me as a boy would stop to say hello!

I went round to my nan's house to see her and uncle Brian. It was a difficult reunion, and I think they felt as tense as I did. Nanny made a cup of tea, and we all sat around the table making polite conversation. She wanted to know about my life as a model, the places I had been, the people I had seen. As I talked I sensed that they weren't really taking it in, they were so busy accustoming themselves to my new appearance. It must have been a real shock. But it didn't take them long to relax, and soon I found myself cracking jokes about my situation. Even uncle Brian, who had worried about my effeminacy when I was a child, behaved brilliantly.

'I expect you're every bit as nervous as me,' he said, when he saw me as a woman for the first time. He was very complimentary about my looks, and it was great to see him again.

Tolerance and understanding came from the unlikeliest of places. The men at Dad's garage were magnificently supportive. One of his mates came up to him and congratulated him on having such a lovely daughter.

'I think she's been given a really tough time,' he said. 'And I'd like you to know that I admire her bravery and determination. She's a stunning girl.' Dad had always feared the reactions his workmates might have, and nothing could have made him happier than hearing that heartfelt and unrehearsed speech.

As I walked across the fields that weekend, and enjoyed the peace and tranquillity of the Norfolk countryside, I felt clear-headed and resolute. I had faced the worst and survived. I would continue to earn my money as a model, and try to live a life of some dignity. I wished to be left alone, untroubled by media interest. 'I've taken enough from them,' I thought. My greatest hope at that moment was to find a man who would love and accept me for what I was. Little did I know it, but that dream was to cost me dear.

15

Glauco and a New Start

I returned to London and forced myself back to work, but it was by no means easy. The exposé had rocked my confidence, and I became more and more reclusive. I went to no parties and avoided everybody except my closest friends. Most evenings I stayed at home in my flat in Maida Vale, and at the weekends I would travel back to Norfolk to be with Mum and Dad. I still felt very damaged by what had happened.

When I was away on a shoot, I would keep myself to myself, preferring to stay in my hotel room rather than going out with the other models. I dare say they thought I was a bit of a snob. If anyone ever questioned me about my transsexuality, I would suggest they buy a copy of my book. 'It's all in there,' I would say. I didn't want to enter into any kind of discussion.

Just at the point when my social confidence had reached rock bottom, I met Glauco.

I had been sent to Italy to model ski and sports wear and the shoot was due to take place on the slopes above a town called Gressoney. When I arrived at the airport I was told that an unusually heavy snowfall would prevent me from travelling up the mountain to join the other models, and I was to be taken to a hotel where the advertising agent would be waiting to greet me.

The agent was a tall, elegant Italian with blue eyes and golden-brown hair. His name was Count Glauco Lasinio, and he had a smile that could have melted an iceberg. 'I am so pleased to meet you,' he said. 'I apologize for the atrocious weather, and hope that you will allow me to entertain you while we wait for the roads to become passable.'

That evening he took me out to dinner. He was witty and charming, and I felt relaxed in his company. Half-way through the meal he surprised me with an extraordinary question.

'Is it a publicity stunt?' he asked.

'I beg your pardon,' I replied, completely mystified.

'All these rumours about you being a sex change. It's all just a publicity stunt, isn't it?'

For the first time since the exposé I was able to laugh about my situation. 'No,' I said. 'I only wish it were. But I'm afraid it's all true.'

Glauco's attitude to the whole subject was so relaxed and open-minded that I found it surprisingly easy to talk to him. His behaviour towards me did not change in any way; he remained as attentive as he had been earlier. He said that in Italy transsexuality was widely accepted.

'In the red-light district of Rome there is as much interest shown in the transsexual and transvestite prostitutes as there is in the heterosexual ones.' He told me that transsexuals even had the right to marry.

I was surprised that a European government had been fair-minded enough to bestow legal rights on transsexuals. 'The situation is very different in England,' I said.

The next day the roads were still blocked by snow and once again Glauco put himself at my disposal. 'I don't want you to feel lonely and deserted. Would you like to have dinner with me again tonight?'

This time there was a definite hint of romance in the air. He presented me with a red rose, and kissed my hand several times during the evening. I remained wary. I liked him, but it was hard for me to believe that his attentions sprang from anything other than curiosity. Glauco was the first man I had been out with who had known from the very beginning about my past. Besides, this was business, and I had no desire to get involved.

On the third day the snow had still not cleared, and I flew back to London. I was booked for a week to work on a milk commercial and couldn't break that contract. Take Two arranged for me to fly back to Italy as soon as I had finished filming. Glauco was there at the airport to meet me. I had been so busy that I had given him little thought, but as we drove in his Range Rover up into the snowy Alps, I was reminded of how charming and attractive he was.

He dropped me off at the ski lodge where the models were

staying and, after I had unpacked, I was taken up to the slopes where the shoot was to take place. It was a long day's work and by the time we had finished my toes were beginning to freeze. That evening we all relaxed together in the cabin, seated around a warm fire.

'Have you met Glauco yet?' Monty, the photographer, asked me.

'Yes,' I replied. 'He seems like a nice man.'

'He's OK. But I should warn you, he's a bit of a playboy. He loves models and he's bound to make a play for you. He's got a well-established routine. He takes you out a few times and then he asks you to come and stay in his house in Venice.'

'Does he now?' I thought to myself, grateful for the tip. It would take a lot more than a trip to Venice to seduce *me*.

The next evening Glauco came calling. He drove me to another beautiful restaurant and told me a little more about himself. He was an Italian aristocrat, with several lucrative businesses. His family had been champagne exporters and he was continuing the tradition. Advertising was a sideline for him. We were getting on famously, and I was beginning to wonder whether Monty had been right about Glauco. Then, over coffee, he came out with his famous line: 'Have you ever been to Venice, Caroline?' His face was a picture of innocence.

'No,' I replied, trying to suppress a smile.

His big blue eyes widened in disbelief. 'You've never seen Venice? That's terrible. It is the most beautiful city in the world. I have an apartment there if you . . . '

I could contain my laughter no longer and began to chuckle.

'What is so funny?' he asked.

'I'd been wondering how long it would take you.'

'How long it would take me?' He was mystified.

'How long it would take you before you invited me to Venice. I hear it's your trump card. If you haven't managed to get a girl into bed by the third date, then you whisk her off to Venice. It's guaranteed to work.'

Glauco threw back his head and roared with laughter.

'I like you a lot,' he said. 'You're smart and you're funny. So, will you come?'

'Maybe one day,' I replied, 'when I have the time, and when I have decided what I think of you.'

Glauco took up the challenge, and when I returned to England I was inundated with flowers, letters and phone calls. He flew to England at the weekend and booked himself into a hotel. He was persistent but charming, and he made no sexual overtures. He took me out to lunch and to the opera, where he introduced me to the works of Mozart. He was passionate about opera and Mozart in particular.

Glauco spent the next three weekends in London, and the more time I spent in his company the more I liked him. Then, one Friday night, he phoned me from the airport. It was nearly midnight.

'The flight was delayed. Can I come straight to you rather than stopping off at the hotel?'

I told him to get a cab and drive to my flat. When he arrived I let him in.

'Can I stay the night?' he asked.

I narrowed my eyes and gave him a long, speculative stare. 'I hope this wasn't just a ploy,' I said.

I told him he could sleep on the sofa in the sitting room. It was getting very late and I was tired, so I kissed him goodnight and went to bed. Ten minutes later, as I emerged from the bathroom, we collided in the hall. Glauco whooped with laughter.

'Look at those pyjamas!' he exclaimed. 'And there was me imagining you in a silk negligee or a cute little baby-doll nightie.'

I blushed with embarrassment. The cause of his mirth was the large pair of striped men's pyjamas I was wearing. I felt mortified.

'Cheer up,' he laughed. 'You look delicious whatever you put on. Now, how about a proper goodnight kiss?'

We embraced. And then, taking my hand in his, he led me into the bedroom.

Despite all my reservations and anxieties, making love with Glauco provided an enormous release. After the tensions caused by the exposé, it was incredible to be able to express myself in a physical way. He was a marvellous lover, and I had no sense that he was pruriently curious about my sexuality. He treated me as though I was a normal and desirable woman.

We spent the next day looking around art galleries and

antique shops. Glauco was fascinated by the Far East, and was a great collector of Japanese and Chinese art. He knew a lot about Eastern philosophy, and over dinner that evening he talked to me about his experiences at a retreat in a Tibetan monastery.

At the end of that weekend we made plans to meet the next week. I drove him to the airport, and he gave me a passionate kiss before he left.

Driving back to my flat, I thought about what had happened and decided to rein in my feelings. If this man was a playboy, his interest wouldn't last long. I had to protect myself from any rejection. 'I must be cautious,' I thought to myself.

But Glauco's interest didn't fade. If anything he became more ardent. We spent weekends together over the next few weeks, and when he repeated his invitation to go to Venice, I accepted. I had been working hard and felt I deserved a break.

The apartment was on the top floor of a modest palazzo. It had a small balcony which looked over the rooftops of a maze of ravishing Venetian buildings. Inside was a treasure chest of antique furniture and fine art. The elegant chairs, tables and richly coloured carpets were laid out on a fine marble floor. The effect was both grand and inviting. As Glauco had predicted, I loved Venice, and those few days we had there really cemented our relationship. We spent the time shopping, drinking cappuccino in the many little restaurants, or simply wandering beside the canals and over the bridges.

As time passed, and we grew closer and closer, Glauco invited me to Milan to meet his mother. He was an only child.

'My father is dead,' he told me, 'and consequently my mother is rather protective. You may find her difficult to get on with.'

But nothing could have been further from the truth. She was an elegant Austrian woman, and living as a foreigner in Italy made her particularly sensitive to how I, as an outsider, might feel. She did all she could to make me feel at home, and we got on immediately.

'My God,' said Glauco, as we left the restaurant where we had been having dinner. 'I've never seen my mother put her arm around any girlfriend of mine before. I think she really likes you.'

And she did. She knew about my past, but it never seemed to bother her. We spent hours chatting about Glauco, and sometimes we would gang up on him and complain about his chauvinistic behaviour! Glauco was a little spoilt. He liked his women to run around after him, and he didn't expect them to complain.

'You and my mother are the only two women who give me a hard time,' he would moan.

But for all that, he was very much in love. He told me that before we met he would never sleep the whole night in the same bed as any woman. It was different with me; we slept wrapped around each other, and I would wake each morning in his arms. Whereas before he had disliked kissing anyone on the mouth, now he became thoroughly uninhibited, enjoying the foreplay every bit as much as the intercourse.

Glauco was a very strong-minded man, and he enthused me with his confidence. 'You should never apologize for who you are,' he would tell me. 'You are a fine person – beautiful, loving and moral. Learn to hold your head high.'

He was also extremely cultured, and led me into a new world of books, art, music and conversation. Not that he was a Pygmalion, with me as his malleable statue. But Glauco *did* change things about me. He encouraged me to dress immaculately. Working in the advertising world had given him a natural eye for clothes and he knew which colours and styles suited me and which did not. And I wasn't the only one to change. Glauco had been a very conservative dresser, always wearing a suit and tie. I encouraged him to wear more casual clothes – baggy trousers, shoes without socks, sloppy jumpers.

At first he found it difficult to relax. 'Oh God,' he would moan. 'I look like a truck driver!'

During the first year of our relationship I had continued to model, and divided my time between Italy and England. The work rolled in steadily, most of it low key, and out of the media spotlight. Then I was asked to perform in a video that the rock group Duran Duran were making with Robert Palmer. They were recording together under the name 'Power Station'. They were well aware of my past, but liked the way I looked, and were more than delighted when I accepted their offer. Filming was great fun, and I got on well with John Taylor and

Robert Palmer. They both made no secret of the fact that they found me very attractive, and I was flattered by their attentions. All was going well until the media homed in on me like a pack of hungry wolves. I suppose I should have known that the job was too high profile and would attract attention. Once again 'Transsexual Tula' was splashed across the tabloids, with the story of how 'The sex change model has fooled rock group Duran Duran.'

Even with Glauco's support, I found it hard to bear being exploited yet again by insensitive and inaccurate journalism. I tried to get statements from the group refuting the paper's claims, but it was all too late. The story had been printed and the hacks had moved on. I had a further experience with an advert I had done for lingerie. The poster had a shot of my behind, and it was deemed by a number of feminists to be offensive to women. They complained to the Advertising Standards Council, and the newspapers got on to the story. When they found out that the model in question was 'Transsexual Tula', they had a field day. Here was an opportunity to knock feminists and transsexuals in one story.

These two jobs left me with a bitter taste in my mouth. Obviously, no matter how careful I was, the press were watching my every move. Glauco suggested that I become even more selective about my work.

'But I have to make a living,' I protested.

'Yes, I know that,' he replied, 'but not at the cost of your peace of mind. Clearly you will have to hit upon another backup profession. But until you have decided what you might want to do, you must let me help you out with your mortgage.'

I had never been dependent on anyone for money, and I found this a difficult proposition to accept. But then again, I had to recognize that if I wanted to make this relationship with Glauco work, I was going to have to give up more and more time to him. As it was, I was already practically living in his apartment in Milan. I worried about the problem for several days. Finally we agreed on a compromise: I would only do those jobs with which I felt comfortable, and Glauco would provide a kind of financial safety net if I got into trouble. I was tremendously moved by his generosity.

A few days later, Glauco and I were having dinner together

when he asked me if I had given any thought to the idea of changing the law in England regarding transsexuality. As things stood, while it was possible, legally, for a transsexual to be given the surgery that would allow them to function in the sex that they felt themselves psychologically to be, it was not permissible for them to marry. Nor could they change the information on their birth certificate, which recorded their original sex and not the gender in which they now lived. This placed transsexuals in a kind of legal no man's land. In the eyes of the law I was still a man. Therefore, if I broke the law and received a prison sentence, I would be obliged to serve my time in a man's prison and not in a female gaol. I could not be legally raped, and I was not entitled to a pension under the same terms as a woman.

'They are denying you your basic human rights, Caroline. In Italy transsexuals are allowed to marry. Why should the law be any different in England? It seems to me that the law is lagging way behind society. As each year passes people are understanding more and more about gender reassignment, and yet transsexuals are still treated like second-class citizens. You should fight against such prejudice. Stand up for your rights.'

I knew that what he said made sense. If I had been able to produce a birth certificate which stated that I was female, the *News of the World* would never have been able to go to print with that article. And so often in life we are asked to produce a birth certificate: for job applications, medical examinations, insurance. Each time I had to supply that piece of paper I was vulnerable to prying, questioning and prejudice.

'It violates your right to privacy,' Glauco continued. 'And, since you can neither legally marry a man nor consummate a marriage with a woman, as far as marriage is concerned, they are sentencing you to a life without legal status. Basically, they're telling you to keep quiet and know your place. Perhaps they reckon that transsexuals have forfeited their right to a happy domestic life? Maybe they think you should be punished for a mistake of biology?'

His words hit home. But I was still unsure that I could present any kind of case. I knew that the transsexual model

April Ashley had tried and lost some years earlier, and she had been married.

'But, Glauco,' I said. 'I don't have a partner who wants to marry me. Why should they take my petition seriously?'

He took my hand over the table. 'Yes, you do,' he said softly. 'You have me.'

I realized at that moment just how serious Glauco was about our relationship. But I couldn't quite believe that he would be prepared to marry me. Underlying all my happiness was a deeply rooted fear: I might be able to offer Glauco companionship and sexual happiness, but there was one very important thing that I could never give him – children.

My inability to procreate made me feel desperately insecure. Lust was lovely, but a long-term commitment would involve Glauco recognizing that he would be sentencing himself to childlessness. I had been brought up in a very close family, where the birth of children had brought the parents into an even closer relationship. Glauco and I might possibly have been able to adopt, but we would never know the joy of producing a child between us. And so when Glauco suggested that I present my case to my MP, citing him as my fiancé, I advised caution.

'Glauco, are you sure that you could live a life without kids?' I asked.

His response was immediate and definite. He admitted that he had never felt any strong paternal urge: 'I like other people's children well enough,' he said. 'But I have no desire to have any of my own. To be honest with you, Caroline, I think I am far too self-centred to be a father.'

Even with that reassurance I couldn't quite believe that Glauco was serious about marriage. He must have sensed my insecurity, for later that month he proposed in a way that left me no room for doubt.

He had been on a business trip to Japan, and when he returned we decided to spend a few days at the apartment in Venice. It was late spring, the weather was balmy, and the city was not yet too crowded with tourists. On our second evening there Glauco told me to dress up, as he was taking me somewhere special. First we went to hear an orchestra playing Vivaldi in one of the many beautiful churches, and then we had a candle-lit dinner, sitting beside a canal. The flames flickered in the light breeze as we drank sambuccas and watched people taking their evening stroll. It was a moment of quite perfect happiness, and I felt light-headed with wine, love and the night air.

'Come on,' said Glauco, reaching for my hand. 'The evening isn't over yet. I have a surprise for you.'

The 'surprise' was moored beside the Accademia Bridge: a gondola with gondolier and serenading violinist. Glauco helped me down into the boat, and then off we went, floating down the Grand Canal. It was so unutterably romantic that I didn't know whether to laugh or cry.

'Caroline,' said Glauco, taking my hand in his, 'will you marry me?'

'Yes,' I replied without hesitation. 'But,' I added with a giggle, 'in this situation I would probably say "yes" to anything!'

And so it was settled. Glauco and I were to marry. We would divide our time between Switzerland, where we intended to buy a flat, Milan and Venice. As soon as the Italian press got hold of the news they were desperate to feature the two of us together. I was worried about how Glauco would react to the publicity, but he seemed utterly unfazed.

'Sweetheart,' he said, 'as far as I am concerned you are a complete woman. I love you and am proud to be with you, and I don't care about public opinion.'

He introduced me to all his friends. Again I was anxious lest they give him a hard time, but they all accepted me without difficulty. Even Glauco's old friend Mario, who had seen some of the articles and had teased Glauco about the relationship, was impressed when he actually met me.

'He told me that I was a lucky man,' Glauco informed me later. 'And he thinks you are a very beautiful woman.'

If I was to become Glauco's wife, I had to think about my legal position. From the first, Glauco had encouraged me to stand up and fight. If I didn't contest British law, my marriage would never be considered legal in my own country. To be protected by the law, I would have to become an Italian citizen.

Did I want to give up British citizenship, or was I prepared to enter the fray? I spoke to my parents and asked their opinion. Dad's advice was clear and concise.

'If you don't feel up to a legal battle, I would understand. But I think Glauco is right. Until this thing is settled, you'll always be at the mercy of gutter journalists and ignorant bureaucrats. If you are to marry, you should do it legally. One day you may need the protection of the law.'

And so I began the long, slow haul that was eventually to lead me to Strasbourg and the European Court of Human Rights. Because the legal process was so long drawn out (in all my case ran for seven years), it is hard to chart. Months would pass while the wheels of bureaucracy turned, and correspondence, lawyers' briefs, memoranda and written testaments accumulated in files and on desks, and added to solicitors' bills.

To begin with the process was relatively straightforward. I went to see a solicitor, Henri Brandman, who has acted on my behalf ever since, and he advised me on what course of action I would have to take.

'First you must write a letter to your MP and ask him to inquire of the Director and Registrar General of Births, Deaths and Marriages whether you could validly marry a man. You will also need to ask whether it is possible to be granted a birth certificate showing your sex as female. Once you have a response to those requests – and here I should say the response *will* be negative – we can take the case to the European Commission.'

I knew nothing about the work of the Commission and asked him to explain.

'It's a part of the Council of Europe, and was established in 1953 for the protection of human rights. It works independently of the parliaments or governments of individual countries, and it's an important source of legal principles.'

He went on to explain that a barrister would have to present my case to the European Court, and would do so on the grounds that the British Government, by refusing to change the information on my birth certificate and by not allowing me to enter into a valid relationship with a man, were violating articles eight and twelve of the European Convention on

Human Rights. He read out the relevant sections from both articles. Article eight states that:

Everyone has the right to respect for his private and family life, his home and his correspondence. There shall be no interference by a public authority with the exercise of this right, except that which is in accordance with the law, and is necessary in a democratic society in the interests of national security, public affray or the economic well-being of the country, for the prevention of disorder or crime, for the protection of health or morals, or for the protection of the rights and freedoms of others.

'Well, I'm hardly a threat to national security, am I?' I joked.

'No,' he replied. 'But their refusal to change your birth certificate does threaten *your* security, laying you open to prejudice and hostility.'

He went on to explain article twelve: 'It provides that . . . "Men and women of marriageable age have the right to marry and to found a family, according to the national law governing exercise of this right."'

'Do you think I have a chance of winning?' I asked.

He couldn't give me an answer. It was even too early to know whether the Court would accept the case. He did warn me that I would have to supply a medical report with my application.

That report was written by Dr David Herbert. He was a consultant plastic surgeon, and he conducted the examination in the presence of two witnesses. The experience made me feel awkward and embarrassed. I knew it was necessary, but I felt like a circus act with my legs in stirrups and two doctors describing what they could see. At one point he stuck a ruler inside me to verify that my vagina was large enough to accommodate a penis. He wrote a very favourable report, stating that he found me to be 'a pleasant young woman with a gracefully female attitude to life', and he confirmed that a genital examination showed me to be 'female in all respects'.

But having gathered all the necessary papers, I discovered that, for the time being, my case would not even get a hearing. The Commission was passing judgement on the case of a female to male transsexual, and my case would be either accepted or rejected depending on the outcome of that one. The man in question was one Mark Rees, who had been born a girl and at the age of thirty-two had undergone gender-reassignment surgery. Like me, he was claiming the right to marry and change the birth certificate. But, unlike me, he did not have a partner to whom he was engaged. The decision on that case was to take some while. Still, I felt happy to have set the ball rolling. Glauco and I could now start planning for our future.

Glauco began flat hunting in Switzerland. We wanted to stay close to Italy, and both fell in love with Lake Lugano. We found two flats, one with a beautiful view of the water, the other with an atomic bomb shelter! Glauco was vastly impressed by the shelter, but I told him that in the event of a nuclear attack, I would prefer to die looking out at the lake, and he agreed to settle for the view.

Having found a place to live, I now had to decide what I was going to do with myself in Switzerland. I had always had a job and I couldn't see myself declining into endless shopping trips and coffee mornings with the ladies of Lugano. No, I would have to keep myself occupied and earn my keep.

Around this time I met a friend of Glauco who ran a clinic for alternative medicine and therapies. Like Glauco, he was fascinated by oriental culture and philosophy, and he suggested I take some courses at the Oriental School of Medicine. I was excited by the idea.

Unlike some, who feel a natural suspicion towards alternative medicine, I had always found much sense in its doctrines. When I had been under the greatest stress from press attention, I had learnt how to meditate. It had had a profound effect on me, enabling me to find peace of mind in an otherwise intolerable situation. Glauco had introduced me to the healing power of crystals and to several homoeopathic remedies for stress. Much of the Chinese medicine in which he was interested formed the basis of modern medicine, and was centuries old.

I decided that I would apply for a course in acupressure, a form of massage that concentrates on certain pressure points. The Chinese believe that our energy travels along pathways called meridians. When we are tense, unhappy or ill, these pathways can get blocked, and will need stimulating if they are to run freely once more. I also took a course in Reki in which I learnt about chakras – centres of energy in the body which have been used in healing for centuries by oriental medicine. My teacher was a Chinese man called Dr Chang, who was tremendously patient with me. It had been years since I'd had to study, and it didn't all come easily. I had to do a crash course in anatomy and physiology, and I often ended the day with a headache. But Dr Chang encouraged me, and I felt that though the theory might cause me some grief, the practice wouldn't – when I was working as a beautician I had often been asked to massage necks and heads, and many clients had praised my skill. I have strong hands with long fingers, and found it easy to locate and relieve pressure from tense muscles.

The plan was to use my diplomas from the Oriental School of Medicine along with my qualifications in electrolysis and Slendertone, and my experience in beauty therapy to set up a clinic offering women total body care. The relief that I felt at the idea of being able to leave modelling and step out of the public eye was immense. By now, as far as the papers were concerned, I was married off and living in Switzerland, and their interest in my life had evaporated. 'The circus is over,' I thought, and breathed a sigh of relief.

Then, just as my life seemed to be sorting itself out at last, a few small but ominous clouds appeared on the horizon. Glauco and I came from very different worlds: he was an Italian aristocrat and I was a working-class girl from Norfolk. To begin with the differences between us had enhanced the attraction – I found his sophistication fascinating and he loved my irreverence and sense of humour. Occasionally his snobbishness would irritate me – if he went to a restaurant the food had to be cooked to perfection and he would never stay in anything but the best hotels. But we were in love, and to me these were little things. I am a fairly strong-willed person, and I knew that we both needed to compromise, he as much as I. Given time we would find a way to accommodate our differences.

But there was one area of difference between us that did cause me to feel some disquiet. Although Glauco was very fond of his mother, he was an only child and he didn't share my passion for family. My family was still more important to me than anything else. Glauco sensed this, and I think he resented it. But it was impossible for me to feel differently, for it was my family who had supported me through all those trying years, who had given me the strength to carry on. It would take some time and a sea of love to convince me that anybody else could love me as much or as unconditionally.

I needed to be in close contact with Mum and Dad, and visits to Brooke were a vital part of my life. Initially, Glauco had been very curious about Norfolk, and when he asked if we could go there together I was tremendously excited. But the trip was not a success. He was restless all weekend and, I felt, anxious to get away. Suddenly I found myself looking at my home village through his eyes, and I didn't like what I saw. The house seemed small and the countryside flat and dull. Glauco was perfectly charming to Mum and Dad, and Mum thought he was adorable. He always won over women with his wit and his big blue eyes! Dad liked him well enough, but I don't think he really felt he could relate to him – they didn't have anything in common.

The real drama began when I tried to find a decent restaurant for him to eat in. Glauco, in common with many Italians, cared passionately about his food. Sometimes he would send a meal back to the kitchen two or three times and I would be cringing with embarrassment. Glauco suffered no such agonies.

'We eat in very expensive restaurants,' he would say. 'For these prices we deserve the best.'

Norfolk was hardly up to his exacting standards, and for the first time I felt tense and strained in his company.

That weekend made me realize that although Glauco would be happy to see any of my relations if they cared to visit, he would not go out of his way to forge a strong bond of kinship, and he showed no desire to return to Norfolk. I suppose that we would have worked something out if it had not been for Christmas.

For me, Christmas is a very important festival, and I had always spent the week with my family. It meant wood fires, long walks over the fields, midnight mass . . . The first Christmas that Glauco and I had been together our relationship was quite new, and naturally I assumed we would spend the holiday apart. But by the second year, we were engaged. Sensing that there might be trouble, I broached the subject as early as November. I told him that I intended to go home and hoped he would come too. He remained vague about his plans. Then, two weeks before Christmas Day, he announced that he was going on a business trip to South America and would be away until 6 January. Would I come with him?

'But you know I always spend Christmas with my family,' I said, dismayed.

He flew into a childish rage and demanded that he come before anyone else in my life, and we found ourselves having an argument. Finally he snapped: 'Oh, do what you want to – you usually do!'

He left for the airport the next day without our having made up.

I went home as planned, and heard nothing from him for two weeks. I was hurt, but I also sensed that it had been important for me not to give way on this issue. All the same, I was delighted when he rang me from the airport to tell me he was back. We met for dinner that night and he was clearly relieved to see me. I put our quarrel to the back of my mind and began to enjoy the meal. We swapped stories and then, for no real reason, I asked: 'Have you been a good boy while you've been away?'

I almost didn't wait to hear the answer, so sure was I that he wouldn't even contemplate infidelity. His answer shocked me.

'No,' he said. 'As a matter of fact I haven't.'

He carried on eating his dinner as though nothing had happened.

'What did you say?' I asked, hoping I had misheard.

'Well, there was this beautiful girl at a party and she made it clear that she wanted to sleep with me and so . . . '

I put my knife and fork down and stared at the tablecloth. I could feel the tears pricking the back of my eyes.

'What's the matter?' asked Glauco. 'Aren't you hungry?'

'I think I just lost my appetite.'

'Oh, come on, Caroline. You did ask, and so I told you.'

I stayed silent, not raising my eyes.

Finally he sighed. 'Look,' he said. 'I did it for spite. I wanted to get back at you. You made me feel insecure. Don't take it so badly.'

I stood up to leave.

'Where are you going?' he asked.

'Home.'

'Sit down,' he said, pulling me back into my seat. I sank into the chair feeling as weak and helpless as a baby. Glauco had clearly underestimated my reaction and was now attempting to backtrack.

'It wasn't serious,' he protested. 'I didn't even come.'

'For Christ's sake, is that supposed to make me feel better?'

'We were just fooling around! I didn't enjoy it. I felt too guilty.'

But I didn't want to hear any more. I told him he could stay in a hotel that night and that I was going home.

Glauco's reaction to my anger was to sulk. He didn't contact me for a week. That gave me time to think. Could I accept a man who was capable of infidelity? 'If he's done that while we are still engaged,' I thought, 'what chance would our marriage have?' Maybe I was being naïve, but I had been brought up to believe in the sanctity of marriage. I may have loved Glauco, but that didn't mean I was prepared to put up with his philandering. Also I had to consider my own vulnerability. It had taken me years to build up confidence about my sexuality. All women can feel pain about an infidelity, but as a transsexual, I felt inferior in so many ways that I didn't need a wandering man to exacerbate the situation.

After a week had passed Glauco rang me and asked if we could meet. He was desperate to repair the damage, and for a while I did try to make things right between us. But although I still loved him, I was too disturbed by what had happened. It killed much of the sexual feeling I had for him.

And so we parted. To begin with I felt too distressed to talk to him, but as time has passed he has become a real and very valued friend. He has continued to give me support and encouragement, and he occupies a very special place in my heart. Perhaps we met at the wrong time. Who knows?

The end of that relationship left me without a clear future. I had given up modelling, and all my contacts in the business imagined that I was living in Switzerland with Glauco. I felt far too proud to go knocking at their doors, yet I had to earn some money: I had bills to pay and a sizeable mortgage. The idea of returning to the world of modelling filled me with terror. Living a quiet and private life had given me peace of mind. Just the occasional assignment might be possible, but that wouldn't provide anywhere near enough money. I talked the problem over with some friends. One suggested that I put an advert in several of the health and beauty magazines offering my services as an acupressurist.

'You're qualified, and you're good at it. I bet you'd soon build up a regular clientele,' she said.

The more I thought about it, the more I liked the idea. Obviously I couldn't work from home – I didn't have a licence – but I could make house calls.

I worked out the wording for an advertisement:

HEADACHES, BACKACHES, TENSION? WHY NOT TRY
ACUPRESSURE MASSAGE?

The following week it appeared in the magazine *Health and Fitness*. I got an immediate response. I decided that since I would be working in people's homes, I would accept inquiries from women only. I didn't feel comfortable working by myself with men, and, besides, I received a number of calls from gentlemen who clearly had something other than the merits of acupressure on their minds.

I bought myself a collapsible massage bed from John Bell and Croydon. Since I was so tall I had to have one specially made for me. I also applied for several more courses, including one in hypnotherapy. I didn't want to practise as a hypnotherapist *per se*, but I did feel that it would be a useful skill to have when dealing with people who needed to know how to relax.

The course was in Scarborough. It was expensive but it was also intensive. For months I had to devote every spare moment to it. At the end of the tuition, we sat an exam in which, among other things, we had to send a volunteer into a trance.

With my qualification in hypnotherapy, along with my experience as an acupressurist and my skills as a beautician, I felt able to offer a whole range of services to my clients. They

157

were mostly foreign: Jewish and Arab women who preferred to be treated in their own homes. For work I wore a white tracksuit, pulled my hair back into a ponytail, and went easy on the make-up. I can honestly say I enjoyed the work. I felt I was good at it, and able to help people with muscular problems. Soon I had a regular clientele and was earning a reasonable living.

Then one day a woman telephoned inquiring about my work, and asked if I would be willing to see a male friend of hers. I had been recommended to her by one of my most trusted clients, and she was wondering if I would be willing to break my 'women only' rule.

'The gentleman in question is a businessman suffering from the condition polymyalgia rheumatica. He has been on tablets and has been receiving cortisone injections. I thought that acupressure might be able to help him.'

I had heard of this ailment. It was a puzzling and debilitating condition that often affected businessmen, causing all the muscles in the body to suddenly and inexplicably cramp. It was like rheumatics of the muscle rather than the joints, and doctors were unsure of its cause. It sounded like a challenge, and I told her I would be happy to see him if she wanted to ring back with an appointment time.

A few days later she called again. 'Mr Fattal would be pleased if you could visit this Wednesday,' she said. 'He lives in a penthouse suite in Regent's Park. Will that be convenient?'

I replied that it would, and put the phone down. And that was how I was introduced to Mr Elias Fattal, the man who was to cause me both the greatest joy and the worst heartache of my life.

16

Elias Fattal

Elias Simon Fattal. The man I married. How to begin to describe the years we spent together? How to begin to describe the happiness I felt with him? Memories come back to haunt me: his laugh, that would send tears of mirth running down his face; his body wrapped round mine in sleep; watching him shave – a towel wrapped round his middle and his feet bare and familiar and adorable. Never before had I felt such contentment with a man. Every day was an adventure – he made the ordinary seem fantastical: cooking a meal together, walking in the countryside, even watching the television. We were everything to each other – parent, lover and friend. When love is good and true it feels destined, and we did feel as though we were meant to be together, that ours was a marriage made in heaven to be played out on earth. When such a love is lost it leaves a scar in the brain and a crack in the heart. Elias and I gave each other the greatest gift: peace of mind. With that peace gone, I wonder if it will ever be found again.

It was a Wednesday morning like any other. I had struggled out of the taxi with my portable massage table, the address of a Mr Fattal scribbled on the piece of paper I was clutching. He lived in a penthouse in Nottingham Terrace, but when I rang the bell I was informed by the security guard that my client was delayed. Would I wait in the lobby? I waited while the clock ticked away twenty minutes, then, not prepared to hang around any longer, I turned to leave. At that moment Mr Fattal came through the door.

'I'm sorry I'm late,' he said, and held out his hand. His politeness could not disguise the look of cynicism in his eyes. Clearly he had been expecting someone older and more robust.

We travelled up in the lift together. Neither of us spoke,

and I had a chance to observe him closely. He was a well-built man, with a broad chest and a strong, muscular neck. He had dark hair and an olive complexion, and although I knew he was Jewish, he looked Italian. He was dressed immaculately but conservatively in a dark suit and tie.

As he opened the door to his penthouse, he told me the history of his illness. He had consulted a number of doctors in Harley Street, and had received treatment from several physiotherapists. They had failed to give him any relief from the pain. At present he was on a course of tablets and cortisone injections. He found this prescription painful and debilitating.

'Frankly, I doubt that acupressure can make any difference. But since you are here, we may as well give it a go.'

His scepticism acted as a spur. 'I'll show him,' I thought, and threw myself into the treatment. By the time I had finished I was hot and sweaty, and Mr Fattal was pleasantly surprised.

'I feel great!' he exclaimed, climbing down from the couch. 'Would you be able to see me two or three times a week?'

Feeling vindicated, I agreed, and he went to fetch his diary. While he was gone I looked around me. The flat was large and open plan, with huge french windows leading on to a roof terrace. The terrace seemed bigger than most people's gardens, and I walked towards the doors to have a look. I was amazed to discover a pond, complete with ducks paddling up and down on the water.

'They come from Regent's Park,' said Mr Fattal, appearing at my shoulder. 'They seem to like it up here and have built a nest.'

We settled on a time and date for my next visit and then I left. I liked Mr Fattal in that he was polite and seemed a gentle, introverted man. I had assumed from the rather spartan feel of his apartment that he was a bachelor. But I was still very sensitive about Glauco, and a new relationship was the last thing on my mind.

For the next few months I worked hard to wean him off the cortisone. The results were tremendous, and the cramping slowly disappeared. We learnt to relax in each other's company, and we would chat and joke as I worked. Then one day he asked me if I would have dinner with him.

'I don't mix business with pleasure,' I replied, trotting out that old cliché, scarlet in the face with embarrassment.

He laughed. 'I've made you feel awkward, Caroline. But I'm so grateful for all you've done. I wanted to say thank you. Please say you'll come.'

It would have seemed churlish to refuse such a gracious invitation, and so I agreed.

We spent a lovely evening together in a quiet restaurant, and Elias told me a little more about his life. He came from a strict, Orthodox family, and, though born in India, had been educated and brought up in England. His family name, Fattal, meant spinner, and his father had owned a number of carpet factories in Iraq. They had fled to England during the 1940s, because when Israel was granted nationhood, the situation for Jews living in Baghdad had become increasingly precarious.

Elias was the youngest of three children. He had a brother called William and a sister called Lydia. It was clear from the beginning that his family was of great importance in his life. He and William had gone into business together at an early age. They were given a thousand pounds each by the family and told to make of it what they could. Elias had bought land in Tunbridge Wells and made a sizeable increase on his investment by building and then selling property. From this auspicious start, he went on to form a number of companies.

High finance was a closed world to me. I knew nothing of business, and had no sense of the relative size of companies. There was one company of his that I had heard of – Roboserve – a vending-machine franchise that had machines all over the world – but other than that I had no idea of the magnitude of his financial empire. He didn't brag and I didn't pry.

The next day I received the largest bunch of flowers I had ever seen, and the courtship began. He discovered that orchids were my favourites; sometimes he would play tricks and three bunches instead of one would arrive. One stem would carry a card saying 'With love from Elias' and the other two would be anonymous. Calling to pick me up for dinner, he would ask, all wide-eyed innocence: 'Oh, who are those from then?'

I played along with the game despite the fact that the florist had told me several days earlier that the sprays were all sent by the same person.

We grew ever closer and I could feel myself beginning to turn from liking to love. One evening, after a candle-lit dinner in a Greek restaurant, he asked me to come back to his penthouse for coffee. The subtext was obvious – he wanted to sleep with me. I felt that we had known each other long enough by now, and that I could trust him to treat me with respect, so I said yes.

Our first sexual encounter was a disaster. I suppose we were both too anxious to please. To begin with all went well, and then Elias produced a Durex.

'Is that protecting you from me or me from you?' I asked.

I had told Elias that I couldn't have children, and so I felt it was fear of disease that made him cautious. (I should add that this was a few years before the threat of AIDS had hit the headlines.)

'I want you to make love to me when and if you feel safe to do so,' I told him.

After that we lay together talking and exploring each other's bodies in a more gentle and loving way. He asked me to stay the night, but I had no change of clothes and no toiletries, so, kissing him softly on the lips, I let myself out of the apartment and took a taxi home.

When we met the following evening the atmosphere between us was intimate and relaxed. The physical expression of desire had brought us closer together, and we both felt that the time was right to ask each other a few questions. Elias asked about my past relationships and I told him about Glauco and the engagement. He in turn told me about a German girl he had been in love with in his early twenties.

'The timing was wrong,' he said, with some sadness. 'I was far too ambitious for my career.'

I looked at this kind, gentle and caring man and wondered how he had remained alone for so long. 'When was your last relationship?' I asked.

There was a long pause. Then, stuttering with embarrassment, he told me the truth. 'I do, in fact, have a girlfriend at the moment.'

His reply shocked me. I felt foolish and cheap.

'But why didn't you tell me?' I demanded.

'You never asked,' was his rather lame reply.

'What the hell gives you the right to ask me out when you are already committed to someone else?'

'I suppose I imagined you might have guessed. There are some of her things in the apartment. Didn't you notice?'

'No, I didn't,' I snapped. 'I'm afraid I'm a great deal more naïve and trusting than you may have imagined.'

We drove home in silence and when we reached my flat I got out of the car without wishing him goodnight. I was angry and hurt, and I had no intention of seeing him again.

The next day there was a bouquet of flowers on my doorstep with a note saying 'Please call me. Love, Elias.' Over the next two weeks he sent a number of messages, each time asking me to call him. I never did, and eventually communication ceased. I imagined I had heard the last of him.

I threw myself back into my work and, to cheer myself up, joined a health club in Chiswick. There I could swim, take yoga classes and use the sauna and jacuzzi. The club was quiet and, not being in the centre of London, I hoped it wouldn't attract anyone from the modelling or theatrical world. I began to attend regularly and the exercise was very therapeutic. Then one day I bumped into Twiggy in the gym. I turned right round and went back into the changing rooms. Driving home, I debated whether to give up my membership – not on account of Twiggy, who had never met me and had no reason to know the first thing about me, but because I didn't want, after all these months of privacy, to be thrown back into the public gaze.

I began to visit the club during those hours when it was least crowded, and I never stayed to drink in the bar and socialize with the other members.

There was one woman with whom I did strike up a friend-ship. We met one day in the jacuzzi and got chatting. She was an attractive blonde with a warm, friendly manner, and I felt able to relax a little in her company.

'I've seen you in the club a couple of times,' she said. 'But you always seem to be in such a hurry to get away.'

'I like to beat the rush hour,' I told her.

I learnt that her name was Myra and that she was married with one daughter, Rebecca.

'Are you married?' she asked.

'No,' I replied. 'I'm just recovering from a relationship that went badly wrong.'

I told her a little about Glauco and she was very sympathetic.

The following week I was sitting in the jacuzzi, my mind blissfully free from thought, when an extraordinarily handsome man stepped into the water.

'Hello,' he said, smiling.

I blushed to the roots of my hair, and muttered, 'Hi.'

I have always found myself crippled with shyness when confronted with an attractive member of the opposite sex. He continued to smile at me whilst I stared at the bubbling water, feeling the steam join the perspiration on my face. Luckily, Myra chose this moment to make her entrance. She slipped into the jacuzzi beside us saying, 'Hello, Steve. Hello, Caroline. Have you two met?'

'Yes,' I replied, and, as she began to chat about Steve's experiences on a recent holiday in Florida, I made my escape. Walking with two left feet, I staggered towards the pool and slipped gratefully into the cool water. After ten minutes Steve left, and Myra joined me in the pool.

'What on earth happened to you?' she asked.

'I'm sorry,' I stammered. 'Whenever I meet attractive men, I clam up. I must have seemed rude.'

Myra laughed. 'You are a strange girl, Caroline. You seem so cool and sophisticated. I would never have guessed you were so shy.'

She told me that the man in question was a professional footballer who played for Chelsea.

'He's married with two children,' she added. 'So he's spoken for, I'm afraid.'

We both giggled, and, feeling emboldened by our chat, I plucked up the courage to ask her if anyone at the club had been talking about me. Myra paused for a moment or two and then said, 'I'm not going to lie to you, Caroline. There are some people asking if you are the model Tula.'

'I am,' I replied.

'Well, what you choose to tell me about your life is your business. I like you as a person, and that's enough for me.'

I decided that I would confide in Myra and began to tell her the story of my past. But Myra told me that she had read my book some years before. 'I can't say I recognized you from the pictures,' she said. 'They made you look so much darker.'

Knowing that she was familiar with my history made me feel that much more comfortable. But I found the idea of other people in the club knowing difficult to handle. Myra sensed this and begged me not to withdraw my membership. 'The people here like you very much, and they will guard your privacy. Besides, if you stop coming I shall be cross with you.'

From that day on Myra became a close friend. She introduced me to her husband, the actor Peter Egan, and I got on just as well with him. Peter and Myra have shown me such love and care in the time I have known them that they have my eternal gratitude and affection. They accepted me as I was without question, and showed me that there are people in this world who live lives free of prejudice and full of generosity.

Weeks had passed since I last heard from Elias. But one day he called me.

'How are you?' he asked.

'Overworked and underpaid!' I replied, surprisingly pleased to hear his voice. I told him about the health club and the new friends I had been making.

'Any boyfriends?' he asked.

I laughed. 'None of your business!'

'I've missed you, Caroline. I'd like us to meet and talk.'

'Talk about what?'

'Let's have dinner,' he suggested. 'I'll tell you all about it then.'

And so we met for a meal.

He seemed tired and anxious. 'You've been working too hard,' I told him. 'You should tell your girlfriend to take better care of you.'

'There is no girlfriend, Caroline. I ended the relationship some time ago.'

My face flushed with pleasure. I had missed him too, more than I had been prepared to admit.

And so we started again from the beginning. This time we were both cautious and took things slowly, really allowing ourselves time to get to know each other. We both liked what we discovered and before long we were falling hopelessly in love.

It was the easiest of love affairs. We shared similar pleasures and very rarely quarrelled. In his work, Elias was a high-powered business executive, but in his private life he was a quiet, home-loving man, down to earth and unassuming. We were soon spending every night together; we ate together, played together and slept together. At the weekend we would visit the health club or go to the theatre or cinema. But best of all, we would rent a couple of videos and I would cook Elias his favourite meals. Unlike Glauco, Elias didn't stand on cere-mony. He was happy to eat sitting in front of the TV with his feet up on a chair.

There were so many things that I grew to love about him: his ready humour, the scent at the back of his neck . . . I even found myself washing his dirty socks! I'd never known love like this before. If he hurt his finger or stubbed his toe, I felt the pain as though it were mine. In sleep, after incredible love-making, we would twine our limbs around each other as though we couldn't bear to be parted even in dreams.

'Do you love me, pet?' he would ask, twice or three times a day.

'You know I do,' I would reply, kissing the back of his neck.

For a man as worldly and as confident as he was, I found his insecurity about love curiously touching. He needed to feel looked after, and I began to suspect that at some point in his life he had been starved of affection. Simple things like a freshly ironed shirt, a massage, or a surprise dessert would bring him tremendous pleasure. Whatever I cooked for him, he would make a point of asking for a second helping.

'You're just like a little kid,' I would laugh.

Under the warm gaze of his love, my confidence grew ever stronger – he was so appreciative of me. If he were engrossed in the newspaper and I passed by on my way to the bathroom dressed in my underwear or draped in a towel, he would put his reading aside.

'Oh, pet!' he would groan and lead me into the bedroom. Sometimes it was impossible for me to get dressed!

But the passion was mutual. Often I would sneak into the bathroom to watch him shower. Just the sight of his naked back made me ache with desire. As time went by our sex life

grew stronger and stronger. There was such a sense of rightness when I lay in his arms.

I had introduced him to my parents very early on in the
relationship. Mum and Dad had come to visit me and Elias
offered to take us all out to dinner. After my experience with
Glauco, I was a little apprehensive. But I need not have worried.

They all three got on like a house on fire. Watching my
father and the man I loved deep in conversation over a glass
of wine gave me a burst of real pleasure. Elias was very
involved in the day-to-day activities on the shop floor of his
factories, and he could connect with my dad's life in a way
that Glauco never could.

'What a great guy,' said Dad at the end of the evening when
Elias had left. 'He's the kind of man you need, Caroline. He's
down to earth and caring. You could really plan a life with
someone like that.'

'Oh, Dad,' I protested. 'We haven't known each other long.
In any case, marriage isn't a possibility – he's an Orthodox
Jew.'

I believed what I said. Despite my feelings of belonging, I
had never imagined a long-term future with Elias. Firstly, he
didn't know about my past, and I wasn't sure that I had the
courage to tell him. I hoped that he might have guessed. He
knew I didn't menstruate, and on several occasions I had been
approached in the street by people who wished to congratulate
me on my bravery. One time in a department store, two
women had come up to me and praised my paperback, *Tula –
I am a Woman*.

'We think you are very courageous. And we would like you
to know that we wholeheartedly support what you are fighting
for.'

Elias was standing a few feet away and I wasn't sure whether
he had heard. Afterwards he asked, 'What was that all about?'

'A book that I wrote.'

'Can I read it?'

'One day. But not just yet. It's full of some rather painful
experiences that I'd rather forget.'

But more importantly, his Jewishness would always be a
stumbling block. Elias kept me very much in the dark regarding

his family. Friday nights were sacred to him, and he always spent them with his father and mother. There was no question of my being invited along. I had met his brother William once or twice. They shared the penthouse. But although William was always polite, I felt that in his eyes I was just another girlfriend.

If his family was a closed book to me, mine was the exact opposite to him. Mum and Dad encouraged us to come and stay as often as we liked, and Elias loved the simple life style of Norfolk. He and my dad would go to the pub together while Mum and I cooked lunch. My pleasures were ordinary ones, but not the less poignant for that. I even got him on a bicycle and we went pedalling off across the Norfolk countryside! He appreciated the closeness that we had as a family.

'Not many families are like yours, Caroline,' he said one evening, as we were driving back to London. 'Some pretend to be, but in fact they are not. I love the way you hug and kiss each other. You can show your love. I respect and admire that.'

His words were music to my ears. This was a man who, rather than feeling threatened by my family, could celebrate and even envy our love for one another.

Sitting in the car as we sped through the darkness, I thought it would not be possible for me to feel any closer to Elias than at that moment. But I was wrong. A tragedy was about to strike my family that would draw us both into an even stronger union. In the coming months I was to learn just how much I needed the love and support of this special man.

17

11 November 1987: A Sudden Grief

It was such an ordinary evening, unremarkable in every way. Elias and I had gone out to eat at a Thai restaurant. We had been together a good eighteen months, and had become accustomed to staying the night at my flat. He had clothes, books, and even a toothbrush there. We were both tired and looking forward to an early night. As I came through the door, I noticed the red light on my answering machine, signalling that someone had called and left a message. While I rewound the tape, Elias went to the drinks cabinet to pour us both a nightcap. I replayed the message.

How often have I wished that I could turn back time. Then I could re-enter that flat, find no message on the machine, and fall into a deep and happy sleep wrapped in Elias' arms. How strange and unbearable it is that life can be calm and contented one moment, and then shattered into a thousand tiny pieces the next.

It was my mother's voice on the tape.

'Caroline, can you ring as soon as you get in. It's urgent.'

I knew immediately that something was wrong. 'Elias!' I called out as my fingers shakily dialled the number. He came straight over and stood by my side.

'What is it, pet?' he asked.

I didn't answer. The phone was ringing and I heard my mother's voice at the other end of the line.

'Mum, what is it?'

'It's your dad,' she said with a sob. 'He's dead.'

It felt as though at that moment the world had stopped. From a great distance I could hear myself saying over and over, 'Oh, no. Oh, no.'

And from even further away, the sound of my mother crying. With a great effort, I pulled myself together.

'It's all right, Mum. It's all right. We're getting in the car now. We'll be with you in a few hours. Are you on your own?'

'No,' she sobbed. 'Terry is here.'

'Let me speak to him.'

Terry came on the line.

'What happened?' I asked.

'It was an aneurism. No warning. He died instantly.'

'Did he feel any pain?'

'No. It was too sudden.'

As I put the phone down my knees gave way. Elias caught me. The moment I felt his touch I began to cry.

'It's my dad. It's my dad,' I wailed, incoherent with grief. 'He's dead. My dad's dead.'

Without Elias's help I don't think I would have got through that night. He packed my bag, gave me a small brandy and led me gently out to the car. Then he drove through the night to Brooke. I cried solidly. I could see nothing, hear nothing. All I knew was that every passing mile was bringing me closer to home and to Dad.

'I just want to hold him in my arms and say goodbye,' I whispered. I knew that if I didn't see him I would never believe that he'd gone.

Elias drove as fast as he could, but by the time we got there the body had already been taken to the morgue.

'They have to do a post-mortem,' explained Terry.

'Where's Pam?' I asked.

'She's getting the first flight from Rome. She should be home late tomorrow.'

My mum was sitting on a chair, staring into space. Her face was white and stained with tears. I went up to her and put my arms around her. Suddenly she seemed so young and defenceless.

'What will I do without him?' she asked.

She told me how they had been watching the television together. 'He asked me if I wanted a drink. I said yes and he went into the kitchen to put the kettle on. The next thing I heard was this horrible crashing sound. When I went into the kitchen he was lying on the floor. He was dead.'

No one slept that night. We were all too shocked. Elias cradled me in his arms while I cried and cried.

The next morning I drove him to the station. He was due to fly to America on business that afternoon. 'I'll happily postpone the trip if you want me to,' he said as we kissed goodbye.

But I told him he should go. There was really nothing more he could do.

'I know how much this hurts, pet,' he said, as we stood waiting for the train. 'But remember, you've got me. I adore you and always will. I'll be a father, a lover and a friend to you.'

When I got back to the house, I didn't go straight inside. Instead I stood in the garden for a few minutes and looked around me. After we kids had left home, Dad had transformed this plot of land from a vegetable garden to a horticultural extravaganza. He had put his heart and soul into it. Standing there, I felt comforted by the strong sense of his presence that lived on in these well-loved plants and trees.

'My little Italian garden!' he used to exclaim proudly.

He had come up to London to visit and I had taken him to the Italian Gardens in Kensington. He had loved them and rushed home full of plans for planting, pruning and extending. Over the years he had made a putting green with nine holes, and he'd fashioned two ponds, one cascading into the other. They were full of goldfish and decorated with the water lilies he had picked from the mere. He had developed a passion for conifers, and had planted many varieties – one was too close to the house and was threatening to crack the brick with its roots. I gazed about me, my heart full with love and grief. He had been a good man, a kind man. And a loving father. He had stood by me through all my troubles and traumas and now, just when life was getting good and he could look forward to a happy retirement surrounded by his family, he was dead.

I wasn't allowed to see Dad until after the post-mortem. He was in the chapel of rest. People say that it is important to see the dead body in order to come to terms with death. But that wasn't the case for me. I wished that I had remembered him as he was, pottering around his garden or cleaning his car. The corpse that I was shown was nothing like the man I remembered. Death had altered him: he was yellow and cold and the post-mortem had left stitches round his neck. I have a vivid memory of the ridiculous lace cap that they had put on his head. The experience left me deeply traumatized and I went into shock.

As time has passed, the pain has eased. But I still miss my father terribly. I often find myself talking to him in times of trouble. I try to imagine what he would have said to me, what advice he would have given. I suppose that you never really lose someone you love – they live on in shared memories. Terry, Pam and I often get together at the house in Brooke and talk about Dad until late into the night. We remember little things he did, funny things he said. Sharing memories in that way helps to release a lot of grief.

I still feel troubled by the notion that I could have done something to prevent his death. If the doctors had known about his condition he might still be alive today. About three weeks before he died, I was cutting his hair and asked him if he had bought himself any BP shares, as I had advised him to do. His reply struck me as strange: 'There's no point. I won't be around to see them come to anything.'

I was alarmed to hear him talking in that way and told him to go and have a check-up. But, as always, he refused to take his own needs seriously and laughed it off. He hated doctors and called them 'quacks'.

Dad died on the 11 November 1987. It was a bleak Christmas that year. Elias supported me throughout. He let me grieve and helped me to come to terms with what had happened. I shall always be grateful for the help he gave.

18

A Moment of Truth

Spring came early and Valentine's Day dawned, sunny and mild. When I awoke there was a large bunch of orchids from Elias and a card. He took me out to lunch and we had a quiet stroll in the park.

'What would you like to do this evening?' he asked. 'Theatre? Cinema?'

'Let's get a video and spend the evening at home,' I suggested.

I drove back to my flat, stopping at the video shop on the way. I opened the door and was half-way out of the car when Elias said, 'I want to ask you something.'

'What is it?'

'Will you marry me?'

I slid back into my seat. 'What did you just say?' I asked incredulously.

'Will you marry me? I know I'm no Robert Redford to look at, but I do love you very much and I think you care about me. I could make you happy. I know this feeling between us will go on getting stronger and stronger. I told you I would be a father, a lover and a friend to you. Well, now I want to be a husband too.'

I was stunned. If he had asked me the question as we were walking in the gentle spring sunshine in Regent's Park it might have come as less of a surprise. But looking at his face, I realized how nervous he was. Tears welled up into my eyes.

'But it's leap year,' I said smiling. 'I should be asking *you*.'

'Just give it some thought, pet. It would make me so happy if you were to say yes.'

Elias asked me not to tell anyone until I had made a decision, but when we got home I was unable to resist sharing the news with my mum. She was staying with me and we all sat down to watch the video together. At one point Elias left the room to make a phone call and I told her what had happened. She was delighted for me, but she also gave voice to thoughts that I had been trying to ignore.

'Darling, you know how much I care for Elias, and I don't want to spoil your happiness, but you know what you must do now, don't you? You must tell him about your past.'

Of course she was right. I had been living in a fairytale. It was one thing to have a love affair with someone, but it was another to marry them. If our marriage was to survive, it had to be rooted in truth. There must be no deceptions between us. I watched the rest of the film in silence, my mind teeming with thoughts and fears.

Next morning, Elias left for work. Mum made me a cup of tea and came and sat down beside me.

'I'm sorry, sweetheart, if I've spoilt things for you by telling you my thoughts. But you mustn't have any secrets from Elias now. If he really loves you he will understand.' I began to cry and she put her arms around me.

'Oh, Mum. I'm so scared of losing him. I need his love so badly.'

I rang Myra. Elias had told me to keep the proposal a secret but I wanted her advice.

'I'm so happy for you,' she said. 'You and Elias are perfect for one another. But I do agree with what your mum says. Marriage is a serious business; it needs a foundation of trust.'

'Myra, I don't think I've got the courage to do this.'

'Yes, you do. I have every faith in you. Why don't you give him your book to read?'

Elias called the next day and asked if we could meet. But I needed more time. I told him that I was unwell and would see him the following evening. All that day and for most of the night I agonized over what I had to do. I had grown so close to Elias in the past few months. All the family loved him, and Terry's two kids, George and Claire, already treated him as though he were a favourite uncle. If he were to reject me or even to become angry, how would I cope?

Elias rang the next morning to ask if I was feeling better.

'There's something I have to tell you,' I said.

'What is it, pet? You sound so serious.'

'I'll tell you when I see you,' I replied, and put the phone down.

I decided to put my book in an envelope and give it to him to take home and read. I waited by the window and when I saw his car draw up, I ran down to meet him. My hands were shaking and I was deathly pale.

'What on earth is wrong?' said Elias, alarmed by my appearance.

'Please, Elias, this is very difficult. There is something in my past that I haven't told you about. I want you to take this home and read it. Don't hate me.'

He took the envelope. 'But what is it?' he asked. 'Have you done something criminal?'

'I haven't done anything wrong. This was something I had no control over.'

By now the tears were pouring down my face. Elias looked utterly bewildered. 'Nothing can be *that* terrible, Caroline. Were you married before? Is that it?'

'No,' I answered. 'Please just go home and read my book. Absorb it and then call me if you want to. But, please, don't hurt me.'

But Elias was already tearing at the envelope.

'What are you doing?' I protested.

It was too late. He was staring at the back cover of the book. There was a photograph of me, aged five, with the caption 'From Tula's personal albums.'

'My God,' he exclaimed.

I waited for the insults, the anger. Instead Elias looked up at me: 'Caroline, I want to read this with you sitting beside me. Let's go inside.'

He took my hand and led me back into the flat. We sat down on the sofa, and, holding my hand, he began to read. I sat there shaking with nerves, my eyes red with crying. 'Perhaps I should have told him from the very beginning,' I thought.

It took Elias about two hours to read *I am a Woman*. At times he would sit back in his seat, run his hands through his hair and sigh. When he reached the section covering the operation, he began to sweat slightly.

'Did you have to put in so many gory details?' he asked.

As he reached the last page, he breathed out and took my hand. 'Well, you've certainly got balls, pet!'

'WHAT!' I cried. It was an unfortunate choice of words in the circumstances! He turned puce with embarrassment.

'Oh God, I'm so sorry. I didn't mean . . . '

Later we were both able to laugh uproariously at the slip of the tongue. At the time, I was horrified. He cradled me in his arms and let me cry.

'This is the way God made you, darling. It's not your fault.'

We made love that night. It felt important for both of us to establish that sexual rapport between us was unchanged. I was relieved. Elias had not yet had time to digest all this new information, but at least he had dealt with it intelligently.

In all it took a week for the dust to settle. He needed time to think and I left him alone. 'He'll contact me when he's ready,' I thought. I knew that he was disconcerted by the fact that all my friends had known about my past when he hadn't.

'It does make me feel a bit self-conscious,' he told me.

I spoke to Diana and Myra on the phone. 'He seems to have taken it well,' I told them. 'But I'm still not entirely sure.'

'Give him time,' they both advised.

At the end of that week we met for dinner. During the meal he seemed awkward and uncomfortable. My heart sank. 'He's going to tell me it's all over,' I thought.

'I want to talk to you about something, Caroline.'

I looked up from my plate and was shocked to see tears in his eyes. 'This is it,' I said to myself.

'I want you to consider converting to Judaism.'

I couldn't have been more surprised.

'My faith means so much to me,' he continued, his eyes still bright with tears. 'It would make me very happy if you would undertake a course in Liberal Judaism.'

'You mean you still want us to get married?' I asked.

'I love you, pet. I know that we are going to have a lot of hurdles to jump, but trust me and have faith. We'll go over them one at a time.'

Over the following weeks we discussed my past on numerous occasions. I needed Elias to understand it all. I also needed to be certain that he didn't feel in any way disturbed about his own sexuality. If Elias were to ascribe his attraction for me to a homosexual impulse, we would both be in trouble. I questioned him about his past. He told me that he had never had any homosexual experience. What did come out of those discussions, however, was a certain similarity in our childhood experiences. As the only Jewish boys in the school, he and his brother had been bullied and persecuted.

'One time somebody wrote "Jewboy" on my locker,' he told me. 'Like you, I felt like an outsider.'

I realized that it would be important for me to understand as much as possible about the Jewish faith before I could make any decision about conversion. So I booked myself into a health farm in the Canaries for a week and took with me a whole pile of books. I don't take naturally to study and expected to feel confused and frustrated. But in truth, I found the subject fascinating. Not only did it help explain so many things about Elias, but I also found Liberal Judaism an inspiring doctrine of faith.

Elias rang every day to ask how I was progressing, and when we met at the end of the week, I was able to impress him with my new-found knowledge. It was the 29 February when I said 'yes' to both his requests: yes, I would marry him, and yes, I would convert to Judaism.

19

Rites of Passage

Our first task was to choose a synagogue. We both felt it was important to find a rabbi who would be sympathetic to converts. We spoke to several before we were introduced to Rabbi David Goldberg. I liked him immediately. He was kind and courteous.

'Conversion usually takes from one year to eighteen months,' he explained. 'It really depends on how eager you are to learn.' Elias told him that it would be preferable if I were to have intensive tuition.

'We want to get married next spring,' he said.

'And in any case, I find it easier to learn by crash course,' I added.

The rabbi suggested a lady who might be able to tutor me. She was called Marjorie Moos and we arranged to meet her and discuss a possible timetable.

Marjorie was a delicate old lady of ninety-four. Her appearance belied her manner: she had a will of iron and an agile mind. She lived in Golders Green in a home for the elderly, and I visited her for three hours in the afternoon, three times a week. She was to teach me the history of the Jewish people, the meaning of their ceremonies and how to observe them, and, most important of all, the Hebrew language. Of course it would have been impossible for me to become fluent in Hebrew in such a short space of time; I had only nine months until my examination. But it was feasible for me to be taught the alphabet, the pronunciation and the main prayers. At first it seemed impossible, and I thought I'd never make sense of the script she placed in front of me. But with time, I grew accustomed to the sight and sound of the language and I was soon able to stumble through a rendition of the Shema, the most important Jewish prayer.

Marjorie was a tough and demanding teacher. She was strict with me and wouldn't leave a particular lesson until she was truly confident I had grasped the meaning.

Elias and I began to attend services together. We went to Rabbi Goldberg's synagogue in St John's Wood. The original synagogue was being rebuilt and so the services were held in a converted church. In some ways this helped me adapt. It was a link with the Christianity of my earlier life. For Elias, the services there were a real delight. His family attended an Orthodox synagogue, where the men are separated from the women. He liked to sit next to me on a Saturday morning and say prayers. The service was an hour and a half long, compared to the five hours he was used to, and Rabbi Goldberg's sermons were topical and inspiring. My dad's death had left me with a real need for God; the Jewish faith assuaged that need. The Jewish belief in direct access to God (without the intercession of a messiah) made much sense to me. I could make use of this notion of perpetual access to the Divine. It comforted me.

And I was sorely in need of comfort. Just as I was immersing myself in the intricacies of the Jewish faith, my mother fell sick. She had been bleeding and, on examination, it was decided that she should have a total hysterectomy, followed by four and a half weeks of radiotherapy. I was thrown into a state of panic. 'What if it's really serious?' I thought. I sat with her in the hospital while the surgeon explained the process. I could tell from her face that she wasn't listening to him. Following so close on my father's death, this latest blow had left her numb.

Mum stayed in hospital for two weeks. Pam, Terry and I visited her every day – sometimes I would be lugging my theological studies in a bag. Elias was magnificent. He provided constant support and a shoulder to cry on when it all got too much to bear.

She had barely had time to recover from the surgery when they began the radiotherapy. At one point, she had to have a caesium implant and was allowed no visitors for forty-eight hours because of the radiation. I stared through the window and saw my mum lying on a bed surrounded by lead screens. The nurses had put chains on the door and a DO NOT ENTER sign was hung from the handle. I couldn't bear to see her so alone.

'I'm going in,' I said, and, ignoring the nurse's protest, opened the door. I walked up to the bed and took her hand in mine.

'You shouldn't be in here, darling,' Mum said.

'I don't care, Mum. You're my mother and you're more important to me than anyone else on this earth. If you are in pain or feeling sad, I want to be with you to make it easier.'

That night I discussed with Elias what we should do for Mum when she came out of hospital. Obviously she would spend some of her time in Brooke, but I didn't like the idea of her being so far away from us all. Pam was in Italy and Terry had his own family to look after.

'Would you prefer it if she had somewhere in London to live?' asked Elias.

'Yes,' I replied. 'But it would have to be nearby. Perhaps I should start looking for a bigger apartment.'

A few days later we were blessed by an extraordinary piece of good fortune. As we were leaving the house, we bumped into a neighbour who told us he was moving out. 'I've just received an offer on my flat.'

Elias jumped at the opportunity. 'Whatever you've been offered, I will offer more *and* pay cash.'

It was the most generous of gestures. I protested, but Elias silenced any opposition. 'Pet, it will make you happy to have your mum near you. And if you are happy, your mother will be happy. We need to get her well and strong again.'

Mum did make a miraculous recovery. For a month or so she seemed very weak, but then her interest in life reappeared and she and I set about decorating her new home.

Time was passing and I was making real headway with my studies. It was late summer and I was studying when everyone else seemed to be sitting in the parks or sunbathing in their gardens. I persevered. But one thing was bothering me. Elias still hadn't introduced me to his family.

'My mother may find it hard to accept,' he explained when I questioned him. 'She's spent a good deal of her life trying to marry me off to the right Jewish girl and I'm afraid she may not be at all happy about my settling down with a Gentile.'

'But I'm converting!' I exclaimed.

'I know, I know. But you have to appreciate my mother is in her seventies and very stuck in her ways. She's used to people doing as she says.'

The more he told me about this woman, the more anxious I began to feel. Elias was forty-seven and although he had a reputation in his own circle for being a bit of a playboy, as far as Mummy was concerned he was still her boy.

'I've never even brought a girl home to meet her,' he told me.

'Phew,' I thought. 'This could be a real battle.'

And what a battle! Early that summer Elias announced his engagement and the gefilte fish hit the fan. There were terrible rows and Mrs Fattal refused to meet me. I suppose she thought her son would renounce me to please her. But once she realized that Elias was not going to budge, her curiosity got the better of her and she agreed to a meeting. Elias and I were summoned to Monte Carlo, where the family had an apartment.

'It will be more relaxing for everybody,' she said.

As the plane landed on the tarmac at Monte Carlo, I for one didn't feel relaxed. I could feel my knees knocking.

'Calm down, Caroline,' whispered Elias. 'Everything will be just fine.'

But looking over at him I could see that he looked none too relaxed himself. He was sweating profusely and a small nerve was turning somersaults under his right eye.

'Just remember,' he muttered as we walked towards the terminal, 'you are a beautician, not a model. Don't mention anything about modelling.'

'Oh, hell!' I thought to myself. 'The Creature from the Black Lagoon had nothing on this.'

I reached into my bag for a cigarette, but before I could light up, Elias had snatched it from my hand. 'You mustn't smoke in front of the family,' he warned. 'Women aren't supposed to smoke or drink.'

My heart sank. 'I'm supposed to get through this ordeal without the help of either nicotine or alcohol?' I murmured under my breath. 'You must be kidding.'

We can't have been in our room for more than five minutes

when the phone rang. 'It's Mummy,' said Elias. 'She's coming right over.'

She certainly wasted no time. I hadn't unpacked or combed my hair.

'You look just fine,' said Elias. 'Come to the balcony. We should be able to see her walking over from the apartment.'

Our room was not at the front of the hotel facing the beach, but at the side, and was overlooked by several large apartment blocks. 'That's the window of our flat, there,' said Elias, pointing.

A horrible thought occurred to me: with a pair of binoculars, anyone could see straight into our lounge. Perhaps that explained the prompt telephone call! But there was no time for further speculation.

'There she is!' cried Elias.

Down below a small figure was walking at great speed towards our hotel.

'My goodness, she certainly moves fast for a lady in her seventies!' I exclaimed.

She disappeared from sight and then there was an agonizing few minutes while we waited for the knock at the door. Elias answered it.

'Hello, Mummy,' he said, ushering her in. She swept past him without so much as a hello. It was me she had come to see. I held out my hand.

'How do you do,' I said, fighting to keep the tremor from my voice. She paused for a moment, staring me right in the eye, then she shook my hand.

'Hello.'

She was a small, stout woman, impressive less for her looks than for her demeanour. She had energy and a willpower the like of which I had never seen.

'Would you like some tea, Mummy?' asked Elias, mopping his brow with a handkerchief.

'No.'

'A cold drink, perhaps?' I ventured.

She accepted and I told Elias to take her out on to the balcony and I would serve the drinks there.

As I sat down beside Elias, I could feel her eyes on me. She didn't miss a thing. My shoes, my jewellery, my engagement ring – all were examined with an eagle eye. She never smiled once but, with a small frown furrowing her brow, proceeded to grill me for twenty minutes. She was anxious to impress on me the importance of Judaism and I had to admire the pride she displayed when talking about her faith. While we spoke (or rather, she spoke and I listened), Elias sat silently by my side, sweat pouring off his face. Every so often he would clear his throat or stand up and pace up and down the balcony.

Then, just as abruptly as she arrived, she got up to leave.

'Please join us for dinner tonight, Caroline,' she said, and then swept out of the door. The moment she was gone, Elias grabbed me and began dancing up and down the room.

'She likes you! She likes you!' he crowed.

'God, I'd hate to see her in action with an enemy,' I muttered.

'I know my mother,' he said. 'And she definitely took to you.'

I had been surprised by the invitation to dinner. It was Friday night, their religious night and traditional family get-together.

'I guess I must have passed the first test,' I said.

The apartment was on the seventeenth floor. As we walked through the door a silence descended. It reminded me of those Westerns when the cowboy strides into the saloon and the piano player freezes. All eyes were upon me. Mr Fattal, a gentle and kind man who seemed older than his wife, came to my rescue.

'Would you like to see the view from the balcony?' he asked. It amused him that I wouldn't stand near the edge. He pointed out the palace and the coastline of Italy. I remained at arm's length from the railings.

'V-very beautiful,' I said, feeling my knees knocking.

'There's really nothing to be scared of, Caroline,' he chuckled.

Dinner was not quite the ordeal I had expected. We were a large group and that made small talk easier. Elias sat beside me, hanging on my every word, and whenever we spoke to each other or touched, I could feel Mrs Fattal's gaze upon me. At one point I decided to stare her out. She had a way of lifting her chin and looking down her nose at people and the next time I caught her scorching stare, I returned the compliment. It felt like the shoot-out at the OK Corral. Who was going to fall first? But truth be told, I was no match for that woman. Our eyes locked for what seemed like an eternity and then, singed by the heat and red with embarrassment, I dropped my gaze and reached for a glass of water.

I was seated next to Elias's sister Lydia. Lydia seemed charming enough and we got into conversation. She asked about my family.

'My father died recently,' I explained.

'Had he been ill long?' she inquired.

'No, he was one year off retirement after working thirty-nine years for a company. He suffered from . . . '

But before I had time to finish, Lydia interrupted. 'Was it his own company?' she asked.

I paused.

'No,' I replied curtly.

These small frictions aside, I enjoyed the evening more than I had imagined I would. They were a lively group of people and it was good to see Elias among his family. I could also understand his fondness for my mum and sister. Elias' relationship with his mother was a fairly formal one. They didn't embrace or show any physical affection. But his respect for her was obvious.

At the end of the meal I made my biggest *faux pas* of the evening. I got up and offered to help clear the table.

'No, no, Caroline,' said Mrs Fattal. 'The maid will do that.'

'Whoops!' I thought and sat down again.

As we walked back to the hotel Elias congratulated me. 'You were superb, pet. They really liked you.'

Buoyed up by wine, I too was prepared to congratulate myself and I reached into my bag for a celebratory cig. I was just about to light up when a voice called out 'Elias!' It was an aunt from Canada who was bearing down on us at full speed.

'Shit!' I muttered and stubbed out the long-awaited cigarette.

More greetings and more introductions. By the time we got home I was too tired to smoke. I fell asleep and dreamt of Jimmy Durante and a pair of staring eyes.

Mrs Fattal dominated the next few days. She decided to take me under her wing and drove us around Monte Carlo, pointing

out the sights. It wasn't all purgatory. I admired her strength
of mind and I felt that, given time, I might earn her grudging
respect. But for all that it was a very tense few days. I rarely
had Elias to myself, and even when we were alone I felt the
presence of his mother coming between us. On our last evening Elias was dressing for dinner.

'What do you think I should wear?' he asked, peering at his
reflection in the mirror. Before I could stop myself the words
were out of my mouth: 'Why don't you ask Mummy?' I said
and walked away.

Elias caught hold of my arm. 'Caroline, what's wrong with
you?'

'I'm sorry. The tension finally got to me. Please forgive me.'

He gave me a kiss and we dropped the subject. But in our
hearts we were both troubled. I realized that I would have to
sort out some ground rules when we returned to England. I
had only just succeeded in finding an identity I could call my
own, and I wasn't about to see it swamped by the demands
of Elias's family. After years spent thinking that I was inadequate as a transsexual, I couldn't allow myself to be regarded
as second-best because I was born a Gentile.

It was a relief to return to England. I was even happy to be
studying again. I had been given an exam date for January
and I knew I would have to work hard. Having met the family,
I was now drawn into a new world. We were invited to dinners
and lunches. With each meeting I felt another chip had been
chiselled from the rock. 'They're getting used to me,' I thought.

Mrs Fattal sent me a present. 'It's a gift from Mummy,' said
Elias, handing me a jewellery box. Inside was an emerald and
diamond set – a necklace, earrings and bracelet.

'Oh, Elias,' I said. 'I can't possibly accept these.'

'Why not?' he asked. 'She likes you and she wants to give
you a present.'

'No, this isn't a present, it's a gesture. And a very extravagant one at that. I don't wear elaborate jewellery like this. I'll
have to send it back.'

He was cross. 'Please Elias,' I begged. 'Don't make a fuss.
This gift will make me feel awkward. I've only known your
mum five or six weeks and she's already been more than

generous. Let me give them back to her. I'm sure she'll understand.'

So the jewels went back and in their place I received a bottle of the most wonderful perfume. I had the feeling that she admired my strength of mind.

One day over dinner Elias declared that he wanted to discuss my past with at least one other member of the family. 'I feel we should prepare the ground,' he said. 'What do you think?'

I paused before I spoke. 'If you tell one,' I said, 'you should tell them all.'

We talked for hours. Uncle Meyer, Elias's mother's brother, who had come over from Israel, was in his seventies but he was a witty and sophisticated man who had trained as a doctor and seemed to have a more liberal outlook on life.

'He would understand, medically, what you've been through,' said Elias.

But the more we thought about it, the more we retreated from the idea.

'I've had enough trouble getting your family to accept me as a convert,' I argued. 'Telling them I had a sex-change operation as well might be the last straw.'

'I understand,' said Elias. 'It's just that I feel so awkward when Mummy starts to talk about all the beautiful children you'll be giving me.'

'We will have children,' I said. 'Just not quite the way she imagines.'

Elias and I had approached my friend Diana and my sister Pam on the subject of surrogacy. They were both delighted to have been asked and more than happy to bear Elias's child.

Finally we came to a decision. We would wait a few years until I had proved myself a good wife and Elias' family were able to see how happy we were together. Then we would tell them about the surrogacy plan and about my transsexuality.

Shortly after that conversation Mrs Fattal invited Elias and me to the Conservative Ball at Grosvenor House. In the past few months we had been invited to a number of her soirées, with guests including Lord Young, Kenneth Baker and John Wheeler. I had always declined the invitations, much to Elias' annoyance.

'But, Elias,' I protested. 'John Wheeler is my local MP, the man I wrote to at the start of my case for the European Commission of Human Rights. What if he were to recognize me?'

This time Elias was adamant. 'Caroline, we cannot duck and dive all our lives. We will face the consequences of whatever happens.'

I don't think he ever really appreciated just how disastrous publicity could be. He was determined to take me to the ball. Mrs Fattal was a captain of industry as far as Margaret Thatcher and the Conservative Party were concerned – she had twenty-four tickets and intended to take along the entire family.

'You can't say no,' said Elias.

In the end he won. Dressed in a hand-beaded top and ankle-length full-circle skirt in black velvet, I went to join the true blues at their annual bash in Grosvenor House. After passing through some tough security checks, the master of ceremonies met us at the door and asked for our names.

'Mr Elias Fattal and Miss Caroline Cossey!' he screamed at the top of his voice as we passed into the ballroom. I shivered with nerves. What if someone recognized the name? Margaret Thatcher materialized with Denis at her side.

'Good evening,' she said. 'Thank you so much for coming.'

I felt the blood drain from my face. Elias hadn't told me that I was going to meet the Prime Minister.

'Thank you very much for asking me,' I stuttered like some dumb schoolchild. I shook hands with Denis, and Elias and I went to our seats.

'Why didn't you tell me?' I hissed.

Elias was grinning. 'Because if I had, you'd never have made it here,' he replied, giving my arm a squeeze.

It was a bizarre evening. The press were too busy concentrating on the political 'giants' of the Conservative Party to pay me any attention, and I was able to relax and look about me. John Wheeler was seated on the next table but he didn't give me a second glance.

The room was full of faces familiar from TV and newspapers. Elias asked me to dance and we waltzed past Michael Heseltine. He glanced at me and raised an eyebrow. 'Now there's a handsome man,' I thought to myself. Half-way through the evening a bottle of champagne was auctioned. As I sat and listened to the bidding jump in thousands of pounds, I realized what a strange world I found myself in. My dad had worked all his life and saved less than these people were prepared to spend on a bottle of bubbly. I believed in hard work and enterprise being rewarded, but somehow looking around the room at the women in their tiaras and ballgowns, I wasn't entirely sure that those rewards had been fairly apportioned.

Mrs Thatcher got up to make her speech. Like many others before me, I was surprised at her gentle, almost motherly manner. She was more feminine and even flirtatious than I had imagined. Once she had finished her speech we were free to leave.

Driving home that night, Elias behaved like a man vindicated. 'I told you it would be fine,' he said.

And it had been fine. But largely due to the anonymous life I had been living for the past three years. I knew how precarious and precious that anonymity was.

That Christmas I begged Elias to come to Norfolk. We were to be married the following spring and I knew that from that day on Christmas would be spent with his family. He agreed. It was a happy time. We missed Dad terribly but the wounds were healing, and Elias brought new love into the house. He showered my family with presents. Mum received the entire Chanel range. George and Claire, Terry's kids, were given a computer. We spent the break walking in the countryside and breathing the clear country air.

In the New Year I took my Judaism examination for the first time. I went to a synagogue in Marble Arch and was grilled by four independent rabbis. I did well on the history and the ceremonies but fell down badly on my Hebrew. I was so nervous I couldn't think straight. They gave me a resit date for six weeks hence. In the interim I studied like mad and passed the second time. Elias was overjoyed. My affirmation service was conducted by Rabbi Goldberg. It was very private, with only Elias, my mum and my sister and Marjorie, my teacher, present. It was a moving ceremony and I felt very proud to have been accepted into the faith that had come to mean so much to me. I was given a certificate signed by Marjorie and my rabbi that confirmed my status as a Liberal Jew, and allowed me to marry in any Liberal synagogue in the world.

Elias's family were pleased and gave gifts to celebrate my

entry into their faith. William bought me a necklace decorated with rubies on one side and sapphires on the other. Mrs Fattal chose a beautiful pair of earrings.

With the completion of my conversion, the wedding plans could really get under way. We had a lot of things to decide: where and when we would marry, where we would live as Mr and Mrs Fattal. And it wasn't only our wishes that were to be considered: there, at every turn, was Elias's mother and her endless stream of demands.

If things seemed complicated then, they were about to become more so. Henri, my lawyer, rang me one morning and told me that after nearly two years of deliberating, the Court in Strasbourg had decided to hear my case. When Mark Rees had lost his fight and had his case dismissed, mine had also been thrown out of court. But with the help of my barrister, the brilliant David Pannick, my case had been re-presented and accepted. It had taken all this time for the Court to get round to hearing it. It couldn't have come at a worse moment. If I were to win, the press would have a field day. I spoke to Elias about it that evening. He listened gravely as I explained the situation.

'I understand what you are fighting for, Caroline,' he said. 'And in the long term it is important that we get the law on our side. But right now the publicity could ruin our chances of happiness. My family mustn't learn about your past from the gutter press. We need to tell them in our own way, in our own time. Wouldn't it be possible for you to change your name to Miss C or Miss X rather than being named as Caroline Cossey?'

I told him that I would talk to Henri about it in the morning.

But before I rang Henri, I spoke to Myra.

'If Henri can't get my name changed, what should I do?' I asked her. 'I've been fighting this for so long that I would feel terrible if I gave up now. But if it meant sacrificing my relationship with Elias . . . '

Her advice was direct and firm. 'Caroline, you've done your bit,' she said. 'You've stood up and you've been counted. Now let someone else take over. You've had so much suffering in your life, don't jeopardize this chance of happiness. If he can't change the name, then pull out.'

I spoke to Henri and explained that I had met someone very special.

'He knows but his family doesn't. I want to protect the relationship from the press.'

'Well,' he said, 'I'll try to get the name changed but I'm not promising anything.'

A week later he rang back with some surprising news. 'They've agreed to change the name to Miss C. The case will go ahead.'

I told Elias and he was delighted. Suddenly everything seemed possible: a marriage to the man I loved, a religion of which I felt proud, and the legal status that would offer me protection from the press.

The news provided a much-needed boost to my confidence. As the wedding date drew nearer, life got tough. I had hoped for a quiet wedding. I felt that the ceremony should be a private matter. Mrs Fattal felt differently.

'You only marry once,' she said. 'If you don't have a proper celebration you'll regret it for the rest of your lives.'

Her plan was to have the reception at the Savoy. 'Nothing big,' she said. 'Only about 300 people.'

I voiced my concern to Elias. 'If we make it a grand society wedding, we'll attract photographers and journalists. Let's keep it quiet. It's far less risky.'

But Elias didn't agree. 'My family are very private people,' he said. 'There will be no journalists allowed in and I will see to it that the photographer we hire is a friend of the family and totally trustworthy.'

I wasn't reassured. I knew that Mrs Fattal intended to invite some seriously wealthy and influential people. The Saatchis, for example, were on the guest list.

In the end Mrs Fattal won. We fixed a date with the banqueting manager at the Savoy. The wedding was to be held on 21 May. My one consolation was that Rabbi Goldberg would conduct the service. I felt I trusted him, and the thought that he would be there gave me comfort.

The weeks sped by in a fury of activity. Elias and I were house-hunting and having a lot of trouble finding somewhere that we both liked. Finally we found our dream home. It cost a cool £1.5 million and I assumed it would be way out of our range.

'Don't underestimate me, Caroline,' said Elias.

He made an offer but we would need to redecorate it before we could move in and time was running out. 'When we come back from our honeymoon,' said Elias, 'we'll stay at my penthouse.'

Mrs Fattal had reached fever pitch in her wedding preparations. She had organized the guest list, presented me with an endless round of parties ('You must meet all the family, Caroline'), and even had a hand in picking my bridesmaids. I was beginning to lose patience.

'I'd really like to cut down on socializing in the week leading up to the wedding,' I told her. 'I think I'll be far too nervous to enjoy myself.'

'Nonsense,' came the swift reply. 'Everyone gets nervous before they marry.'

I took a deep breath and thought hard about Acapulco and the honeymoon. The sooner I got through this wedding the better.

But Mrs Fattal had not finished with me yet. One morning she invited me out for coffee. We had just been to order the wedding cake, and sat down exhausted from the deliberations. Mrs Fattal was a tireless organizer. Without her and her daughter Lydia I doubt if I could have coped. They were seasoned campaigners when it came to society functions.

I had just taken my first sip of coffee when my mother-in-law to be turned to me and said, 'Caroline, I would like you to consider converting to the Orthodox faith.'

After all I had been through, there was still more she wished me to do?

'I know of a course in Canada where they offer intensive tuition. It would make the family so happy, and it would be good for your children, my dear. Israel now only accepts Orthodox Jews as its citizens. I should not like my grandchildren to feel shut out from their homeland.'

I took a moment to collect my thoughts and then I spoke. 'Mrs Fattal, I love Elias very much and I converted to Judaism because I realized how important it was to him. I'm glad I *did* convert. My new religion has become a very important part of my life. But I must explain. I am a *Liberal* Jew and proud to be one. I feel part of the community of Liberal Jews who worship in my synagogue. Israel means nothing to me. I recognize its importance in the history of our faith, but it has no personal significance for me at all. I am an Englishwoman. This is my home. I will never want to live in Israel and abide by laws that were made centuries ago. I want to be a part of the twentieth century.'

By the time I had finished, Mrs Fattal's jaw had almost dropped into her coffee. The blood was pounding in my head. I had never made such a long speech in all the time I had known her.

We left the coffee shop and I drove her home. For several minutes she was very subdued, but finally she rallied. 'What is your wedding dress like?' she asked.

For a moment I was gripped by a wicked impulse to lie. 'Oh, bright red, plunging neckline. You know the sort of thing.' But it occurred to me that she might pass out.

'It's cream with antique lace, a modest neckline and lots of beading,' I replied, struggling to keep the smile off my face.

That evening I told Elias about my conversation. He was unperturbed. 'I'm glad to see you spending time together,' he said. 'Don't get upset about it. You'll soon get used to her ways.'

Elias and I had one more hurdle to leap before the big day: we had to get a marriage licence. It was a tense experience. We went together to the town hall to sign the necessary documents. I was certain that they would ask for a birth certificate.

'What will we do?' I asked Elias, tears welling up in my eyes.

But every time I became cowed or anxious Elias would chivvy me back into shape. 'Stop worrying, pet. We'll face that one if and when it happens.'

When we got there I waited out in the corridor while he went into sign. We'd rung earlier and been told that only one person need come into the office. When Elias emerged a few moments later he was grinning from ear to ear. 'No birth certificate necessary,' he told me. 'We're both British so they don't need one.'

And that was the end of the legal formalities – or at least I assumed it was. That evening Elias seemed agitated. I asked him what was wrong. It transpired that he wished me to sign a kind of pre-nuptial agreement stating that in the event of his death I would inherit only half of the business he ran with his brother, William. I felt insulted by the request.

'Don't you trust me?' I demanded angrily. 'Do you imagine that I'm going to run in and take over your company? For God's sake, Elias. If you died I would expect your brother to look after me. I'd be part of his family.'

He apologized. 'I'm sorry, pet. It's just that I own more than my brother and I care about him. I don't want him to be left in the lurch.'

'Did William ask you to do this?'

He didn't answer. My anger was unabated.

'If anyone should sign anything it's *you*,' I continued. 'What if you were to die in a plane crash and then your mother and father found out about me? It's me, not William, who could be left unprotected.'

He was impressed by the strength of my argument. If the truth were to emerge about our marriage we both knew that legally it would be null and void.

I suggested he sign and date a copy of my book to prove that he had read it. The conversation left us both sleepless and disturbed. I lay in bed staring up at the ceiling. The wedding plans seemed to be forcing us apart, and this new note of distrust that had come between us alarmed me. 'Please God,' I prayed silently, 'don't let this be an omen of things to come.'

I went to see Myra.

'I'm getting cold feet,' I told her. 'I feel as though the entire day is being taken over. Elias and I seem to have been forgotten.'

'Don't worry,' she counselled. 'Weddings are often more about the families than the couple who are actually marrying. And it's quite normal to feel doubtful.'

She was right. I did love Elias and I did want to spend the rest of my life with him. But this was like a roller-coaster ride running out of control.

One evening on the way home from having dinner with yet another herd of relatives, my nerve broke. I started to sob.

'What's wrong?' said Elias, alarmed at my tears.

'I can't go through with it!' I wailed. 'I just can't! I want to call it off!'

'Don't you love me any more, pet?'

'NO!' I screamed. I wanted to hurt him and to break through the barrier that seemed to have arisen between us. He put his arms around me and held me while I cried and cried.

'It's all right, sweetheart,' he murmured in my ear. 'It's all just fine. You are doing so well. I'm prouder of you than I can ever say. I *do* understand what you are going through.'

'I feel like I'm being given the second degree every time I go into your parents' home,' I sobbed. 'I'm losing all my confidence. Nobody thinks I'm good enough to be a Fattal. I've spent so much of my life feeling second-best, feeling despised and ashamed. I can't stand any more!'

'Hush, hush!' he said, rocking me in his arms. 'You've just got first-night nerves, my darling. Everything will be fine and before you know it we'll be on that plane to Acapulco without a care in the world.'

I looked up at him, my face all smeared with mascara.

'Oh, I *do* love you,' I said.

We struggled on. I lost so much weight that the designer, Cynthia Farley, had to alter my wedding dress three times and I cried on average twice a day! But finally it was all done: the wedding invitations had gone out, the cake was made, the ring bought and the bridal suite booked. The night before we were to marry, Elias rang me late.

'I wanted to tell you how much I love you,' he said.

I held the receiver pressed up against my face. 'Oh, Elias,' I thought. 'I wish you were here with me now.'

'I want you to get a good night's sleep, pet,' he continued. 'Don't worry about a thing.'

'I love you,' I whispered. 'See you tomorrow.'

But all through that long night I was tormented by one vision: a vision of Elias and me standing together under the Torah surrounded by a swarm of journalists, their cameras flashing and their voices raised in one deafening cry: TRANS-SEXUAL TULA WEDS! READ ALL ABOUT IT!

20

A Dream of a Wedding

My wedding. A day I had so often dreamt about in those distant times when Pam and I had watched the brides all in white being showered with a storm of confetti outside our local church before climbing into their chauffeur-driven cars and heading off to a life of romance and luxury. They seemed then like princesses from a fairytale. Time and experience had taught me that reality did not consist entirely of long pale dresses and a happy-ever-after. But I had never stopped believing in romance. Nor in the dream of marriage. My parents had loved each other all their married lives and, to me, marriage seemed the right and proper destiny of love.

It was 21 May, a hot day blessed with an incredibly blue sky. A car came to pick up my mum and me and take us to the Savoy, stopping off en route to pick up my wedding dress, which had had to be altered yet again. I was shaking with nerves, but I was also strangely excited. Seeing the cloudless sky and the beauty of the city in the early-morning light, I felt that nothing could harm me. 'It's going to be all right,' I thought.

When we arrived at the hotel, Mum and I were shown to a double room where we could change and leave our belongings. Mrs Fattal had booked the bridal suite for Elias and me, but that was to be left untouched until after we were married. I went downstairs and spoke to the florist and she showed me my bouquet and the flower arrangements for the reception. I was too distracted to absorb what she said.

Mum helped me change and wove my hair into a French plait. Then I climbed into my dress. It was fastened at the back by scores of tiny silk-covered buttons, and I stood waiting patiently for each one to be done up. Then I put my headdress on. I had two large and beautiful orchids at either side of my head, and a veil that covered my face. Even I had to admit that it looked stunning. I wore ballet shoes, as I didn't want to tower over Elias, and silk underwear bought by my mother. I had a necklace borrowed from Diana, and a blue garter from Pam over one of my stockings.

'You look like a dream, darling,' said my mother.

The ceremony was to take place in the Upper Berkeley Street synagogue, and my brother, dressed in top hat and tails, came to pick me up in an old chauffeur-driven Rolls. As we passed through the streets of London I fell silent. I had never felt so nervous in my entire life. Terry gave my hand a squeeze.

'You look beautiful,' he said.

Beautiful or not, I was dying for a cigarette. I fished one out of the little clutch purse I had with me.

'You're not allowed to smoke in here, madam,' said the driver.

'We'll have to stop the car, Terry. I'm desperate for a ciggie.'

'Don't be daft,' he replied. 'You can't get out of the car dressed like that and stand smoking a cigarette by the side of the road!'

I could see his point. But I had another plan. Concealed among the make-up in my purse was a tiny bottle of vodka. I took it out and swallowed a stiff measure.

'Caroline!' hissed Terry. 'I don't want you staggering down the aisle!'

'Don't worry,' I said. 'I'm far too sober to get drunk!'

When we arrived at the synagogue, I was ushered into the bride's room. From that room double doors led into the main hall. There was a tiny window in the door which enabled the bride to look out without being seen by the congregation. I caught my breath. The synagogue was packed with hundreds of people. Diana and Pam helped me with my veil, straightening my train and arranging my bridesmaids and pageboys. By now I was stiff with fear.

A man peered around the door. 'Ready to go?' he asked.

I couldn't speak.

'Are you OK, Caroline?' asked Terry, squeezing my arm.

'Yes,' I whispered.

I heard the music start up and the choir rose from their seats. The doors opened and I walked out holding on to Terry's arm. I had to proceed slowly up an aisle towards the chupa, where Elias, my mum, Mr and Mrs Fattal and William were standing. The music rose to a crescendo as I reached the canopy. I could see Elias's face. 'He looks anxious,' I thought. My mum had tears in her eyes, and I felt a lump in my throat. As the music died down and silence fell I offered up a prayer to God.

'Let me marry this man in peace and happiness.'

As Rabbi Goldberg began the service I was waiting for disaster to strike, for a voice in the crowd to cry out an objection to the marriage. But no one broke the solemn silence, no one interrupted the rabbi's beautiful words. We exchanged rings, we shared the wine and smashed the glass, and then walked up the steps to sign the register. We were pronounced man and wife, and the choir, the organ and the trumpeters combined together in the most spectacular chorus.

It was the happiest moment of my life. I looked into Elias's eyes. He was smiling, his face lit up with love, and I was certain that our marriage would last a lifetime. At last, after years of struggle, pain and turmoil, I had found a partner who not only accepted me as I was but was prepared to make me a gift of total commitment. I was his woman and he was my man.

We drove back to the Savoy high on excitement and dizzy with relief. At the hotel the staff were waiting at the door to greet us.

'Congratulations, Mr and Mrs Fattal,' said the banqueting manager. We were married at last! I could hardly believe it.

The ceremony may have been over but the celebrations had only just begun. The other Mrs Fattal was hot on our heels and she threw herself with near religious zeal into organizing the photographs.

For a full hour we posed in every conceivable permutation: aunts next to uncles, Cosseys shoulder to shoulder with Fattals, men with top hats and men without. Elias and I were snapped from all angles and I dabbed powder on my nose in between shots. Diana ran into the room and threw her arms around me. 'You looked *so* beautiful!' she exclaimed, showering me with kisses. Mrs Fattal, in a fury of creative excitement, glowered. Diana gave me a grin and slipped out of the room.

'This is tougher than any modelling assignment,' I thought to myself.

When the photographer had finished, we began to greet our guests. It took another hour to get everyone in. A master of ceremonies in top hat and tails announced every guest as they moved forward to the receiving line. It was the same man who had announced the guests at the Conservative Ball. Mrs Fattal's eyes shone with delight; this was a social coup of sorts. Needless to say, it was she who stood at the top of the line. My mother stood at the end.

Once all the guests had been announced, dinner was served in the Lancaster Room. Decorated in blue with a dazzle of gilded mirrors, it was large enough to seat all the guests for dinner and there was room for a dance floor. When everyone was seated, Elias and I entered amid applause. The band struck up and together we danced the Horah. I was so anxious lest I trip on my train that I hardly had time to worry about the steps. At one point Elias and I were both lifted on chairs and carried around the room before being brought together above the heads of the crowd to kiss. The satin of my wedding gown made it difficult for me to stay seated, and as the dancers lurched and swung I struggled not to pitch forward on to the floor.

The dinner was lavish and the Savoy performed the great feat of serving all the guests simultaneously with hot souffles. We ate poached salmon, ice-cream truffles, and a dessert served on trays of smoking ice. Between each course we danced, Elias and I opening the ball to the strains of 'Sweet Caroline'. Elias, not normally an enthusiastic dancer, was irrepressible. He moved around the floor, laughing and chatting. I looked at his happy, relaxed face as he asked Myra to dance. 'He's really enjoying himself,' I thought. I was not the only one to notice. All our friends were delighted to see him so gleeful. He was like a little boy at a birthday party; he couldn't stop smiling.

During dinner, Elias and William made speeches. William was witty and self-assured and he complimented me on the changes I had made to Elias's life. 'We all thought he had taken up life-long membership of the bachelor's club,' he joked. I knew Elias was nervous about speaking but in the end he gave a fine speech and thanked my mother for giving him such a beautiful wife. Mum was sitting next to me at the table and smiled with real pleasure.

The rest of the evening passed in a whirl of music, laughter and dance. Elias and I were in perpetual motion, talking to old friends, circulating around the room, drinking champagne. We were full of a kind of dizzy euphoria born of months of worrying and planning. Every so often I would catch his eye and find in his face a secret expression of deep content.

Just before midnight we retired to bed. I hugged Pam and Mum. 'Be happy,' Mum whispered to me. 'It was a wonderful day.'

It had been wonderful, a dream wedding. But I was glad it was over.

Elias took me up to the bridal suite. As soon as he shut the door, he threw his arms around me.

'Now you *are* my wife,' he said, 'and I want you to feel proud. You'll never be ashamed or insecure again. No more worrying – you can hold your head up high and enjoy the wonderful life we are going to have together.'

We both breathed a sigh of relief. I felt exhausted, but the bridal suite was beautiful, with baskets of flowers, cards, and bottles of champagne. We felt like naughty truants who'd just escaped from the classroom.

'Come here,' said Elias. 'Let's see what you've got on under that dress!'

He began chasing me around the room as I shrieked with laughter. When he caught hold of me, he was faced with the challenge of the buttons. 'How on earth am I supposed to get all these undone?' he exclaimed. His large hands were not best suited to the task. We both began to giggle.

'Shall I just rip it off?' he asked.

By the time I was undressed we were nearly hysterical with mirth and exhaustion. We collapsed on to the bed and fell into a profound sleep wrapped in each other's arms.

'Everything is going to be all right,' I thought as I drifted towards unconsciousness. 'I *am* going to live happily ever after, after all . . . '

21

Betrayal

SEX CHANGE
PAGE THREE GIRL WEDS

Pam handed me the paper. On the front page of the *News of the World* was a picture of me posing in a bikini. Mum began to cry.

'The bastards!' I exclaimed, feeling the blood drain from my face. 'They've done it again.'

Not content with having ruined my career and caused untold suffering to me and my family, now they were damaging my marriage. The final sentence stuck a knife in my heart. It read: 'She's really landed on her back this time.' I threw the paper across the room in a rage.

'What are we going to do?' said Elias. He was pale with shock.

'Maybe there's a chance your parents haven't seen it,' I replied. 'Don't panic. Call them up and tell them we're back. That way we'll know what's going on.'

He walked slowly to the phone and dialled the number. His mother answered.

'Hi, Mummy, we're back.'

There was a silence. Then we heard him say: 'No, Mamma. Yes, Mamma. OK, Mamma.'

He put the phone down and turned to face me. 'She knows and she wants to see me straight away.'

He collapsed into a chair. 'What am I going to do? How can I possibly explain?'

We sat and talked for about half an hour. 'Come with me, Caroline. You are better at explaining about your past than I am.'

'The last person in the world your family wants to see is

me. I'm sorry, Elias, but I can't sit and listen to the insults. It's going to take them a while to get used to the idea. It's better they have a chance to get rid of their prejudice privately.'

He fell silent. He had broken out into a sweat and was tapping his foot nervously. 'I could tell them that I didn't know,' he suggested.

'Don't be ridiculous,' I snapped. 'How can you expect your family to have any respect for me if they think I've been dishonest with you?'

The phone rang.

'It's your brother-in-law,' said Pam, holding the phone out for Elias.

'I'm leaving right now,' he said, replacing the receiver.

'What did he say?' I asked.

'Mummy's very upset and wants me home now.'

Elias paced the room while I called a taxi. When the car drew up I walked with him to the door. 'Be strong and be honest,' I said. 'And please protect my dignity.'

'I'll ring you,' he said and walked away.

It was Sunday 11 June 1989, a day I shall never forget. Elias and I had just returned from a glorious honeymoon in Acapulco and were exhausted after twelve hours of travelling. Although tired, we were looking forward to telling our family and friends all about our wonderful three weeks. We had sat in the sun, made love morning, noon and night, and found true peace of mind after the madness of the wedding. I had even been teaching Elias to swim, laughing with tenderness as he clung on to me in our private pool.

And now this. Another dream shattered by the gutter journalists. My privacy torn to shreds.

After Elias had gone I headed for the bathroom and knocked back a tranquillizer. 'At least I can be sure that Elias will stand by me,' I thought. 'With him by my side I can face anything.'

I lay down on my bed and waited for him to call. One hour went by. Then the phone rang. It was Elias.

'How's your mother?' I asked.

'She's in shock,' he replied. 'She looks white and drained. I've never seen her like this. She's been hounded by the press for the last two days.'

'Are you coming home?'

'No, I'm going to speak with my sister and brother-in-law.'

'Where's William?'

'He's abroad, but he'll be home later tonight.'

'OK,' I replied. 'See your sister and wait for your brother. Remember I love you. Be strong. I'll be praying for you.'

I put the phone down and took another tranquillizer. That, combined with the jet lag, sent me into a dreamless sleep.

Pam woke me with a cup of tea. 'You've been asleep for three hours,' she said.

'Has Elias called?'

'He came to pick up his suitcase about an hour ago.'

'Why didn't you wake me?'

'He asked us not to. He said it would be better to leave you sleeping.'

I began to cry. I was tired, confused and hurt. Why were the press still persecuting me? Mum's eyes filled in sympathy.

'That vile newspaper,' she said. 'Why can't they leave you alone?'

The three of us sat on my bed with our arms around each other. I asked Pam how Elias had seemed. She told me he had arrived with William and seemed very agitated.

'I've never seen him like that before,' she said. 'He was in a terrible rush to get his things and go.'

We all spent a restless night. Elias had not called me.

Monday

Rabbi Goldberg rang in the morning.

'How are you?' he asked.

'Terrible,' I replied.

'Just tell me one thing. Did Elias know about your past?'

'Yes,' I replied.

'Good. I'm so relieved. I knew that you would have told the truth.'

He asked me to come and see him at his house in Kentish Town. When I left the flat Elias had still not phoned.

I rang the door bell with a shaky hand. I need not have been anxious. The rabbi was kind and understanding. We sat in his garden and he made me a sandwich. I told him all about my past and apologized for any embarrassment I might have caused.

'How's Elias taking it?' he asked, and I explained that my husband had not been with me last night. This seemed to worry him.

'You ought to stick together,' he said.

The conversation gave me strength. Never at any point had he expressed horror or disapproval at my past. He remained sympathetic throughout.

'I'm afraid I was rather confused when the journalist came round asking questions. He had led me to believe he was acting on behalf of a jilted lover or husband. It wasn't until I read the paper that I understood what had happened.'

Mum and Pam were waiting at the window when I arrived back at the flat. They had been anxious that Rabbi Goldberg might have given me a hard time, and were touched when they heard about his kindness.

I spent another long, long evening waiting for Elias to call. Where was he?

Tuesday

Another day spent waiting. Finally at nine in the evening William phoned to tell me that Elias was exhausted and had gone to bed.

I made the mistake of apologizing: 'I'm so sorry for all the trouble I must have caused. But please don't let anyone give Elias a hard time over this. It was my fault that he didn't tell you before the wedding. I wanted a chance to prove myself as a wife first. I wanted you all to see how happy Elias and I were together. We were both worried about your mum and dad. They aren't young and we were scared that the shock might be harmful . . . '

But William was impervious to any explanations or overtures of friendship. 'I've taken on board as much as I can for the moment,' he replied. 'I don't want to know any more. We will speak another time.'

He hung up and I began to cry. William and I had never been close, but he had always shown me respect. I spent another sleepless night.

Wednesday

The phone was ringing continuously. Journalists wanting a story, friends commiserating, but no Elias. I could stand it no longer; I had to know what was happening. I dialled his number.

'What's happening?' I asked. 'Why haven't you called me?'

'Trust me, Caroline,' he replied. 'I've been acting in our best interests. I've been running around talking to lawyers and dealing with the photographer and the banqueting manager at the Savoy.'

'I miss you,' I said. 'Don't leave me out. Please come and see me tonight. I need to talk to you. This silence is driving me mad.'

'Don't pressure me. I'm too busy this evening.'

'But I'm your wife!' I exclaimed, feeling my stomach knot with tension. 'I need you right now! If you don't come to see me, I'll get in the car and come to your parents' house.'

It was a threat but I was becoming desperate. I was certain that Elias would stand by me and could make no sense of this separation.

'I'll call you back,' he snapped, and hung up.

Ten minutes later the phone rang. It was Elias.

'I'll see you at eight,' he said.

I decided to ring Elias's cousin, Sandra. I had always liked her, and her little daughter had been a bridesmaid at the wedding. I thought that of all the Fattals, she was the one most likely to understand. I couldn't have been more mistaken. Her attitude was cold and hostile. She told me that the family felt hurt and betrayed.

'You've deceived everybody,' she said.

'That's not true,' I replied. 'I told Elias two days after his proposal.'

She remained silent. Suddenly I felt tired of apologizing. 'Look,' I said. 'I can handle the rejection, I've had enough of it, after all. But please, *please*, be gentle with Elias. I love him too much to sit by and watch him being given a hard time.'

I couldn't go on. Sandra's hostility had shattered me. I began to sob and hung up. As I made my way to the bathroom, I caught sight of my face in the mirror. I looked pale and drawn. There were huge dark circles under my eyes. I had to do something about my appearance before Elias arrived. I pulled myself together, washed my hair and put on some make-up. Then I went into the kitchen and began preparing my husband's favourite meal: spaghetti with a spicy bolognese sauce.

The doorbell rang on the stroke of eight. My heart leapt. He was here at last! Things could only get better. I ran to the door to hug him, but he walked straight past me and into the flat. He immediately began to rant about some business at work that had annoyed him. I couldn't make head or tail of what he was saying, but I could see he was in a very agitated state.

'Calm down,' I said. 'Do you want me to massage your neck?'

'No!' he snapped.

'How about a bath?' But he rejected that as well.

'OK,' I said. 'Well, at least eat the meal I've cooked for you. You must be hungry. Come and see what I've made.'

I led him into the kitchen and sat him down at the table.

'What is it?' he asked, his curiosity getting the better of him.

'Your favourite – a spicy spaghetti.'

He couldn't resist it and for a few moments there was calm while he ate.

Then came the explosion.

'Why the fuck didn't you let me tell my parents?' he shouted, flinging a glass across the room. It shattered on the floor. I began to cry. I knelt down and tried to pick up the glass, my tears mingling with the wine. The phone rang. It was Myra.

'Have you heard from Elias?' she asked.

'He's here.'

'Oh, good. Can I speak to him?'

I went through to the kitchen to get Elias.

'Who is it?' he asked.

'It's Myra and Peter. They want to have a word.'

'Why?' he snapped.

'Oh, for God's sake, Elias. They're our friends. They want to help.'

I sat cross-legged on the floor while he spoke. I was shocked at the state Elias was in. I could see that he was in mental torment. In the face of his violence and agitation, I wasn't sure how I should behave.

He spoke for six or seven minutes, and I could hear Peter's

voice. He was full of good advice. 'Bloody journalists . . . just weather the storm and everything will be fine . . . today's news is tomorrow's chip paper . . . '

Elias was replying 'yes' and 'no' but his mind seemed elsewhere. His eyes darted around the room as though he expected reporters to leap out from behind every door. I felt a shiver go down my spine. 'This man is in real trouble,' I thought to myself. 'I have to help him.'

As he replaced the receiver the doorbell rang.

'Who the hell is that?' I asked.

He looked at his watch. 'It's William,' he replied.

'What does William want?'

'He's come to pick me up.'

'What do you mean? I *need* you here. You can't leave!'

'I have some calls to make to Canada.'

'But you can always make calls from here. Please, Elias! Don't leave me on my own again tonight!'

The doorbell rang again – a long-drawn-out peal. Elias picked up the intercom and said, 'I'm coming down.'

By now I was becoming incoherent, sobbing and shaking. For the first time I realized that I could be losing the man I loved. His family had taken control. I waited for him to give me some sign that the old Elias was still there. I expected him to turn to me and say, 'I'm so sorry, pet. It'll all be fine. I just need a few more days.' But instead he was allowing his brother to direct his actions.

'What's more important,' I cried, 'your business or me?'

'Please, Caroline. I have to go.'

My grief turned to anger. 'Go, then!' I yelled. 'Get out!'

'Oh, you're kicking me out, then, are you?' he shouted, and slammed the door.

I sank to the floor, weeping with anger and pain. How could this be happening to me? I knew this man so well. I loved him. Why was he behaving in this way?

I reached once more for the tranquillizers. Before they had had time to take effect, the phone rang again. It was Elias, but his voice sounded strangely robotic.

'If you love me, Caroline, you must let me go. But as far as the press are concerned we are still together.'

I couldn't believe what I was hearing.

When I caught my breath I said, 'You are in shock, Elias. You don't know what you are saying. This is not *you* speaking. I'll talk to you tomorrow.'

I put the phone down and fell into a troubled sleep.

Thursday

I told Mum and Pam about the events of the night before, and I began to feel a real anger growing. When Elias phoned I was firm and direct.

'I don't want any part of your plan,' I said. 'I believe that you will fight for my love and I certainly intend to fight for yours.'

I hung up and switched on the answering machine. Later that day I called Rabbi Goldberg and asked if he had spoken to Elias.

'Yes, I have,' he replied. 'I have seen both him and William. I think you and I had better talk. Can you come to my house tomorrow at eleven?'

'I'll be there,' I told him, and added that I had seen Elias the day before. 'He gave me the strong impression that he doesn't intend to stand by me. What do you think?'

The question was an impossible one to answer but I was desperate for comfort.

'I'm sorry, Caroline. Elias is not behaving in an adult fashion. You may have to be very brave.'

'Am I losing my husband?' I asked.

He replied, 'Come and talk to me tomorrow.'

Another sleepless night.

Friday

I spoke to Peter and told him all that had happened. He offered to take me to Rabbi Goldberg's house and I was grateful for the offer. I was to need all the support I could get.

Rabbi Goldberg confirmed my worst fears. Elias had told him that he wanted an annulment and that I should get myself legal representation.

'Why an annulment?' I asked. 'I thought you told Mrs Fattal that the marriage is legally binding?'

'That is what I thought, but unfortunately the civil marriage holds precedence over the religious.'

I was devastated. It seemed I was to be cast away like an old shoe. Yet again I had no rights. Peter could see my distress and suggested that it might be time to leave. The rabbi held my hand and told me how sorry he was. I gave him a hug and a kiss on the cheek and said how grateful I was for all his kindness. At least one good thing had come out of the meeting: Peter had demonstrated beyond the shadow of a doubt that Elias had known all about my past before the marriage. It was nice to feel vindicated.

Peter drove me home and came in for a drink. He spoke to Mum and Pam. 'It doesn't look very hopeful,' he said. 'I'm so sorry.'

Saturday

Elias had called Peter late on Saturday and asked if they could meet. My spirits lifted. Perhaps Peter could provide Elias with the support and counselling he needed. Suddenly there seemed hope. Myra suggested that I come round to her house so that I could be there the moment Peter returned from the meeting. We waited anxiously for the news, and when Peter's car drew up we both leapt out of our seats. But as he came through the door my heart sank. He was clearly distressed, and, as he looked at me standing there, his eyes filled with tears.

'I'm sorry, Caroline,' he said, choking back the emotion. 'Just give me a minute or two . . . Why don't we all have a drink?'

We all sat down round the table.

'He's not good enough for you,' said Peter. He tried to convince me but I didn't want to hear.

'I want to know what he said,' I replied.

Peter paused. 'There is more, Caroline,' he said, his face tense and pale. 'But I'm not sure that you will want to hear it. After all you've been through . . . '

I interrupted. 'Peter, I want to know *everything!*'

Then he broke it to me. 'Elias says he has woken from a dream. That you bewitched him but now the spell is broken and he's absolutely sure that he wants an annulment.'

I bit my lip to keep from crying. There was worse to come.

'He's says that if he does not get peace of mind, he will

destroy you, and if you screw him for money, he will kill you. He told me that he hated queers and didn't want people thinking he was some kind of freak.'

Peter sighed and reached for my hand. 'I'm so sorry, Caroline. I didn't want to have to tell you all that. He's not worthy of you.'

My mind was spinning. Was the man who had uttered these cruel and barbaric words the same man I had married? The man who had told me on our wedding day that I need never be ashamed again? The man who had sat with me, read my book and told me that he loved and understood me? I was lost in the most terrible nightmare. How could I ever hope to find the Elias that I had loved? It was as though he were dead.

'Do you want to speak to him?' asked Peter gently. 'He told me that he would be at home.'

I walked to the phone and dialled his number. The moment I heard his voice, I broke down.

'What are you trying to do to me?' I sobbed.

'Caroline, if you really love me you will let me go. Our life together is doomed.'

'But what about our vows? What about the three weeks we just spent together? What about the four years of happiness? How can you throw all that away?'

But like a battered old record, he could only repeat: 'If you love me you will let me go. I'm a different man from the person you knew.'

'You're a bastard with no balls!' I screamed and threw the phone down. I ran into the garden, blinded by tears. Myra followed me and we clung together, howling like babies.

Later, when I had cried all the tears I had, I collected my things and left.

'I'm sorry I couldn't help,' said Peter as I kissed him and Myra goodbye. 'He's not good enough for you, sweetheart.'

It had only been a week but it felt like a lifetime. In seven days I had lost the man I loved, the marriage I had believed in, and my own will to live. Without the support of my mum and my sister, I think I would have given up. I still didn't want to believe that Elias was gone for ever, but I knew that I had to take his words seriously. I had the locks changed on my doors and made an appointment to see my solicitor, Henri. Myra came with me and we explained the situation to him.

'Do you want a divorce?' he asked.

'Of course not,' I replied. 'But it doesn't look like I've got any choice.'

He gave Myra his card and asked her to give it to William. 'In future they should communicate with Caroline through me.'

He advised me to see a divorce lawyer and gave me the name of a woman he knew who was very good.

The next day Pam, Mum and I left for Norfolk. They both felt I needed to get away. They tried hard to distract me, but I was lost in a world of my own. All I could think about was Elias. He had left me with so many unanswered questions. Ours was an unfinished story.

Pam forced me to come out jogging with her in the mornings, and Mum took me to Great Yarmouth in an attempt to cheer me up. I remember standing by the prize bingo stall in an amusement arcade, staring at the coloured balls as they bobbed up and down. 'This is the worst moment of my life,' I thought. I felt so isolated by my pain.

I was dreading having to face my nephew and niece, George and Claire. I loved them deeply, but I knew how hurt they would feel by Elias's desertion of the family. I decided to lie and to tell them that Uncle Elias was away on business.

When I finally plucked up the courage to call, Maxine, Terry's wife, met me at the door. She is a lovely warm person and she welcomed me in. The house smelt of cooking. Maxine is a first-class cook, and runs Poppy's Kitchen in Rockland St Mary. She had cooked me an excellent meal and with the food and the kids' chatter, my mind was temporarily eased.

When the children had gone to bed, we discussed the events of the last ten days. Both Maxine and Terry were aghast. 'I could kill him for what's he done,' said my brother.

As I was leaving, Maxine handed me a cooler box packed with little delicacies. 'Get these down yer, gal,' she said, in her broad Norfolk brogue. 'They'll do yer the world agood.'

Henri, my solicitor, rang me the next day to ask if I had decided to go to court to sort things out between us. I felt I had rights.

'I won't stay silent,' I said. I asked him to make me an appointment with the barrister.

My hurt was fast turning to anger. I had been deserted, and now no other course of action seemed open to me. It was the same old discrimination I had suffered all my life. I was a transsexual. Therefore I should keep my mouth shut and consider myself lucky that people didn't spit on me in the street. Any other woman would have been entitled to a fair hearing. I wasn't after Elias's money, but neither was I prepared to be discriminated against. Why should a man be allowed to walk into a woman's life, offer her a future, dissuade her from pursuing her own career, and then, at the drop of a hat, walk out again? It seemed to me that I had given Elias just as much support, care and attention as he had given me. And yet at the point of separation, when I was to be left emotionally wrecked and with no prospects, I was considered nothing more than a gold-digger who could be bought off. Yes, I did want justice. What woman, or man for that matter, wouldn't? And if the court was the only place I could find justice, then that was where I would go. All I wanted at that moment was to see Elias in the witness box. I wanted to watch him take an oath and then swear that he had never known about my past, swear he had been 'bewitched', that I was now odious to him. Given more time, perhaps I would have felt differently, but I was still so raw.

The appearance of one Deborah Sherwood from the *News of the World* on my doorstep when I returned to London made matters worse.

'It's been rumoured that your illegal marriage is over and you are separated. Is that true?' she asked.

She was a short, pushy woman and I longed to swat her like an irritating bluebottle. I rarely become violent but this paper was pushing its luck. I pointed at my wedding ring. 'If you think a four-year relationship could be ruined by your squalid little newspaper, then you are very mistaken!' I slammed the door in her face. 'Oh, Elias,' I thought. 'Where were you when I needed you?'

Our story was not yet over. The next day I received a phone call. It was Elias. Once Henri had spoken to the Fattals' lawyer, he realized that I was not going to be silenced. Elias suggested that he, William and I meet somewhere to discuss a compromise.

'If William is to be there, I want Myra and Peter to be present.'

Elias agreed and we arranged to meet at Myra's house at six the following evening. I was angry that Elias would not see me on my own, but at least we would have a chance to talk. I had still not come to terms with the idea that he no longer loved me. I kept hoping that I would once again discover the old Elias I knew and loved, the man who had promised to stand by me.

We sat round the kitchen table. I asked him to speak to me on his own, but William refused to allow him, and took notes throughout the conversation. It was a terrible experience. Elias would hardly look at me. Whenever he made a comment he would first glance sideways at his brother, as if for approval. We were supposed to be coming to an agreement, but I was unable to stay cool.

'Elias,' I said, trying to reach him with my words. 'How can you behave like this? It was only a few weeks ago that we were in bed together making love. How can you forget that intimacy?'

'The world is the same, but I am changed,' he said. 'I have come out of a dream.'

It was as if he had been brainwashed. I began to panic. Where was the man I loved? I got up and went round the table towards him. Putting my arms around him, I whispered 'I love you' in his ear. Just the scent of his neck made me weep. He put up his hand and caught my wrist.

'Don't, Caroline,' he said. 'Don't.'

'Why are you doing this to me?' I sobbed, and ran from the room.

I sat on the settee, put my head on my knees and began to howl with grief. I was aware someone had walked into the room and I felt them sit down beside me. I looked up and saw Elias there, his eyes full of tears. We were like two lost souls at the end of the world. I leant my head on his shoulder and he put his arm round me.

'Oh, Caroline,' he sighed. 'I love you. I will always love you. But there is no future for us. You must let it go.'

I lifted my head and stared into his eyes. I knew that he was speaking from his heart, and that only made it harder. Our lips met in a kiss and for a moment it was as if time had stopped. Then, blind with tears, I ran into the kitchen, grabbed my bag and made for the door. William held out his hand. I stared at him with such loathing that Peter, frightened of what I might do, stepped between us. And then I turned and walked away. That was the last time I saw Elias Simon Fattal.

22

Annulment

Life is full of ironies. Late in June Henri rang me to say that the European Court in Strasbourg had ruled by ten votes to six that the failure of English law to recognize marriages between transsexuals broke the protection of the right to marry in article twelve of the European Convention on Human Rights. It was an incredible triumph, contradicting as it did an earlier ruling, and represented the end result of nearly seven years of struggle. But the victory left something of a bitter taste in my mouth. It had come too late.

'The British Government is certain to appeal,' said Henri.

'It makes no difference,' I replied. 'I intend to fight this battle to the bitter end. What do I have to lose?'

He was right. An appeal was launched by Her Majesty's Government and a date was set for a hearing in the spring.

Meanwhile the dispute about my settlement with the Fattals continued. I turned to the tabloids to exorcize my fury. I did a piece for the *Mail on Sunday*, revealing that I was the mysterious Miss C. I also consulted the divorce lawyer Henri had recommended, a woman named Judith Hughes. She was excellent, one of the best. She felt that although my marriage was somewhat irregular, I did have a case for being treated like any other woman.

As the lawyers stepped in, any hopes that I might have had of a peaceful reconciliation were dashed. It was war. Mum and I decided to head for Norfolk and the tranquillity of the countryside. We both needed the break. I had been involved in several unpleasant altercations with William and I wanted to step back from the fray. He and Elias were involved in a legal dispute in the States over a 'gentleman's agreement' which an American firm had not honoured. In anger, I threatened to ring up the opposition and tell them just how 'gentlemanly' I considered the Fattal brothers to be!

So we were both relieved when we were finally on the motorway and speeding up to Brooke. As we were driving along, a car drew up alongside me. I glanced over and saw a man frantically waving me on to the hard shoulder. He got out of his car, and, standing back some distance, he shouted: 'There's petrol spraying from your car!'

I was horrified. The car was a new Mercedes.

'Thank God I didn't light a cigarette,' I said to Mum, my heart pounding. 'We would have been blown sky-high.'

'What should I do?' I asked the man, panic-stricken.

'Get it to a garage straight away,' he replied. 'But drive very slowly.'

My mother and I looked at one another and then very slowly and carefully got back into the car. Holding my breath, I turned on the ignition. By now Mum was in tears. I reassured her, gently shifted the car into first gear and crawled to the first garage we could find. I found the manager and told him what had happened and he told me to drive the car to a viewing point. As I moved forward, I was shocked to see three mechanics facing me with fire extinguishers. Clearly they were taking no chances.

There was no possibility of a quick repair and so I ordered a cab. Mum and I went to the Mercedes service and parts centre to order a new fuel pipe. This problem had never occurred before with a Mercedes and so an order had to be sent to Germany. It would take at least six days to arrive and they offered me a replacement car in the meantime. We set off for Norfolk once again, and arrived without incident. It was a tremendous relief to be home in the quiet of the countryside.

In the morning I telephoned my answering service and received a message to call the garage immediately. The news left me shocked and shaken. My car had been tampered with. Someone had tried to cut through the brake cable with a hacksaw and had severed the petrol pipe instead – it appeared that in the Mercedes the two pipes run close together.

'I advise you to inform the police,' he said. 'This was certainly an attempt on your life.'

I began to tremble violently. Surely nobody could hate me

so much that they would wish me dead? I tried to steady my breathing, then reached for the phone and dialled Henri's number. He was stunned by my news. When I had finished talking, he pointed out that as it was a criminal offence, he would have to contact Scotland Yard. My chance of a holiday was gone – I had to return to London immediately. Suddenly my small country retreat seemed very isolated and my mother and I felt alone and unprotected.

On the advice of friends, I hired a bodyguard. Viv was an ex-paratrooper who had made a study of martial arts. He was six feet tall, very handsome, and inspired confidence. Immediately I felt some of my paranoia dissolve. I was confident that this man would be able to look after my safety. I hired him on a twenty-four-hour basis and arranged a bed for him to sleep on.

In the morning I had to go to the police station and give a statement to the detective sergeant. He took me into an interview room and left me there for a few moments while he fetched some coffee. It was a depressing little room with two chairs, a table and an ashtray. I lit a cigarette to calm my nerves. Even though I was there as the victim of a crime, I still felt uneasy. I knew that I would have to discuss my private life and was unsure of the reaction I might receive. I need not have worried. The detective was sympathetic and gentle. But he did need to know about all areas of disharmony in my life. My marriage was discussed and I explained that Elias, my husband, was out of the country and wasn't expected back for two to three weeks.

They never did discover who had sabotaged my car, and that was not the end of the nightmare. For the next few weeks I received a number of anonymous calls. One, which threatened my life, I handed to the police. The voice was not recognizable. The phone would ring in the night at one, two and then three. When I picked up the receiver the line would go dead. The same game was played with my doorbell. Thankfully, with Viv there, I was able to take it all in my stride. I refused to be intimidated by these anonymous callers.

Meanwhile, I had made the final decision to fight on in court. I was suing for an annulment. A date was set for the court hearing. I continued to publicize the break-up of my marriage. In the event Elias *did* state that he had been unaware of my past, and I wanted the real facts to be known to as many people as possible. The idea that the guests at my wedding, especially Elias's family and friends, might believe I had deceived him incensed me. I did features with the *People*, the *Sun*, and the *Sunday Mirror*. I used the only weapon I had in my armoury: the fascination that my transsexuality held for the tabloid press. It was a weapon that had been used against me in the past to terrible effect; now I was harnessing it to help me fight my own battle.

Just before Christmas the case was referred to the High Court. The hearing was to be held in mid-January. In the meantime my mother received a notice to quit. Elias had known that she was still not entirely well. He also must have realized how much I needed my mother near me at that time. If there was one moment when I knew for certain that our love was gone, that was it. Happily, in the event Mum did not have to leave immediately, but I still couldn't believe he could be so cruel.

But love can take for ever to die. Although it was now clear to me that he wanted me out of his life, I still hoped that I would have a chance to see him in court. I longed to talk to him, to find a way of reconciling the past with the present. But it was not to be. The annulment proceedings were a fiasco. Elias was in the court building, but refused to meet me. His lawyer had to act as go-between. It was like a scene from a farce. Finally my lawyer told me that he felt obliged to advise me not to proceed. 'You could face costs of anything up to £80,000. It's a terrible risk.' I realized that if Elias denied knowledge of my past, then the proceedings could drag on for some time.

I was tired, depressed and bewildered. The Commission in Strasbourg had upheld my right to marry and I knew that with the evidence I could supply to show that Elias was fully aware of the facts, and with the European ruling behind me, I did have a chance and was entitled to have my position recognized. But it was a gamble. It only needed a conservative stuffed shirt of a judge and I would be fighting the same prejudice that I was fighting with the British Government's appeal. I was trapped. Feeling cheated, and with a heavy heart, I accepted the wisdom of Henri's words. I decided to retire from the fray and to endure the bitter experience of standing mute before the judge and hearing my marriage annulled on the grounds of my being still legally male.

'Were you born Barry Kenneth Cossey?'

'Yes.'

'Were you born a male?'

'Yes.'

As I stood there, my past laid open for all to see, I struggled to stay silent. Once again I was being told that as a transsexual any marriage I entered into would be declared null and void. In the eyes of that judge and the law-makers of the country, I was a man. It made no difference that I looked, behaved, functioned and felt like a woman. As far as they were concerned, the evidence of their eyes and my soul made precious little difference.

Suddenly I was longing for Strasbourg.

23

Justice?

On Tuesday 24 April 1990 the European Court met in Strasbourg to consider my case. I was present with Henri and my barrister, David Pannick, and we were met at the door of the courtroom by a horde of journalists. Henri had instructed me to stay silent while he gave a brief statement. We were surrounded by TV cameras, flashbulbs and microphones. The world's media had turned out for a glimpse of the transsexual who was fighting the British Government for the right to live a normal life.

As we walked into the vast courtroom, I felt all eyes turn to stare. Looking neither to the right nor to the left, I made my way to my place. David and I were seated on a bench at the head of the room. Beside us were four members of the Commission who originally ruled in my favour. On the opposite side of the gangway sat the representatives of the British Government.

The chamber was cold and I shivered slightly. I had dressed conservatively in an elegant Armani suit. My hair was loose and my make-up subdued. I wanted to look sophisticated yet feminine. Up above was a gallery that ran round the edge of the room, with dozens of tiny windows. Each window framed a figure wearing headphones and peering down on the throng. They were the interpreters.

I felt terrified. The courtroom was packed with spectators and I didn't dare to turn round. As the eighteen judges entered in their robes, everyone rose. 'Here we go,' I thought to myself.

It was to be a long day. David had been right when he warned me that much of what the British Government representatives would say would enrage me. They argued that since the Court had found against Mark Rees in his case, there was no basis for overruling that decision. They claimed there was no difference between the two cases, and maintained that a country had the right to make its own marriage laws. They said that since gender was defined at the latest at birth, I had to be considered male. They stressed the importance of the ability to procreate in marriage. At times I blanked out the words. I found it hard to listen and still remain calm. What possible reason could a government have for wishing to prevent me from leading the life I wanted? My request for justice harmed no one.

When David Pannick presented my case, I listened with fascination. He made everything seem supremely logical.

A world-famous barrister and fellow of All Souls, Oxford, he is a staunch champion of the European Convention on Human Rights. A few days before the hearing he had published an article in the *Independent* criticizing the British Government's record in connection with that Convention. Despite having ratified the Convention in the first place in 1951, English law has fought shy of taking all its obligations seriously. Since 1960, when the first case was heard, the European Court of Human Rights has handed down more than 200 judgements. Nearly forty have involved the United Kingdom, setting a record among the member states of the Council of Europe. David wrote:

> The Court has developed an impressive body of case law that has, in most cases, sensitively recognized and developed fundamental freedoms that an overworked, apathetic or irrational legislature has failed to protect. For the English courts to ignore this growing body of judicial wisdom is perverse. As Lord McNaughten asked in a House of Lords judgment as long ago as 1903, 'With the light before him, why should he shut his eyes and grope in the dark?'

With this sense of purpose, David set out to illuminate the minds of the judges seated before him and, through their ruling, to force the Government to see reason.

In explaining to the Court why article twelve had been breached by the Government's refusal to allow me to marry, his arguments were elegant and concise. He pointed out that in the United Kingdom, gender-reassignment surgery was permitted without legal formality and that the operation was available on the National Health. This surgery, he explained, had made me perfectly capable of sexual intercourse. There was no question that for social, sexual and psychological purposes, I was a woman. I was accepted as such by friends, acquaintances and doctors.

He reiterated the point, made by the majority of the Commission who had found in my favour, that the ability to bear children was not a necessary condition of the right to marry. Many women are unable to procreate yet are permitted to marry. He quoted Justice Matthews:

Certainly a post-operative male-to-female transsexual lacks the capacity to procreate as a woman, but she has also lost that ability as a man. It is of little assistance to apply a test relating to the capacity to procreate in the case of a post-operative transsexual, for she has no capacity to procreate at all.

He explained that by refusing me the right to marry a man, the Government were denying me the right to marry at all. I certainly couldn't marry another woman, as I would be unable to consummate the relationship. He told the assembled courtroom that he could find no good reason to justify the Government's action, and that it was arbitrary to offer me surgery, issue me with a passport in a female name, and allow me to use that name and female identity for all practical purposes, but to refuse me the right to marry a man.

He painted an eloquent picture of the life of the transsexual, describing the trauma of possessing a physical sex contrary to that of the psychological sex. He told the Court how, while waiting for surgery, transsexuals inevitably incur hostility and prejudice and how, therefore, it was of especial importance that the fundamental rights of such people be sensitively defined and applied so as to spare them further ostracism.

In other countries, he pointed out, such rights had been given and, with regard to the Rees case, he argued that the previous decision of the Court was not a binding one. He felt that the matter needed re-evaluation. Since transsexualism was an issue that had only recently come before the courts, the law would have to keep up with developments both in science and in society. He produced a copy of a judgment that had been made in the Court of Appeal in New South Wales. The court had recognized that a man who had had gender-reassignment surgery to become female was a woman in the eyes of the law. In summing up, the Chief Justice had concluded that the 1970 decision of the English High Court in April Ashley's case would 'have to give place to more modern navigational guides to voyage on the seas of problems thrown up by human sexuality'. Unlike Mark Rees, David pointed out, I'd had two opportunities to marry partners who were perfectly aware of my past, and such an opportunity could arise again.

Turning to the issue of the birth certificate and article eight of the Convention, David submitted that once again the Government were denying me my rights. By refusing to allow the certificate to be altered, they were consigning me to a sex that was not my own. If I was required to produce my birth certificate, I would at the same time have to reveal intimate details of my sexual history and identity. This in turn could lead to further prejudice and hostility. It was precisely this type of interference with private life, David argued, that article eight was designed to prevent. He told the Court that he could see no pressing need for the Government to deny me a birth certificate, and judged that they were failing to exhibit the qualities of broadmindedness and compassion which article eight required.

He suggested that the Government might consider providing the transsexual with a birth certificate denoting the new sex while keeping a record on the official register of both the new sex and the old.

I wanted nothing more than my proper rights, he told the assembled crowd. If the Court found in my favour, I would ask for my legal costs to be paid by the Government but would seek no further reparation.

As he talked I stared up at the line of judges before me. A few were frowning with concentration, but their faces remained impassive as they listened through their headphones to the translation of David's words. 'How can they fail to appreciate the rightness of his argument?' I wondered. The Spanish judge caught my eye briefly and I thought I detected some warmth in his expression. Suddenly the law seemed such a heavy and cumbersome vehicle. Surely, if I sat with these people and told them my story in my own words, they could not help but understand and sympathize?

The sounds of the Court faded as, for a moment, I let my mind drift. I thought back over the past and the many trials I had undergone. I thought of my days in London when Polly and I struggled to find our way in a world that was hostile to our cause. I thought of the years I had spent saving and scrimping for my operation. I thought of Bill Rankine and the injury that he and his kind had done to my life. I thought of the Fattals and their more damaging assault on my transsexuality. 'Perhaps it is not possible to make people like that understand,' I reflected.

Then I turned my mind to the future and the trials that lay ahead. What if I lost the case? What would I do then? At the end of this day the Court would be dismissed and I would spend many anxious months waiting for a judgement. In the meantime, I would start work again. I had contacted Yvonne and we had planned a number of photo sessions. I also intended to write this book. All of these things would keep me busy, but still, what if I *did* fail? How would I bear it? I closed my eyes and saw before me the image of my father. He had taught me to be a fighter and I knew that whatever happened, I would go on fighting. I would raise petitions, I would write to politicians, I would appear on chat shows, I would not let the issue drop. No one should have to go through what I had gone through.

I had been blessed with my dad's stubborn spirit and it was that and the love of my family that had kept me going through the darker moments. But not all people would be so fortunate as I. The prejudice, cruelty and ignorance that transsexuals had to face could easily break a personality and leave it fractured beyond repair. I had hoped for a different life, a life of domestic peace and tranquillity with a man I could love. I had never wanted to take up the banner that I was now holding. But fate had given me no choice. Time and time again I had been forced into the public arena and treated with disrespect as some kind of sexual freak.

Seated in that courtroom on an April day in 1990, I finally accepted my destiny. I would be a voice speaking out for those who had been silenced by their fear of exposure. I would champion the rights of men and women who, like me, had been born into a sex to which they did not belong. Somehow I would find the courage to carry on. I would not be silenced.

I thought of Elias and felt my heart contract. I had wanted his love so badly and knew that I would go to my grave longing for a glimpse of his face, for the sound of his voice. Some wounds would never heal. But, curiously, at that moment, it was his words that came into my mind and offered comfort. 'We'll take it one step at a time,' he had once said to me. And that was what I intended to do. I would walk slowly and cautiously back into my life. I would speak out about my experience. I would work again, as a transsexual model. Maybe, in time, I would even learn to love again.

Step by step I would find my way to a better future. I had come so far, why falter now? With the justice of my cause in one hand and the love of my family and friends in the other, I was moving forward, into the light.

Epilogue

At 8 a.m. on Thursday 27 September 1990, my lawyer telephoned to tell me that the European Court had made its decision. By ten votes to eight it had found against my right to change my birth certificate. By fourteen votes to four it had found against my right to marry.

'I'm so sorry,' said Henri.

Numb with shock, I replaced the receiver. On the television the newscaster was telling early-morning Britain the same news that I had just heard. To most viewers the decision was a matter of small interest, but for me and other transsexuals it was a shattering blow. Legally it left us at a dead end. There was no higher court or authority who could review the case. Any transsexual wishing to marry would find their case thrown out by the European Court and their lawyer referred to Cossey versus the United Kingdom.

What, I wondered, were the other implications of the ruling? Does it mean that I will not receive a pension until I am sixty-five – the retirement age for men – even though male-to-female transsexuals pay a female insurance stamp? Perhaps I should get myself arrested to see how the courts deal with my being sent to a penitentiary crammed with men detained at Her Majesty's pleasure.

Perhaps a change of government, or else the Europeanization of the UK, will bring this backward-looking country into line with its more progressive neighbours. I believe that one day governments all over the world will recognize the rights that transsexuals should possess in their new sex. And I shall not give up the struggle, however long it takes. However long.